WATTERS • LEYH • SOTUYO • LAIHO

LUMBERJANES™

TIME AFTER CRIME

BOOM! BOX™

BOOM! BOX™

LUMBERJANES Volume Eleven, March 2019. Published by BOOM! Box, a division of Boom Entertainment, Inc. Lumberjanes is ™ & © 2019 Shannon Watters, Grace Ellis, Noelle Stevenson & Brooklyn Allen. Originally published in single magazine form as LUMBERJANES No. 41-44. ™ & © 2017 Shannon Watters, Grace Ellis, Noelle Stevenson & Brooklyn Allen. All rights reserved. BOOM! Box™ and the BOOM! Box logo are trademarks of Boom Entertainment, Inc., registered in various countries and categories. All characters, events, and institutions depicted herein are fictional. Any similarity between any of the names, characters, persons, events, and/or institutions in this publication to actual names, characters, and persons, whether living or dead, events, and/or institutions is unintended and purely coincidental. BOOM! Box does not read or accept unsolicited submissions of ideas, stories, or artwork.

For information regarding the CPSIA on this printed material, call: (203) 595-3636 and provide reference #RICH – 830537.

BOOM! Studios, 5670 Wilshire Boulevard, Suite 400, Los Angeles, CA 90036-5679. Printed in USA. First Printing.

ISBN: 978-1-68415-325-1, eISBN: 978-1-64144-178-0

THIS LUMBERJANES FIELD MANUAL BELONGS TO:

NAME:_____

TROOP:_____

DATE INVESTED:_____

FIELD MANUAL TABLE OF CONTENTS

A Message from the Lumberjanes High Council............4

The Lumberjanes Pledge............4

Counselor Credits............5

LUMBERJANES PROGRAM FIELDS

Chapter Forty-One............6

Chapter Forty-Two............30

Chapter Forty-Three............54

Chapter Forty-Four............78

Cover Gallery: Time After Crime Badge............102

LUMBERJANES
FIELD MANUAL

For the Intermediate Program

Tenth Edition • November 1984

Prepared for the

**Miss Qiunzella Thiskwin
Penniquiqul Thistle Crumpet's**
CAMP FOR ~~LADIES~~  HARDCORE
LADY-TYPES
"Friendship to the Max!"

A MESSAGE FROM THE LUMBERJANES HIGH COUNCIL

miss Quinzella Thiskwin Penniquiqul Thistle Crumpet's
Camp for
HARDCORE LADY TYPES
FRIENDSHIP to the MAX!

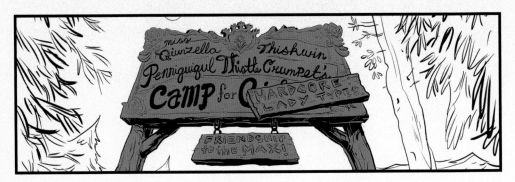

To be a Lumberjane Scout, you do not need to pass a test, or nail an interview, or go out for an audition. There are no grades and no prerequisites, no levels you must pass, or initiations you must go through to prove your worth before you don your beret and sash. And even these traditional trappings of scouthood are becoming less important now than they once were, and in many places, your uniform pieces may be provided for you, or handed down from scout to scout, or deemed unnecessary for every day Lumberjaning.

All you ever need to become a Lumberjane is genuine interest, and all you need to be a Lumberjane is to try your best to live up to the words of our pledge. Yes, there are often badges and uniforms, troops and ceremonies, but these aren't what make you a Lumberjane.

There are two things that are most vital to being a Lumberjane. The first is your interest in experiencing the world around you, and in learning everything you can about the topics and ideas that thrill you most, be they macrame or particle physics. The horizon of our knowledge is ever-expanding, and the depth of our understanding is ever-deepening, as we all discover more about the world and universe around us. There is so much to explore, and we hope to encourage you to seek things out and to strive to understand what they mean; to find out what interests you and to grapple firsthand with new and exciting ideas.

The other most important element of what makes you a Lumberjane is your drive to treat others with kindness and compassion, to stand up for what you believe in, and to fight to make the world a better place. Just as our knowledge is ever-growing, so too should be our hearts. We in the High Council hope that you will learn to extend your friendship and love as best you can to all, and to fight against injustice and prejudice when you see it in the world. Stand up for the downtrodden and offer them comfort, whenever you're able.

Remember: badges are vehicles for learning and for self-improvement, but learning for its own sake is equally vital and wonderful, and just as much what makes you a Lumberjane as your uniform or your troop. Your hunger for knowledge and understanding is what makes you a scout, even if there isn't yet a badge for every subject you may wish to examine, and your kind heart and willingness to do the right thing is what makes you a Lumberjane, even if there may not be a troop near you just yet.

THE LUMBERJANES PLEDGE

I solemnly swear to do my best
Every day, and in all that I do,
To be brave and strong,
To be truthful and compassionate,
To be interesting and interested,
To pay attention and question
The world around me,
To think of others first,
To always help and protect my friends,
[redacted]
And to make the world a better place
For Lumberjane scouts
And for everyone else.

THEN THERE'S A LINE ABOUT GOD, OR WHATEVER

LUMBERJANES™

TIME AFTER CRIME

Written by
Shannon Watters
& Kat Leyh

Illustrated by
Ayme Sotuyo

Colors by
Maarta Laiho

Letters by
Aubrey Aiese

Cover by
Kat Leyh

Series Designer
Kara Leopard

Collection Designer
Chelsea Roberts

Assistant Editor
Sophie Philips-Roberts

Series Editor
Dafna Pleban

Collection Editor
Jeanine Schaefer

*Special thanks to **Kelsey Pate** for giving the Lumberjanes their name.*

Created by **Shannon Watters, Grace Ellis, Noelle Stevenson & Brooklyn Allen**

LUMBERJANES FIELD MANUAL

CHAPTER
FORTY-ONE

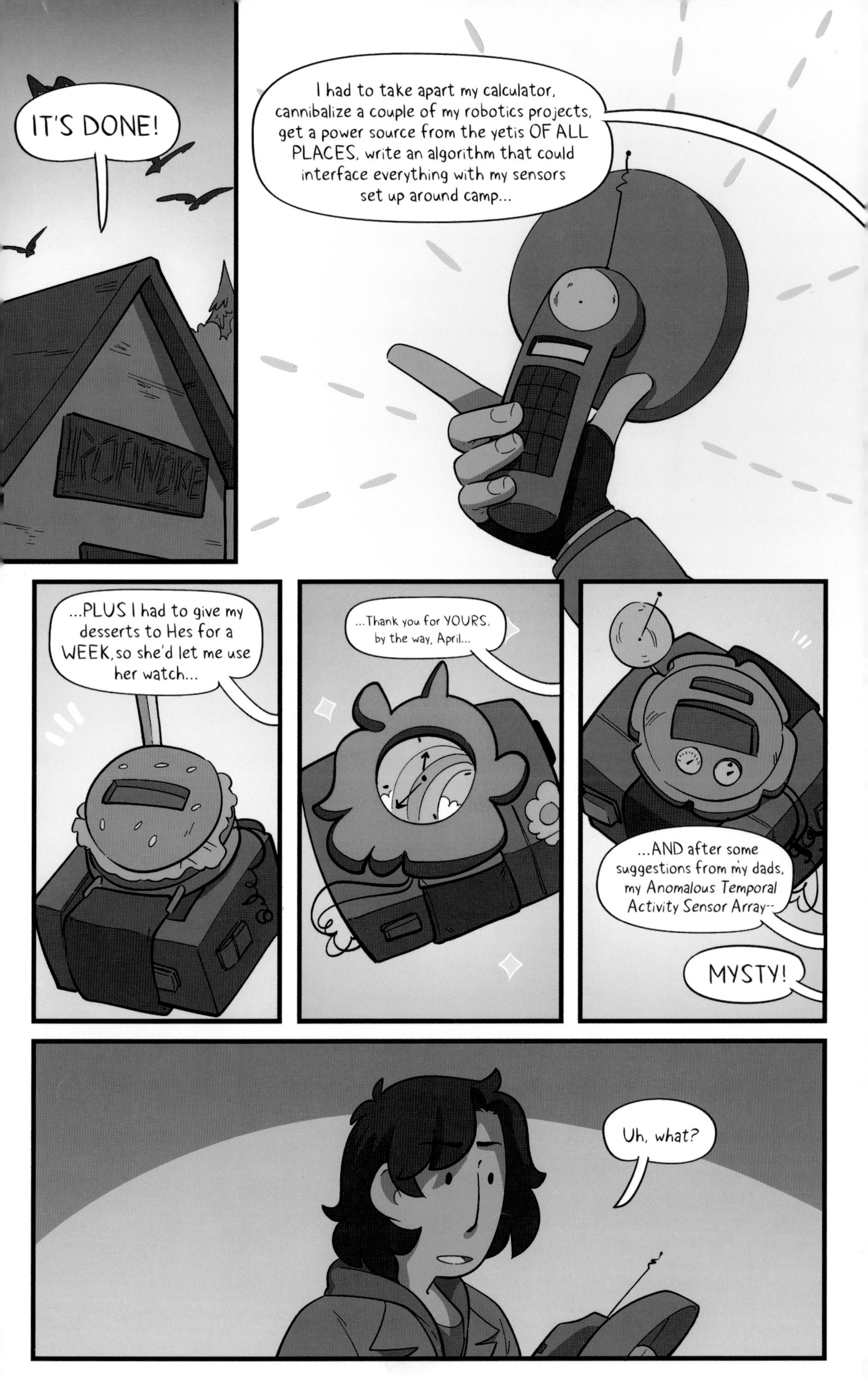
IT'S DONE!
I had to take apart my calculator, cannibalize a couple of my robotics projects, get a power source from the yetis OF ALL PLACES, write an algorithm that could interface everything with my sensors set up around camp...
ROANOKE
...PLUS I had to give my desserts to Hes for a WEEK, so she'd let me use her watch...
...Thank you for YOURS, by the way, April...
...AND after some suggestions from my dads, my Anomalous Temporal Activity Sensor Array--
MYSTY!
Uh, what?

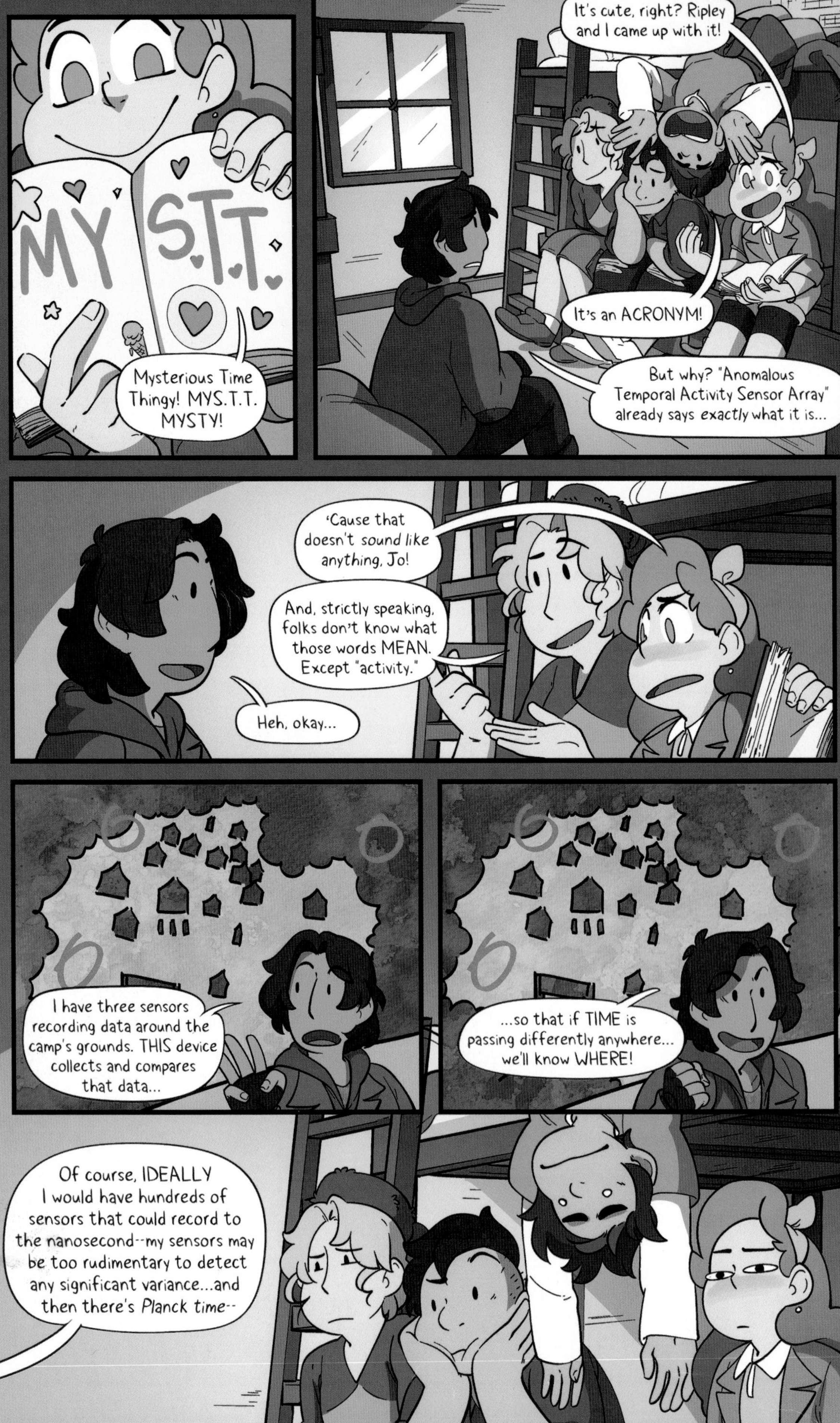
MY S.T.T.
Mysterious Time Thingy! MYS.T.T. MYSTY!
It's cute, right? Ripley and I came up with it!
It's an ACRONYM!
But why? "Anomalous Temporal Activity Sensor Array" already says *exactly* what it is...
'Cause that doesn't *sound like* anything, Jo!
And, strictly speaking, folks don't know what those words MEAN. Except "activity."
Heh, okay...
I have three sensors recording data around the camp's grounds. THIS device collects and compares that data...
...so that if TIME is passing differently anywhere... we'll know WHERE!
Of course, IDEALLY I would have hundreds of sensors that could record to the nanosecond--my sensors may be too rudimentary to detect any significant variance...and then there's *Planck time*--

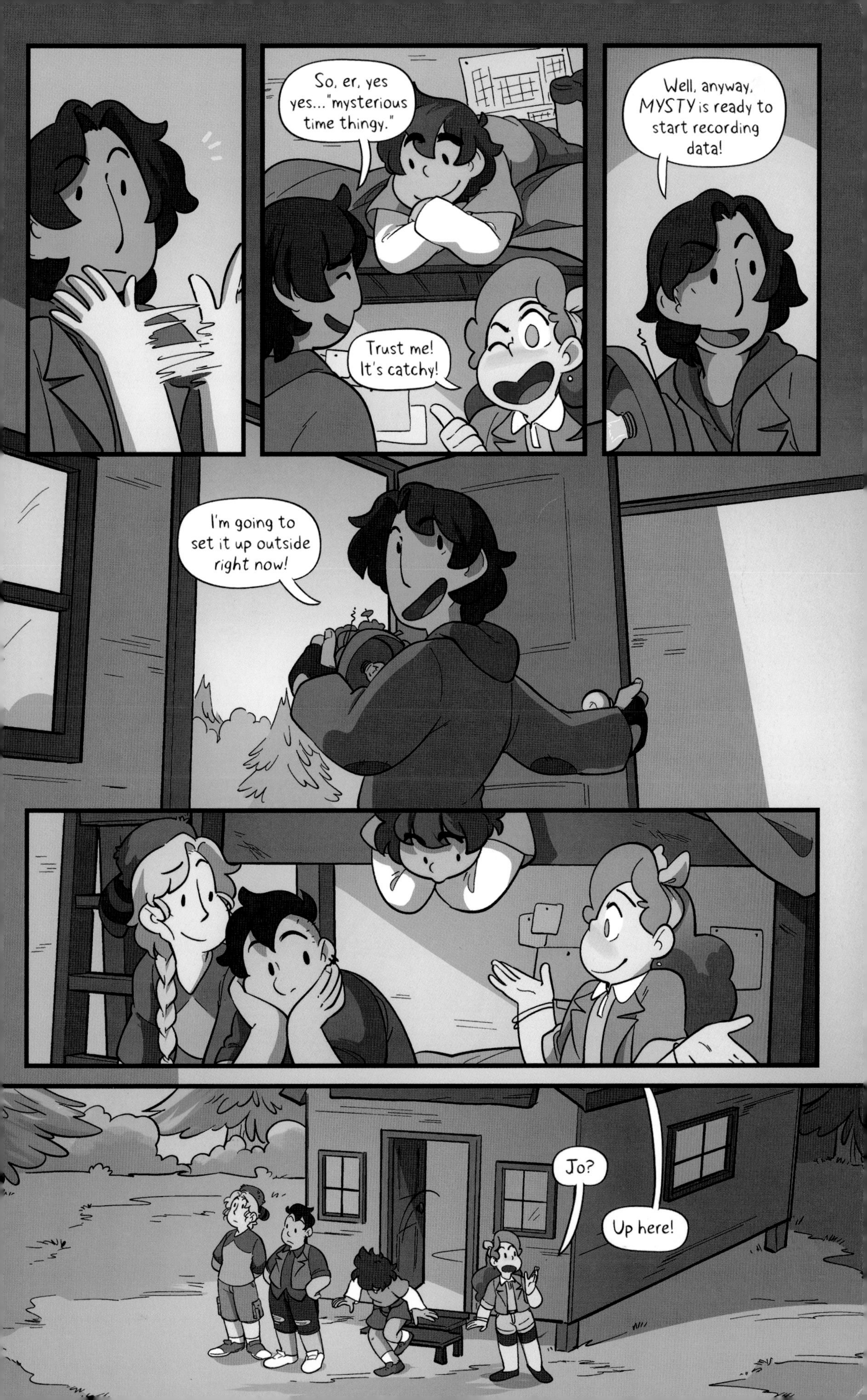
So, er, yes yes... "mysterious time thingy."
Trust me! It's catchy!
Well, anyway, MYSTY is ready to start recording data!
I'm going to set it up outside right now!
Jo?
Up here!

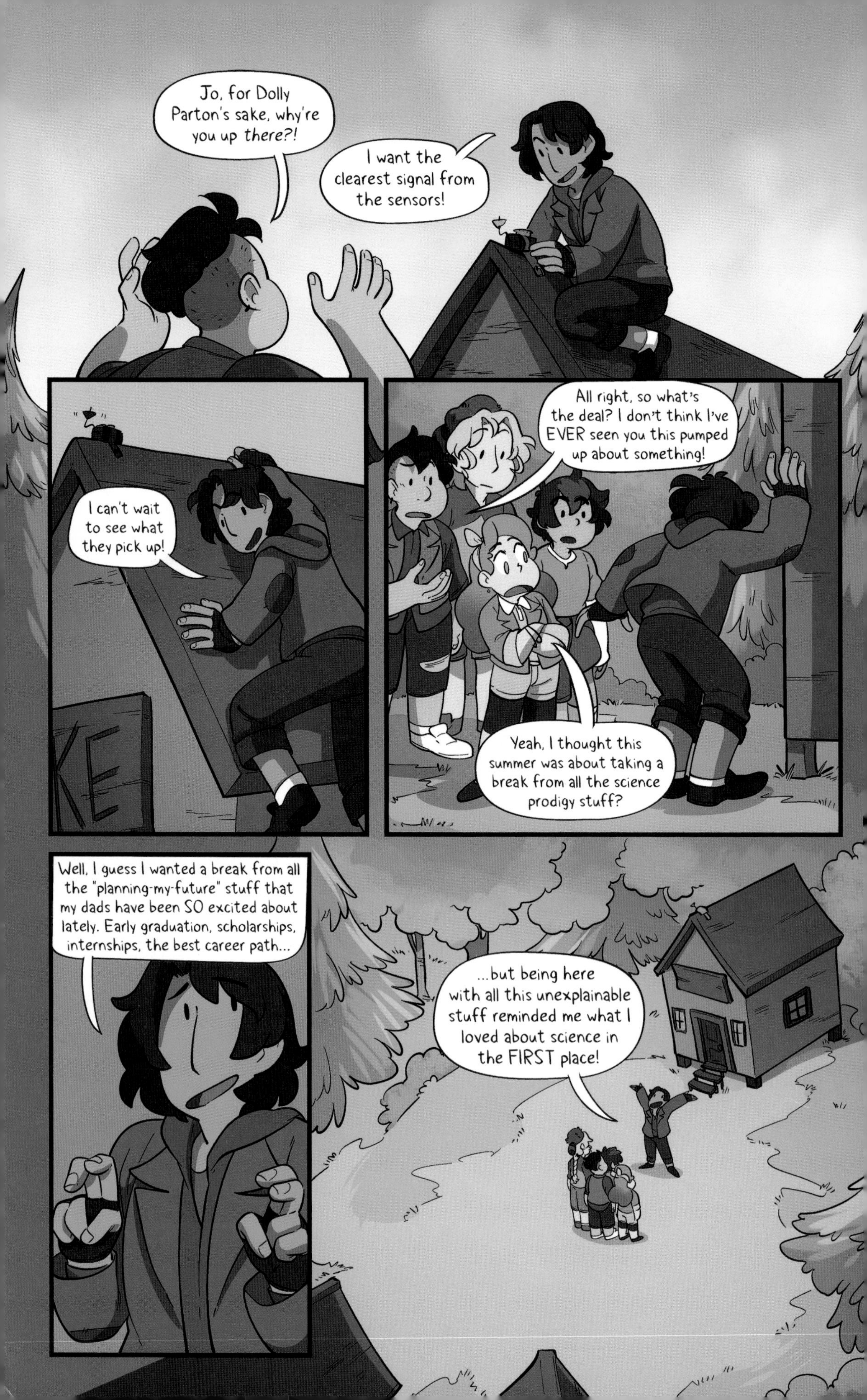
Jo, for Dolly Parton's sake, why're you up there?!
I want the clearest signal from the sensors!
I can't wait to see what they pick up!
All right, so what's the deal? I don't think I've EVER seen you this pumped up about something!
Yeah, I thought this summer was about taking a break from all the science prodigy stuff?
Well, I guess I wanted a break from all the "planning-my-future" stuff that my dads have been SO excited about lately. Early graduation, scholarships, internships, the best career path...
...but being here with all this unexplainable stuff reminded me what I loved about science in the FIRST place!

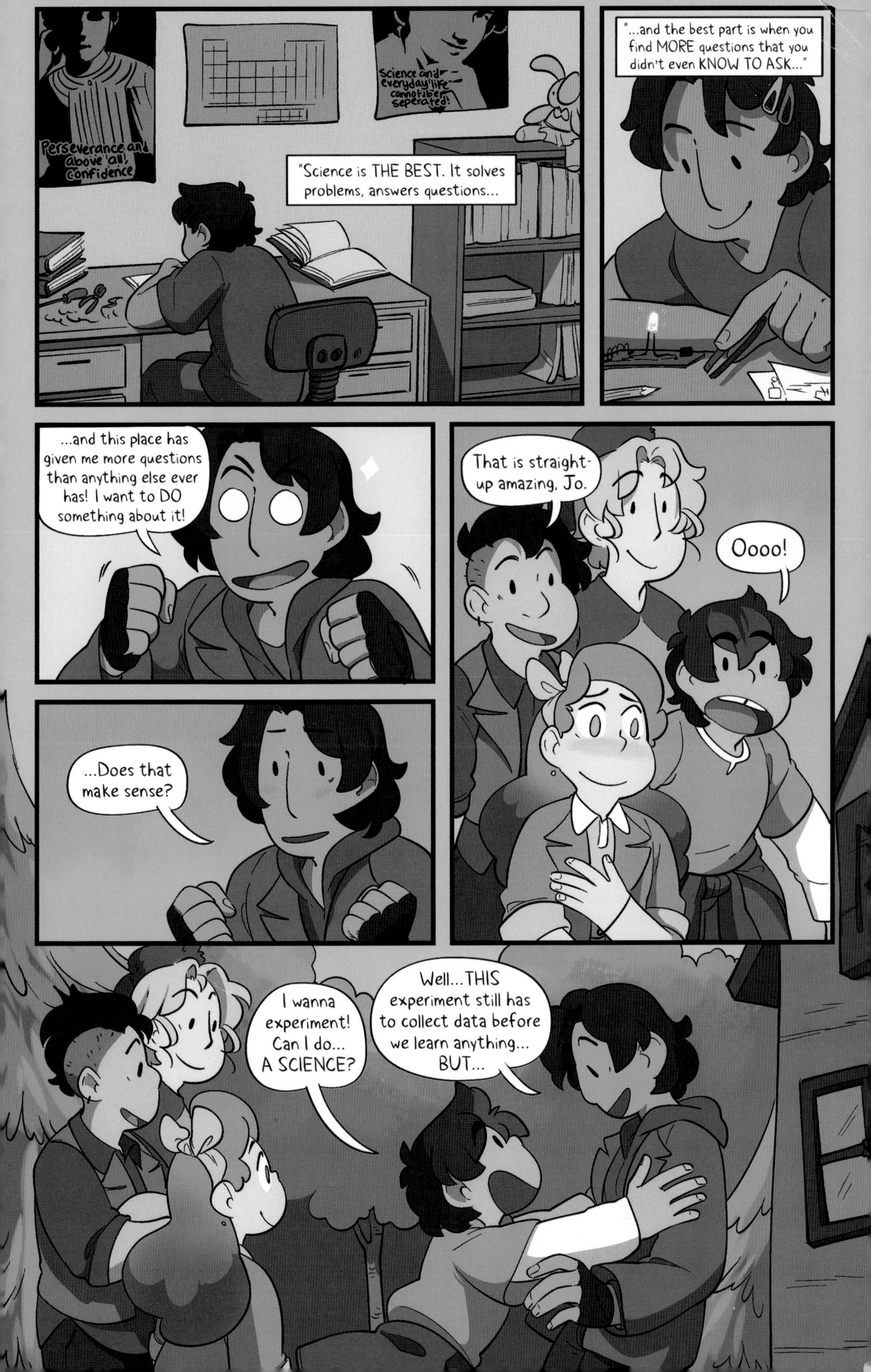
Perseverance and above 'all', confidence
Science and everyday life cannot be seperated!
"Science is THE BEST. It solves problems, answers questions...
"...and the best part is when you find MORE questions that you didn't even KNOW TO ASK..."
...and this place has given me more questions than anything else ever has! I want to DO something about it!
...Does that make sense?
That is straight-up amazing, Jo.
Oooo!
I wanna experiment! Can I do... A SCIENCE?
Well... THIS experiment still has to collect data before we learn anything... BUT...

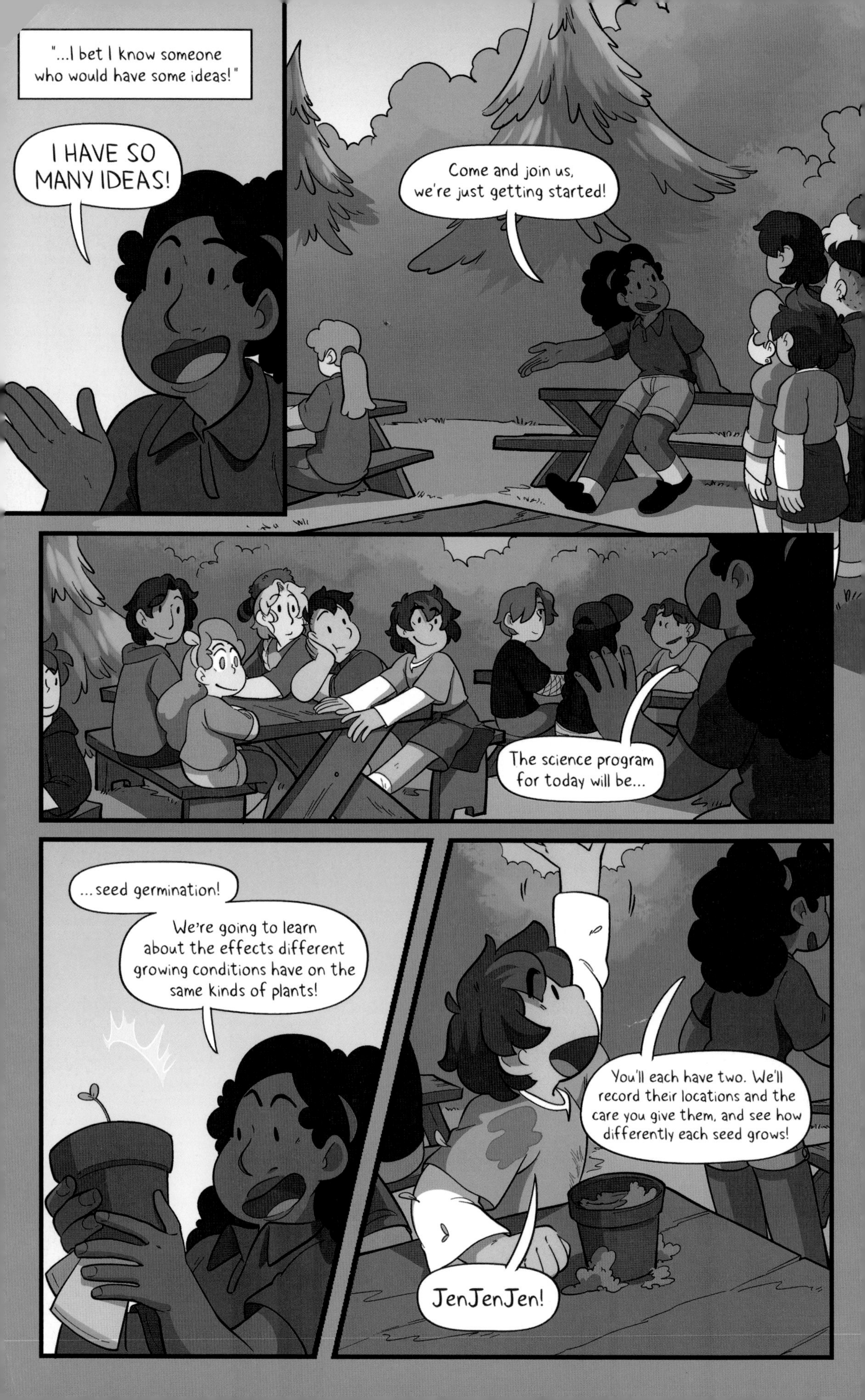
"...I bet I know someone who would have some ideas!"
I HAVE SO MANY IDEAS!
Come and join us, we're just getting started!
The science program for today will be...
...seed germination!
We're going to learn about the effects different growing conditions have on the same kinds of plants!
JenJenJen!
You'll each have two. We'll record their locations and the care you give them, and see how differently each seed grows!

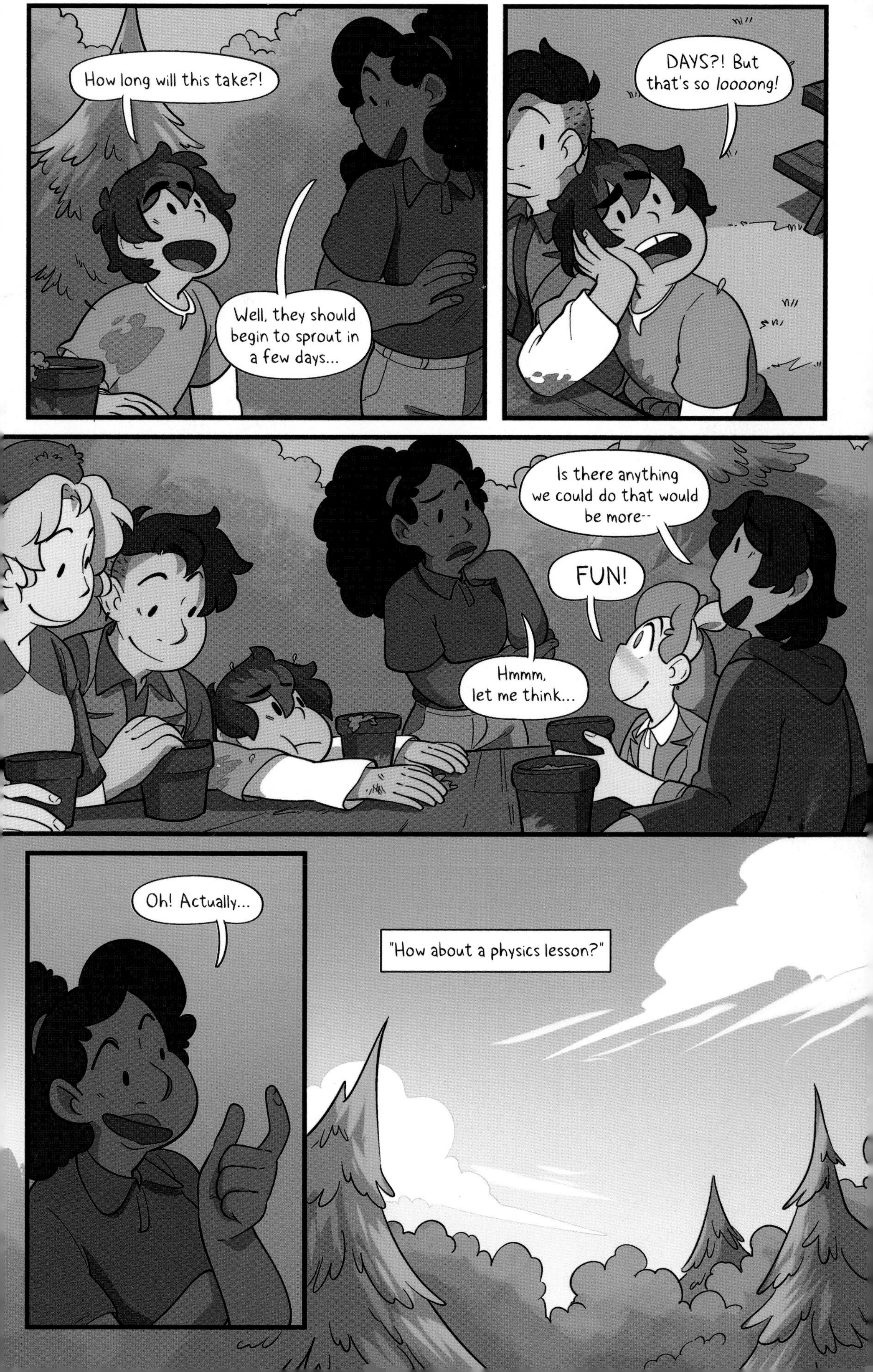
How long will this take?!
Well, they should begin to sprout in a few days...
DAYS?! But that's so *loooong*!
Is there anything we could do that would be more--
FUN!
Hmmm, let me think...
Oh! Actually...
"How about a physics lesson?"

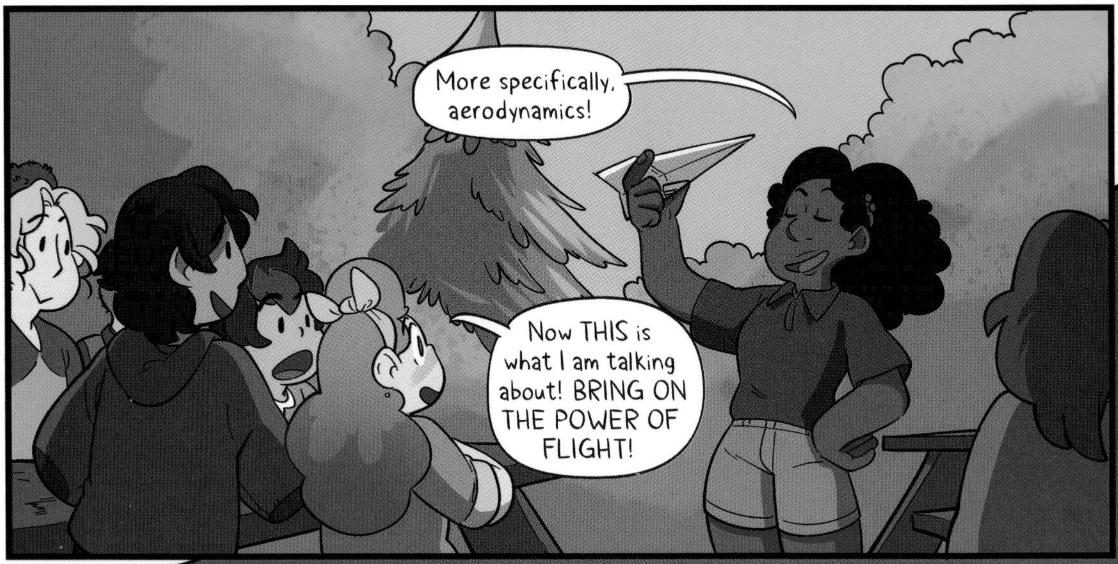
More specifically, aerodynamics!
Now THIS is what I am talking about! BRING ON THE POWER OF FLIGHT!

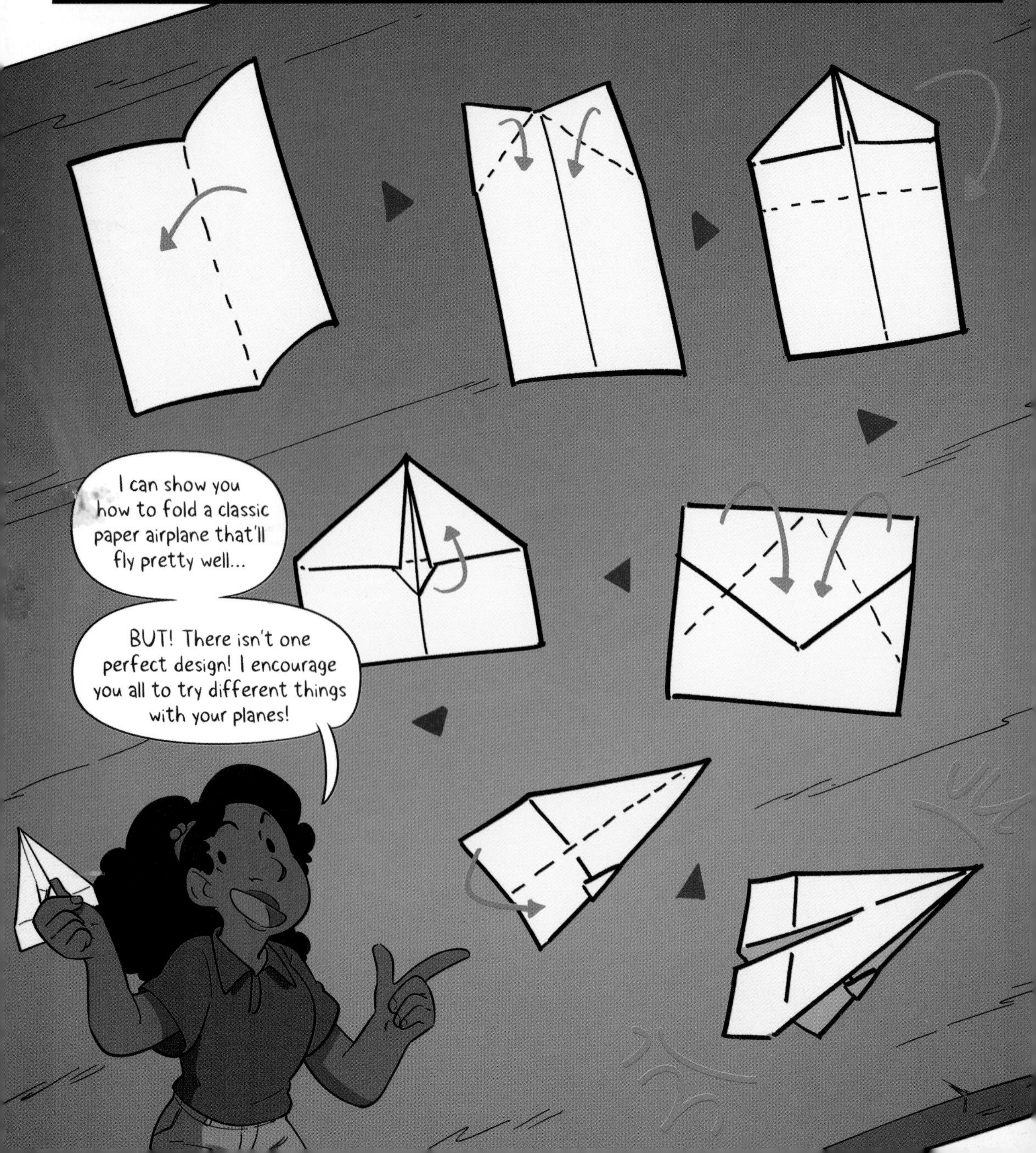
I can show you how to fold a classic paper airplane that'll fly pretty well...
BUT! There isn't one perfect design! I encourage you all to try different things with your planes!

Prepare to be CRUSHED!

I have spent EVERY study hall in the history of my EVER perfecting the PERFECT paper airplane!

You guys'll see, it's ALL about the paper quality and balance!

BWAHAHA!

Let's do this!

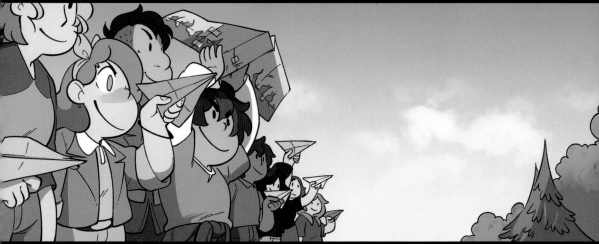

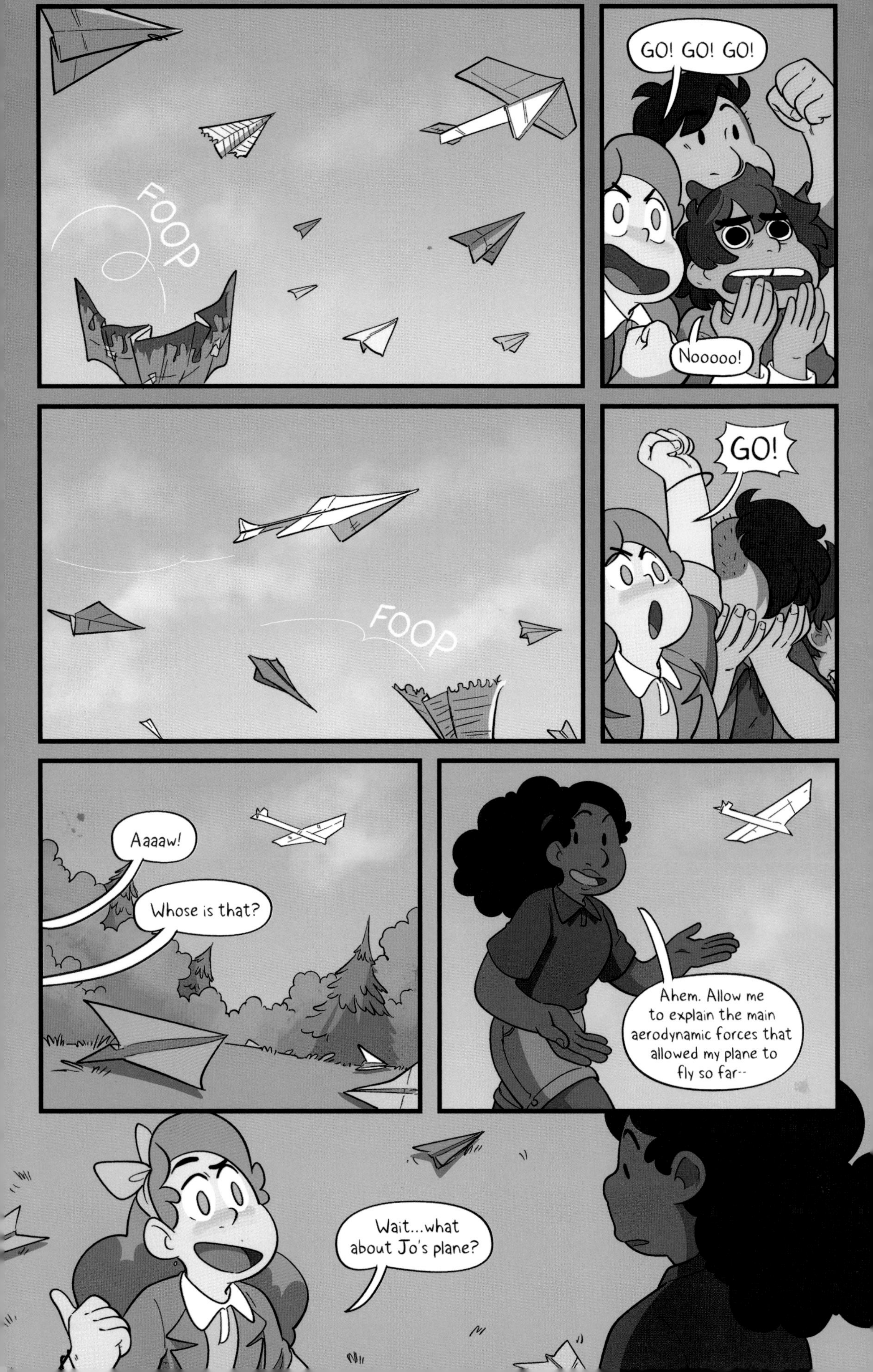
FOOP
GO! GO! GO!
Nooooo!
GO!
FOOP
Aaaaw!
Whose is that?
Ahem. Allow me to explain the main aerodynamic forces that allowed my plane to fly so far--
Wait...what about Jo's plane?

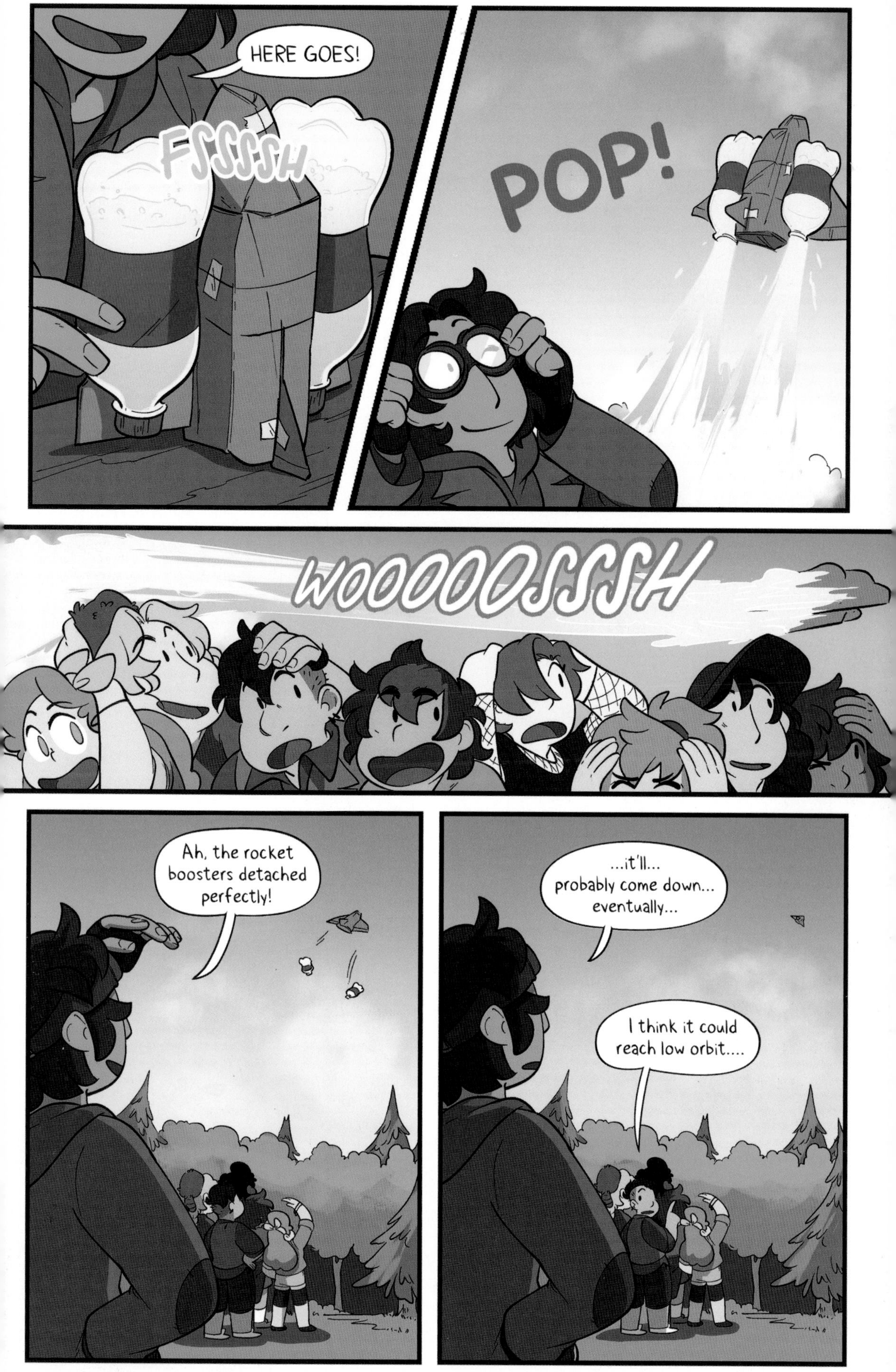
HERE GOES!
FSSSSH
POP!
WOOOOOSSSH
Ah, the rocket boosters detached perfectly!
...it'll... probably come down... eventually...
I think it could reach low orbit....

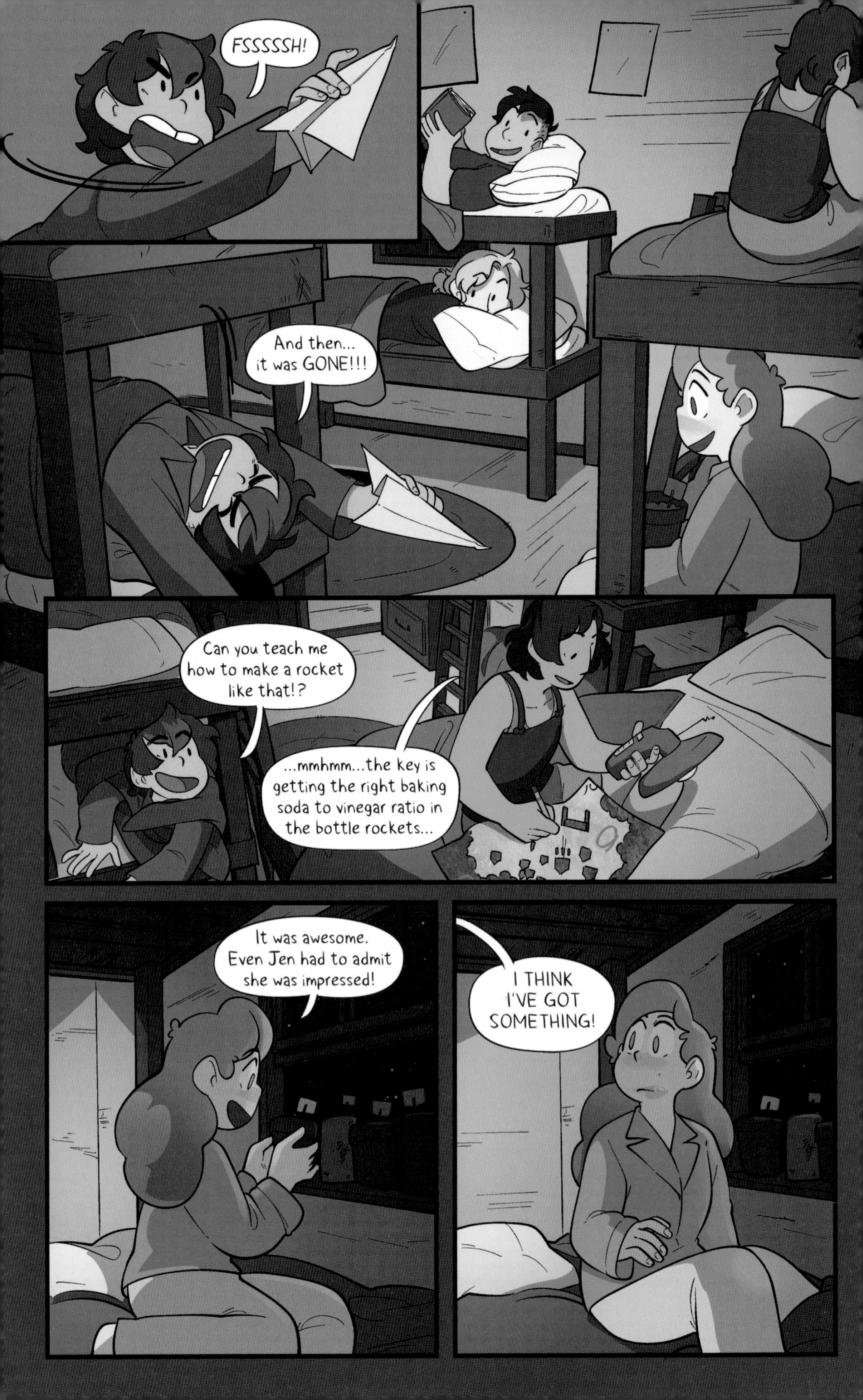
FSSSSSH!
And then... it was GONE!!!
Can you teach me how to make a rocket like that!?
...mmhmm...the key is getting the right baking soda to vinegar ratio in the bottle rockets...
It was awesome. Even Jen had to admit she was impressed!
I THINK I'VE GOT SOMETHING!

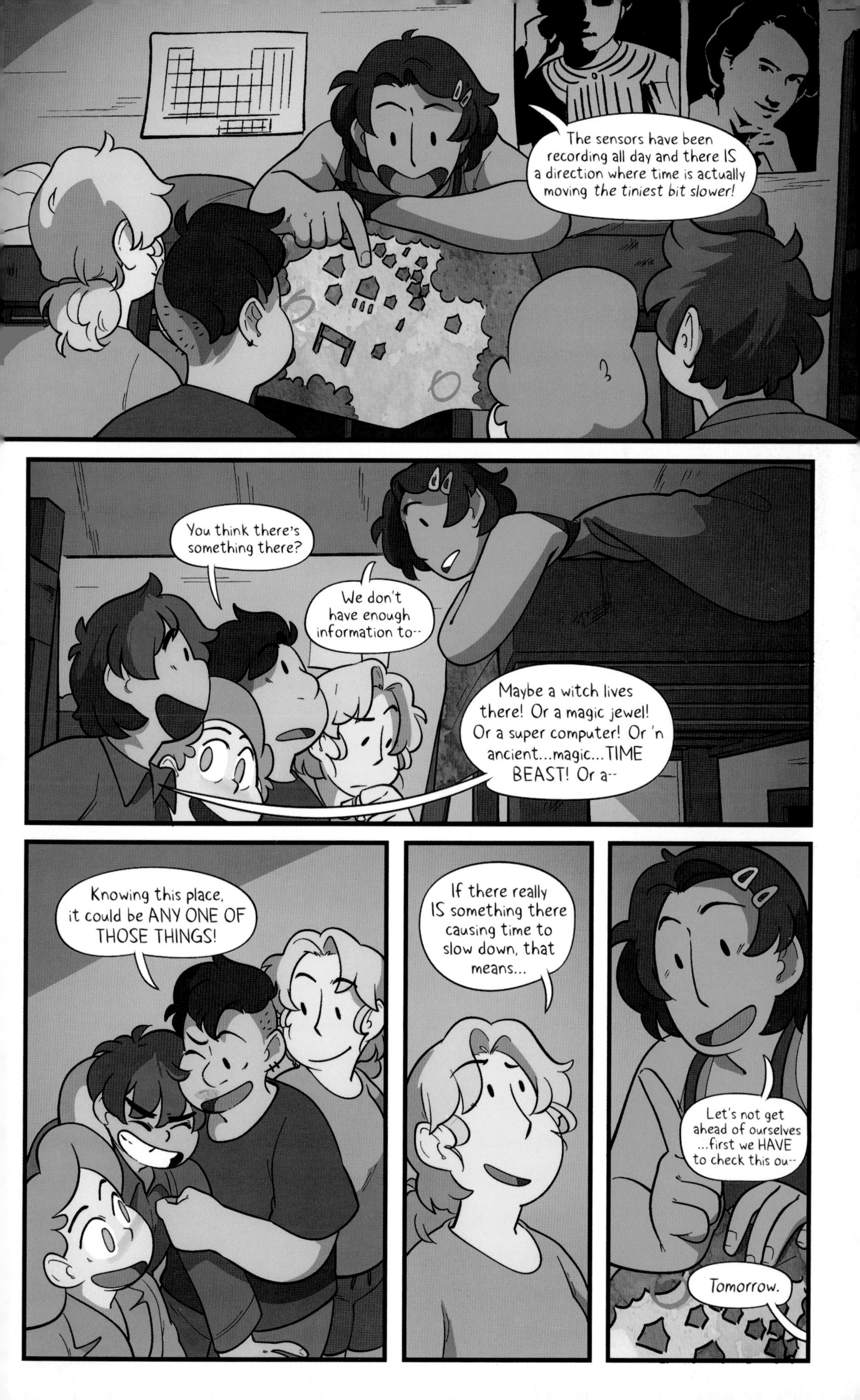
The sensors have been recording all day and there IS a direction where time is actually moving *the tiniest bit slower!*
You think there's something there?
We don't have enough information to--
Maybe a witch lives there! Or a magic jewel! Or a super computer! Or 'n ancient...magic...TIME BEAST! Or a--
Knowing this place, it could be ANY ONE OF THOSE THINGS!
If there really IS something there causing time to slow down, that means...
Let's not get ahead of ourselves ...first we HAVE to check this ou--
Tomorrow.

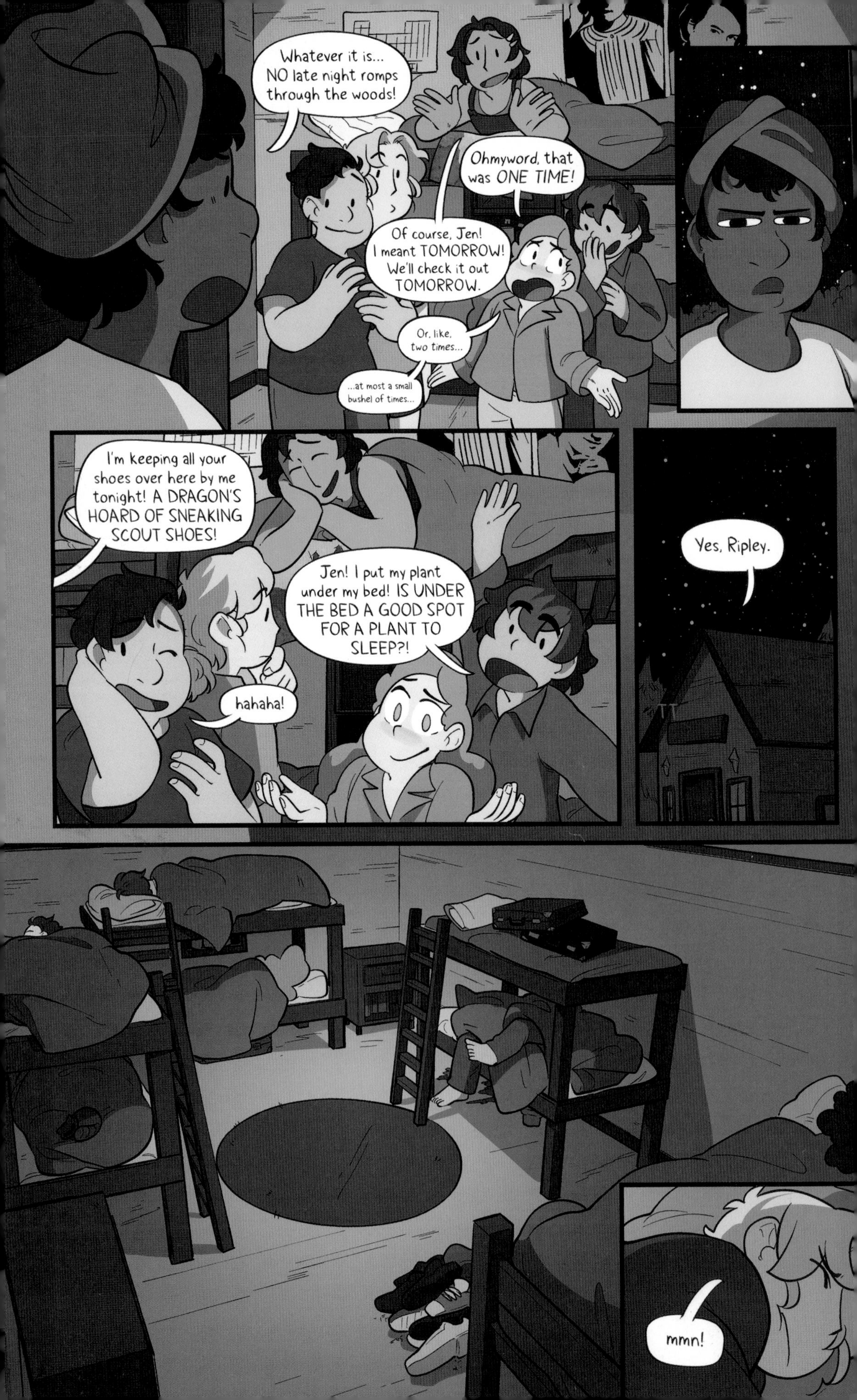
Whatever it is...
NO late night romps through the woods!
Ohmyword, that was ONE TIME!
Of course, Jen! I meant TOMORROW! We'll check it out TOMORROW.
Or, like, two times...
...at most a small bushel of times...
I'm keeping all your shoes over here by me tonight! A DRAGON'S HOARD OF SNEAKING SCOUT SHOES!
Jen! I put my plant under my bed! IS UNDER THE BED A GOOD SPOT FOR A PLANT TO SLEEP?!
hahaha!
Yes, Ripley.
mmn!

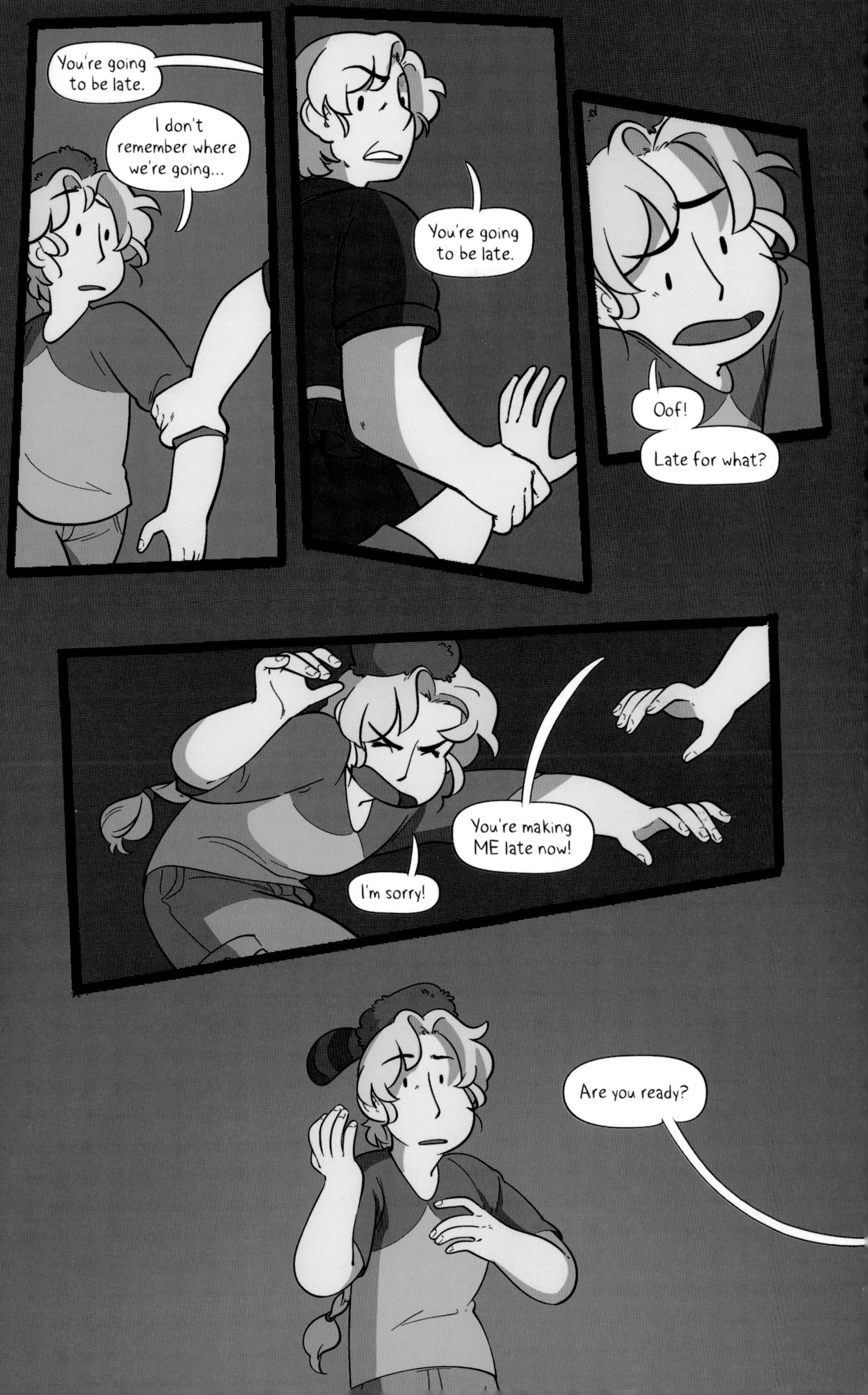
You're going to be late.
I don't remember where we're going...
You're going to be late.
Oof!
Late for what?
You're making ME late now!
I'm sorry!
Are you ready?

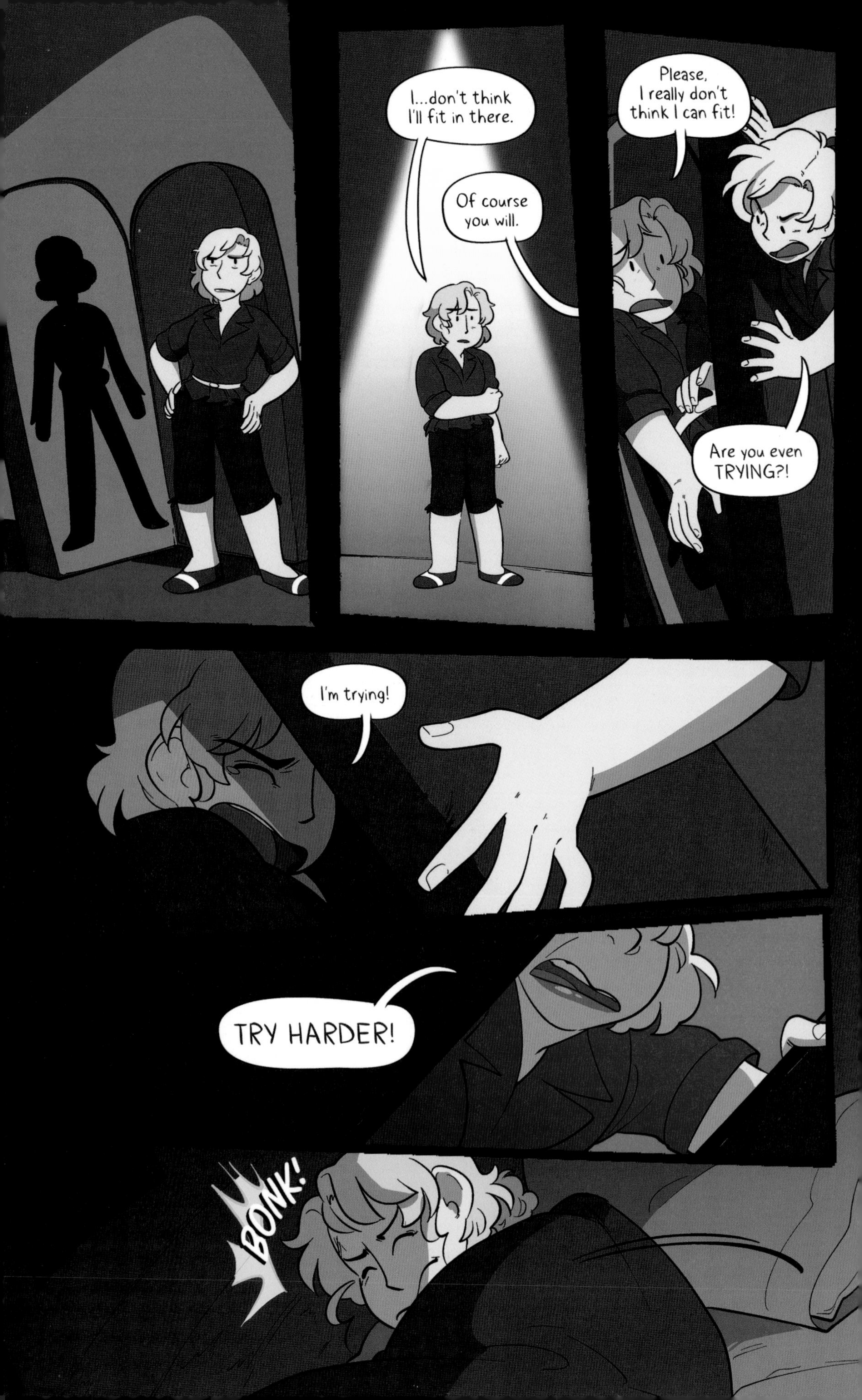
I...don't think I'll fit in there.
Of course you will.
Please, I really don't think I can fit!
Are you even TRYING?!
I'm trying!
TRY HARDER!
BONK!

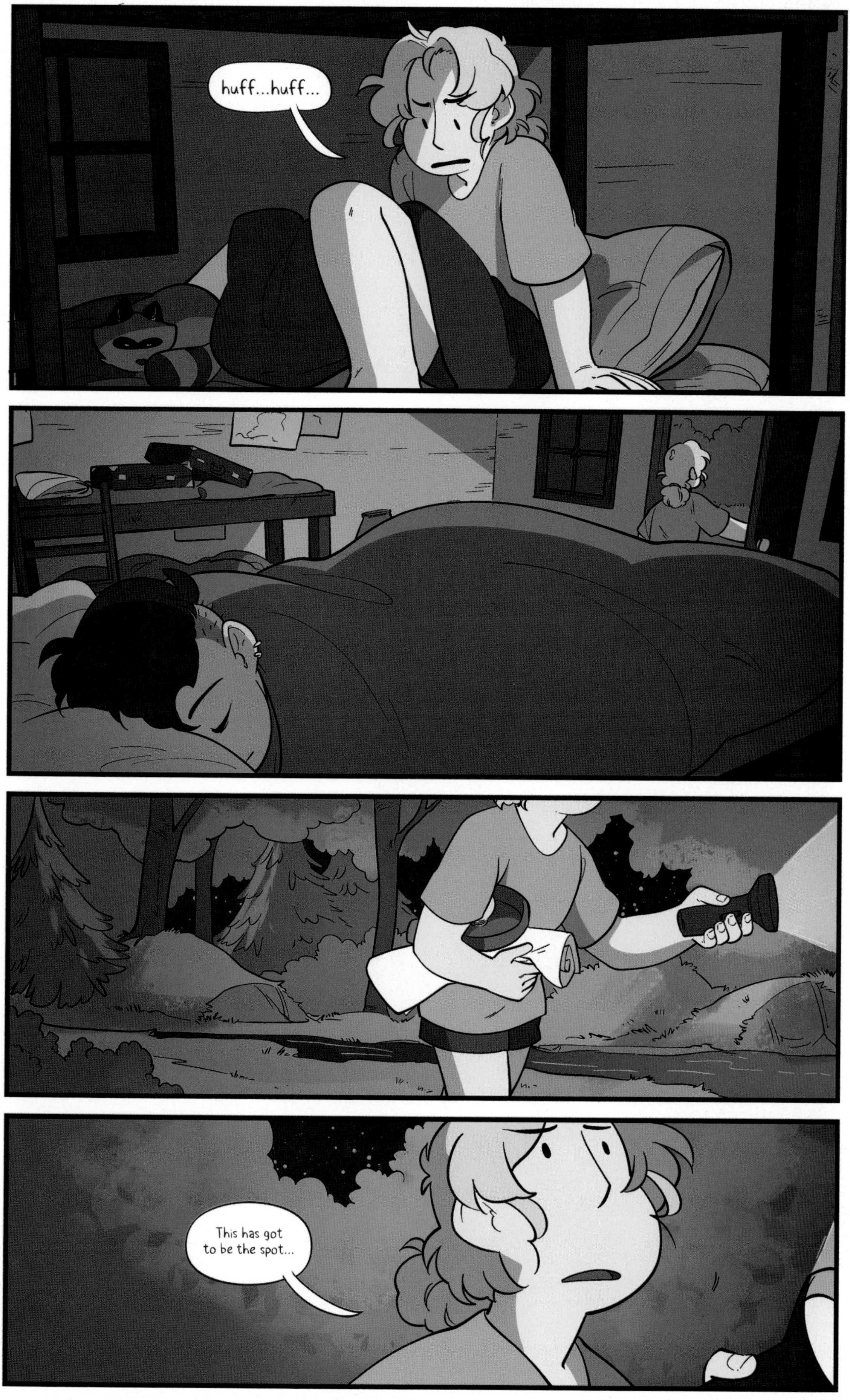
huff...huff...
This has got to be the spot...

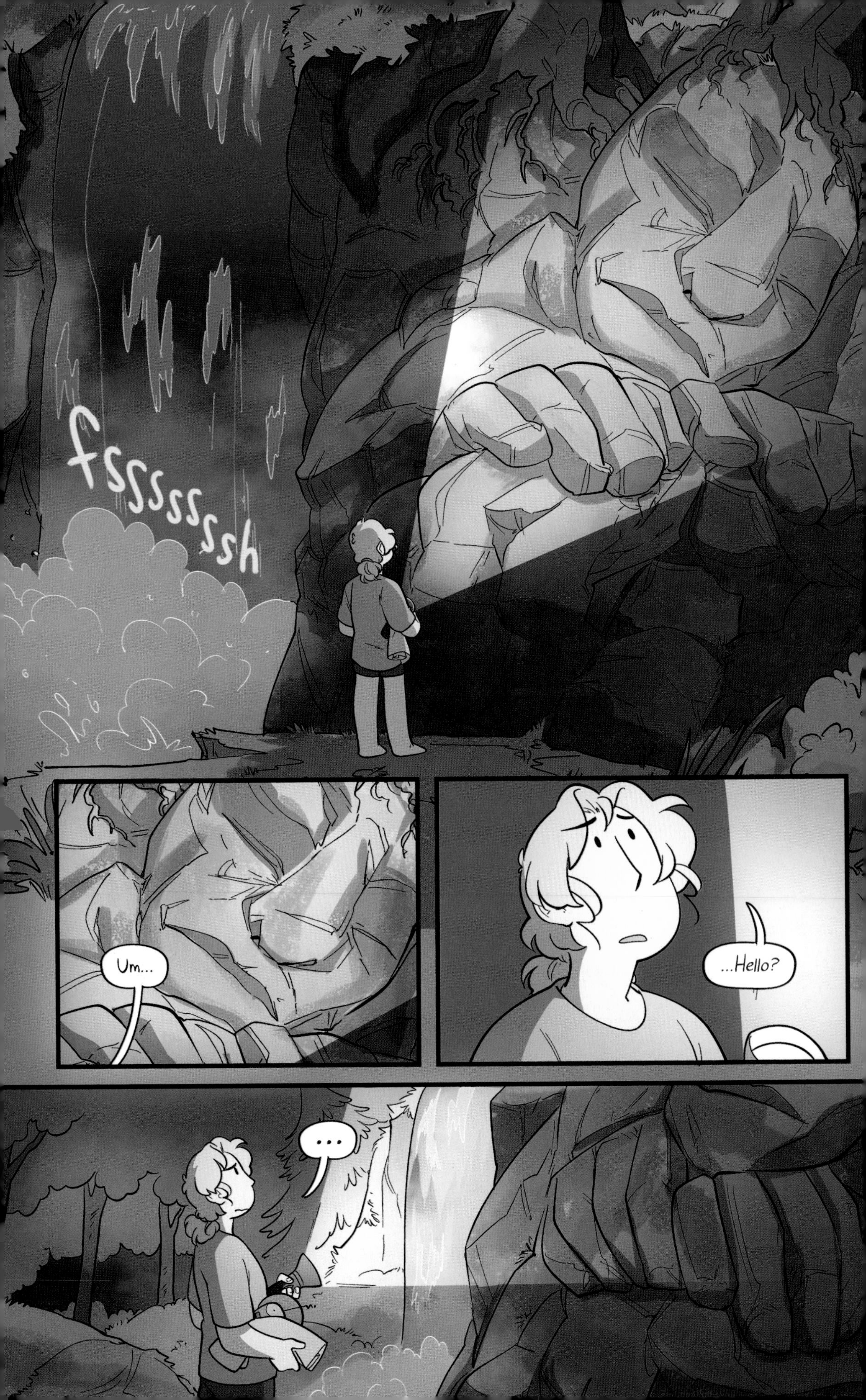
fsssssssh
Um...
...Hello?
...

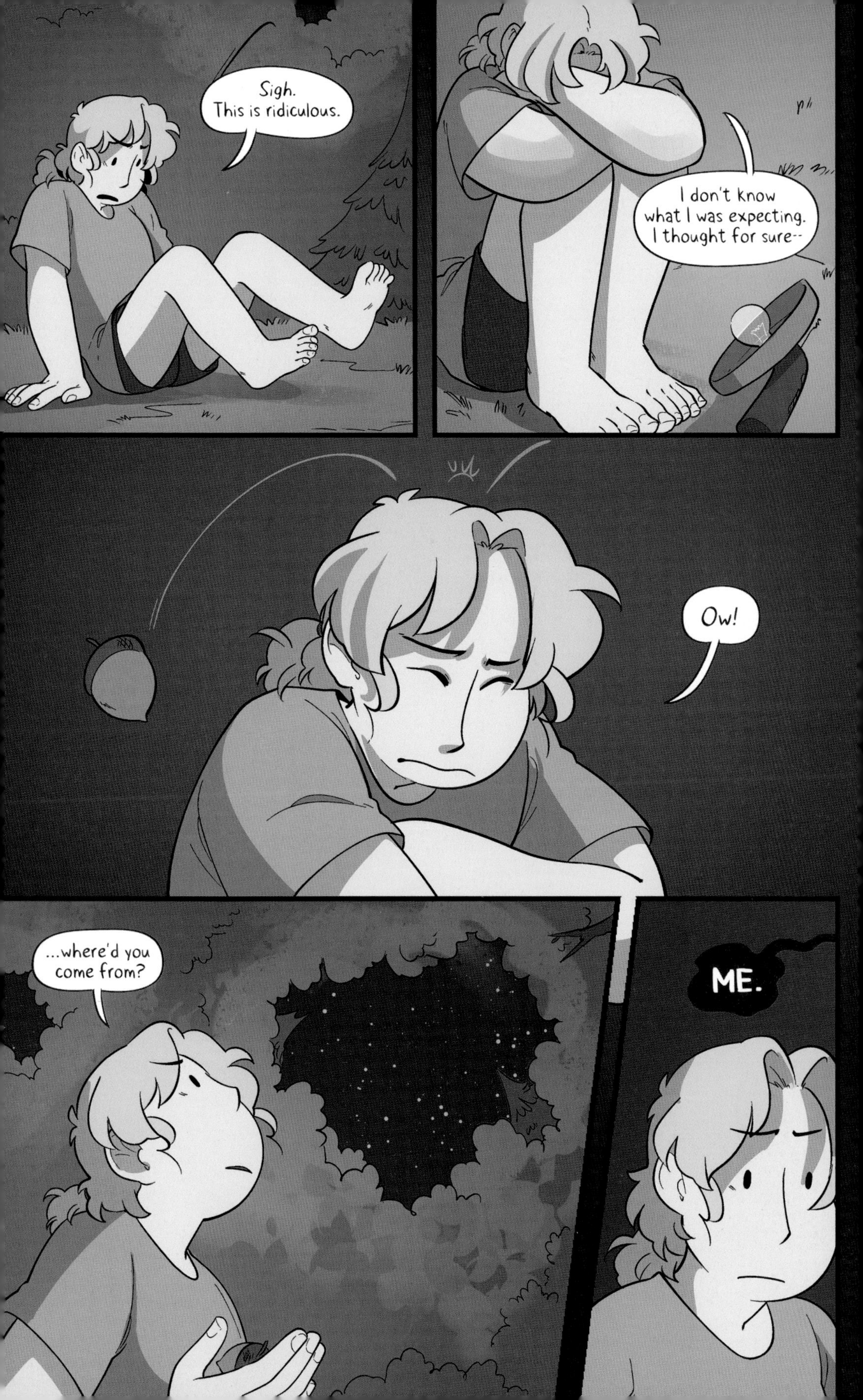
Sigh.
This is ridiculous.
I don't know what I was expecting. I thought for sure--
Ow!
...where'd you come from?
ME.

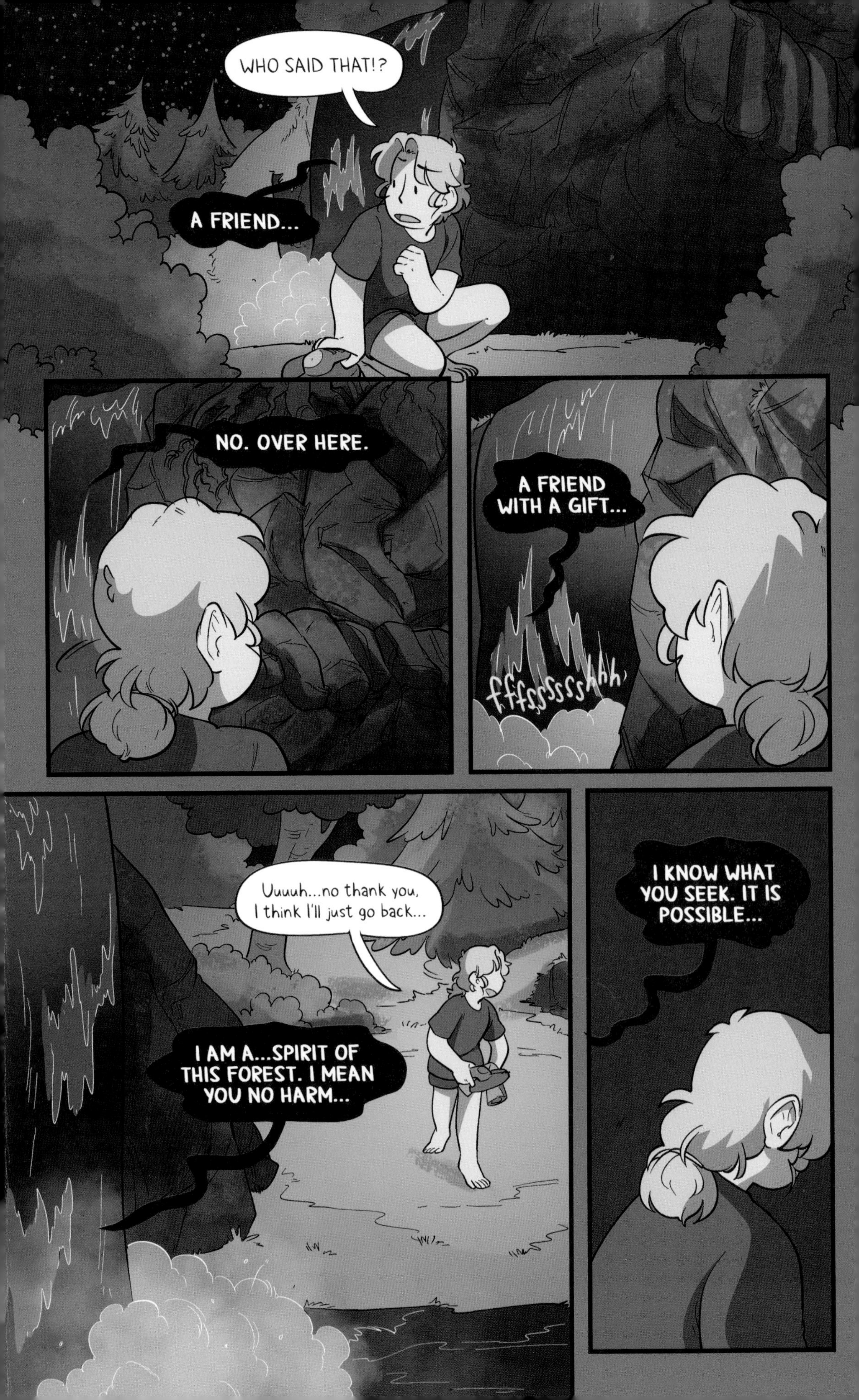
WHO SAID THAT!?
A FRIEND...
NO. OVER HERE.
A FRIEND WITH A GIFT...
ffffsssssshhh
Uuuuh...no thank you, I think I'll just go back...
I AM A...SPIRIT OF THIS FOREST. I MEAN YOU NO HARM...
I KNOW WHAT YOU SEEK. IT IS POSSIBLE...

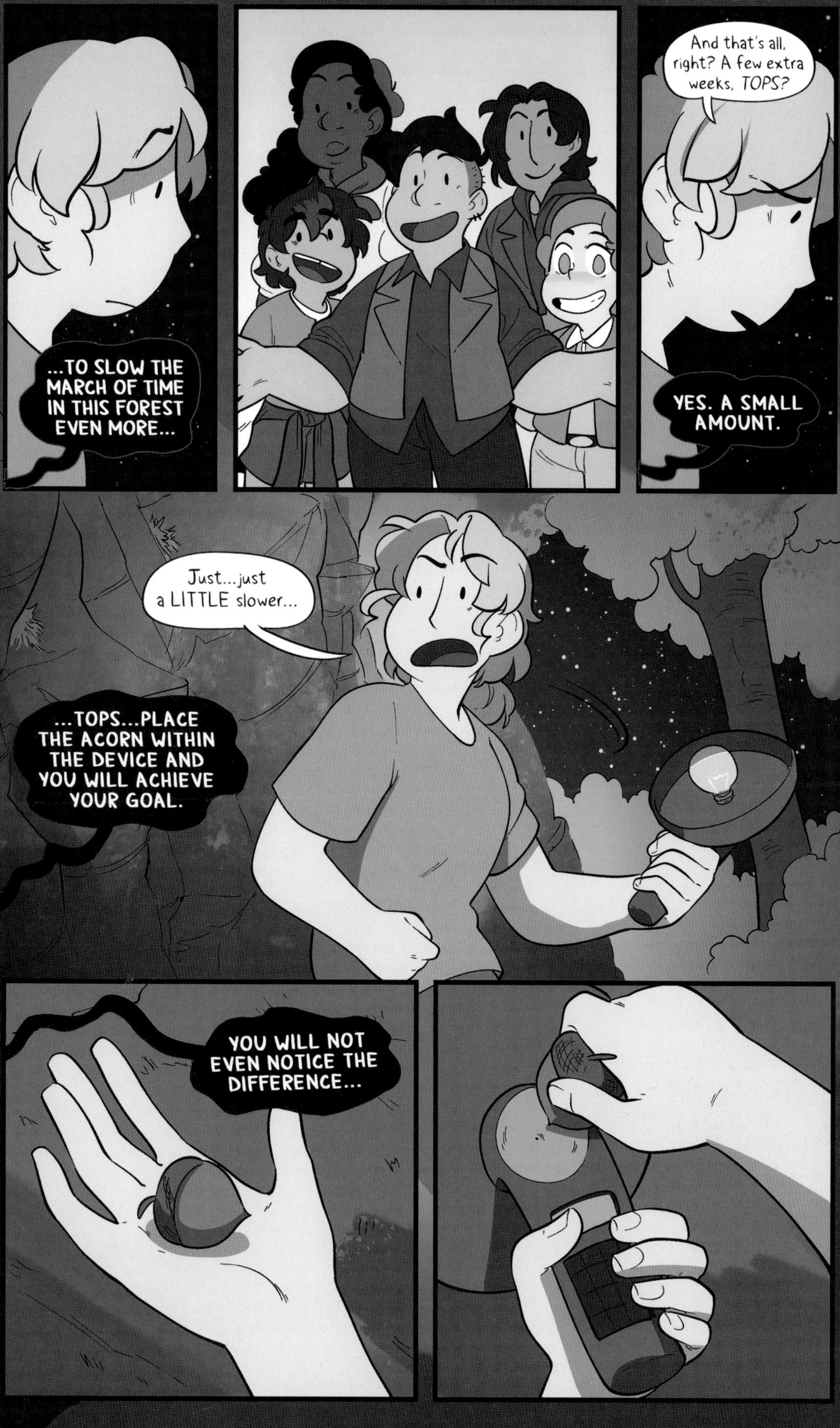
...TO SLOW THE MARCH OF TIME IN THIS FOREST EVEN MORE...
And that's all, right? A few extra weeks, TOPS?
YES. A SMALL AMOUNT.
Just...just a LITTLE slower...
...TOPS...PLACE THE ACORN WITHIN THE DEVICE AND YOU WILL ACHIEVE YOUR GOAL.
YOU WILL NOT EVEN NOTICE THE DIFFERENCE...

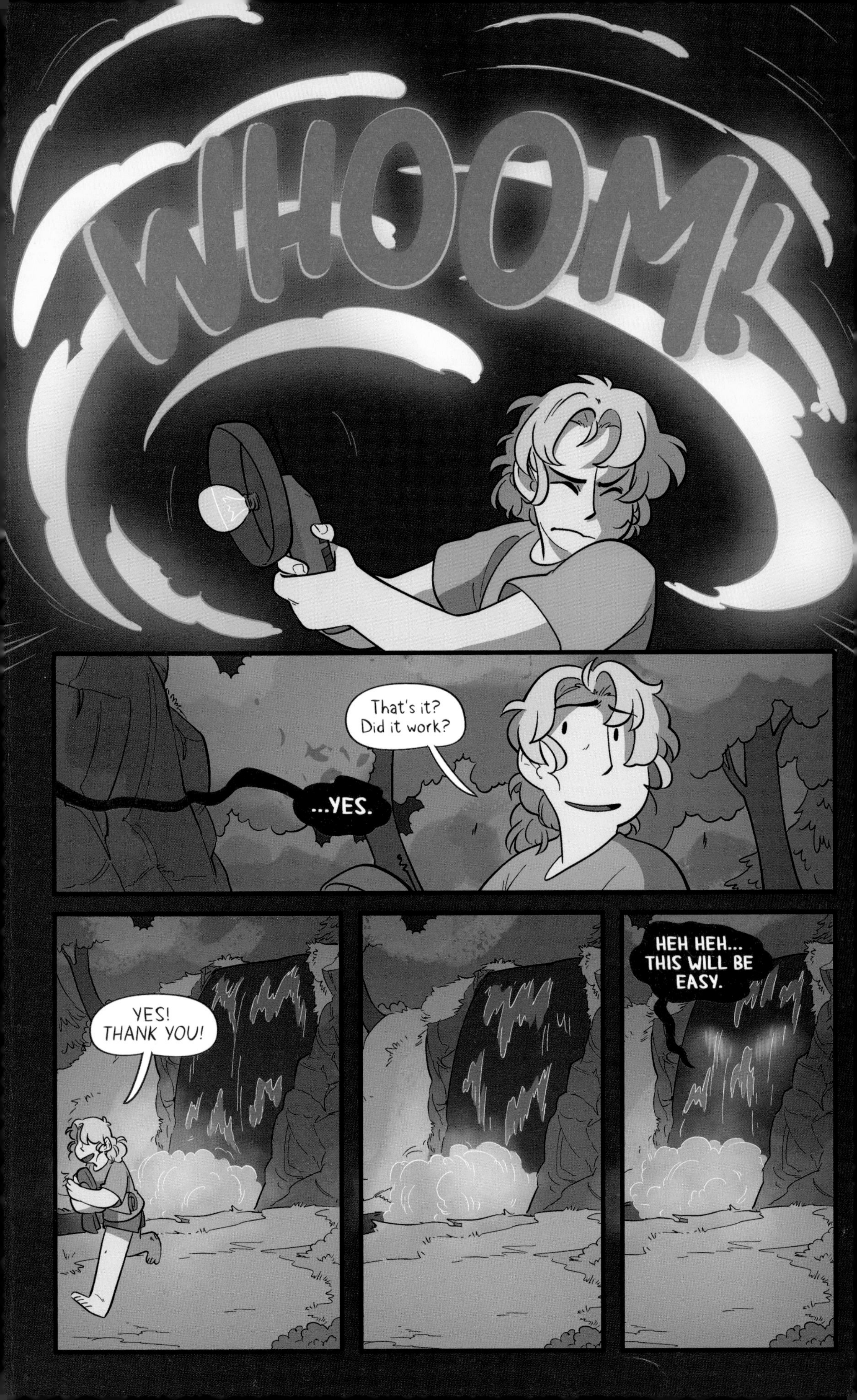
WHOOM!
That's it? Did it work?
...YES.
YES! THANK YOU!
HEH HEH... THIS WILL BE EASY.

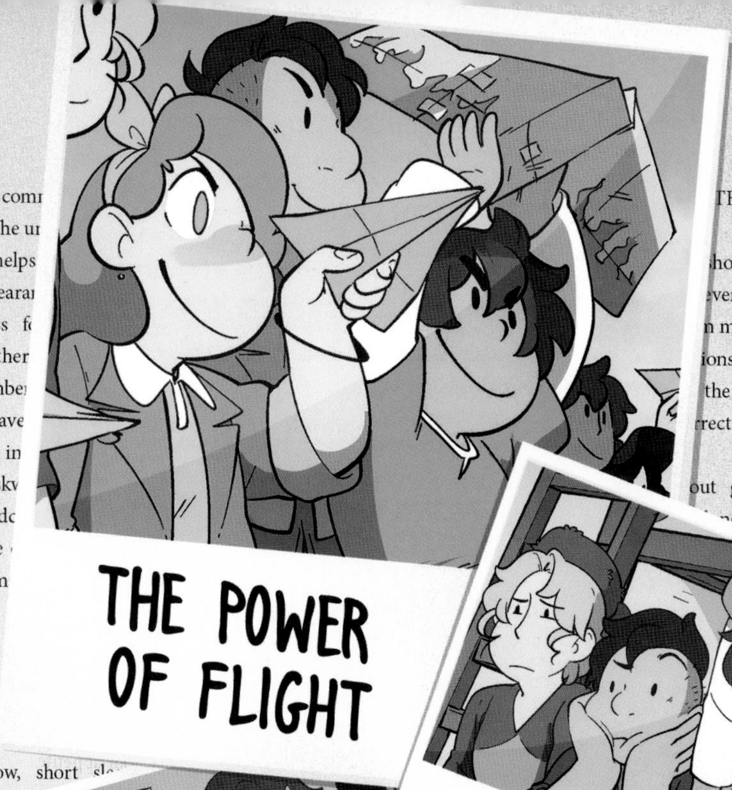
THE POWER OF FLIGHT

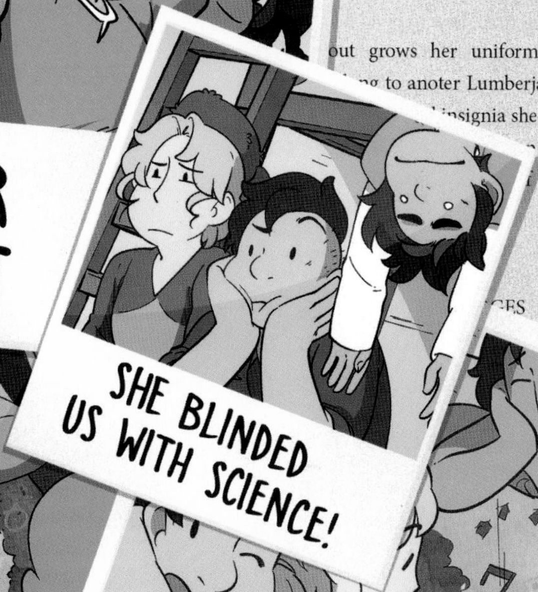
SHE BLINDED US WITH SCIENCE!

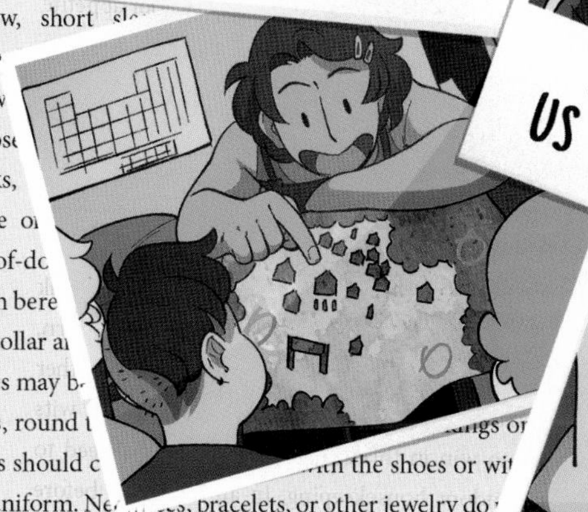

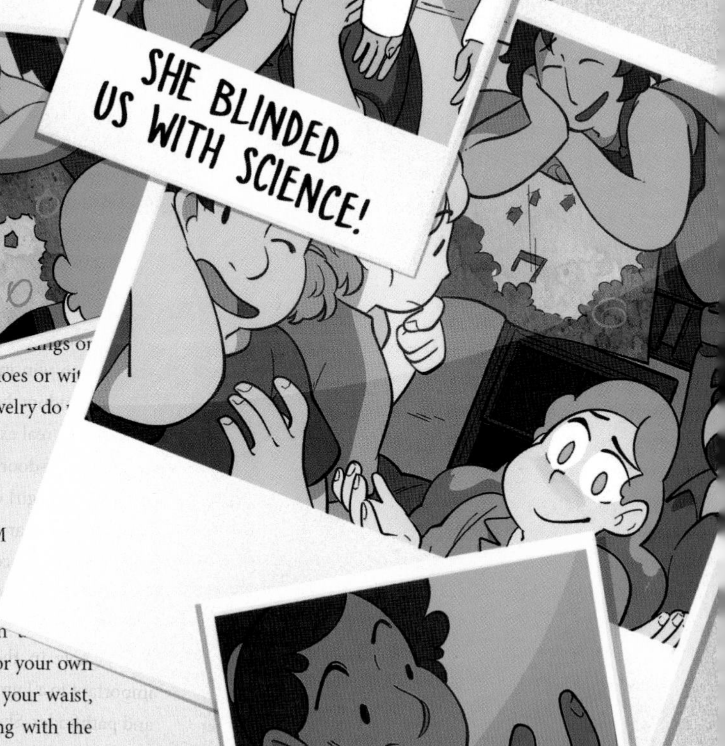

will comm
The un
It helps
appearan
dress fo
Further
Lumbe
to have
part in
Thiskv
Hardc
have
them

THE UNIFORM

hould be worn at camp
events when Lumberjanes
n may also be worn at other
ions. It should be worn as a
the uniform dress with
rrect shoes, and stocking or

out grows her uniform or
ng to anoter Lumberjane.
insignia she has
her
her

GES

The
yellow, short sl
emb
the w
choose
slacks,
made o
out-of-do
green bere
the collar a
Shoes may b
heels, round t
kings or
socks should c with the shoes or wi
the uniform. Ne ces, bracelets, or other jewelry do
belong with a Lumberjane uniform.

HOW TO WEAR THE UNIFORM

To look well in a uniform demands first of uniform be kept in good condition—clean pressed. See that the skirt is the right length for your own height and build, that the belt is adjusted to your waist, that your shoes and stockings are in keeping with the uniform, that you watch your posture and carry yourself with dignity and grace. If the beret is removed indoors, be sure that your hair is neat and kept in place with an insonspicuous clip or ribbon. When you wear a Lumberjane uniform you are identified as a member of this organization and you should be doubly careful to conduct yourself in a way that will show everyone that courtesy and thoughtfullness are part of being a Lumberjane. People are likely to judge a whole nation by the selfishness of a few individuals, to criticize a whole family because of the misconduct of one member, and to feel unkindly toward and organization because of the

The unifor
helps to cre
in a group.
active life th
another bond
future, and pr
in order to b
Lumberjane pr
Penniquiqul Thi ore Lady
Types, but most jones will wish to have one. They
can either buy the uniform, or make it themselves from
materials available at the trading post.

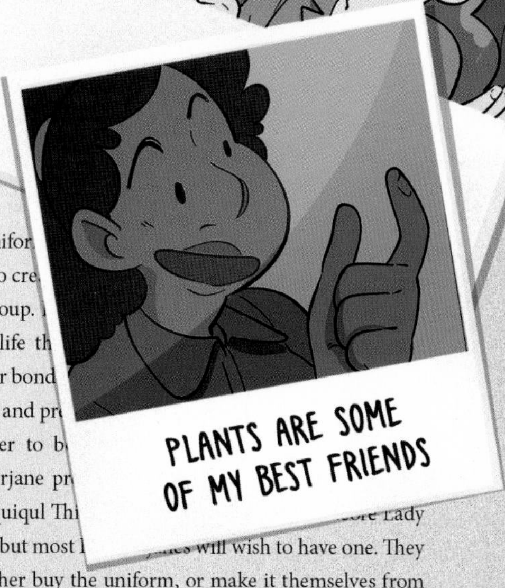
PLANTS ARE SOME OF MY BEST FRIENDS

LUMBERJANES FIELD MANUAL

CHAPTER
FORTY-TWO

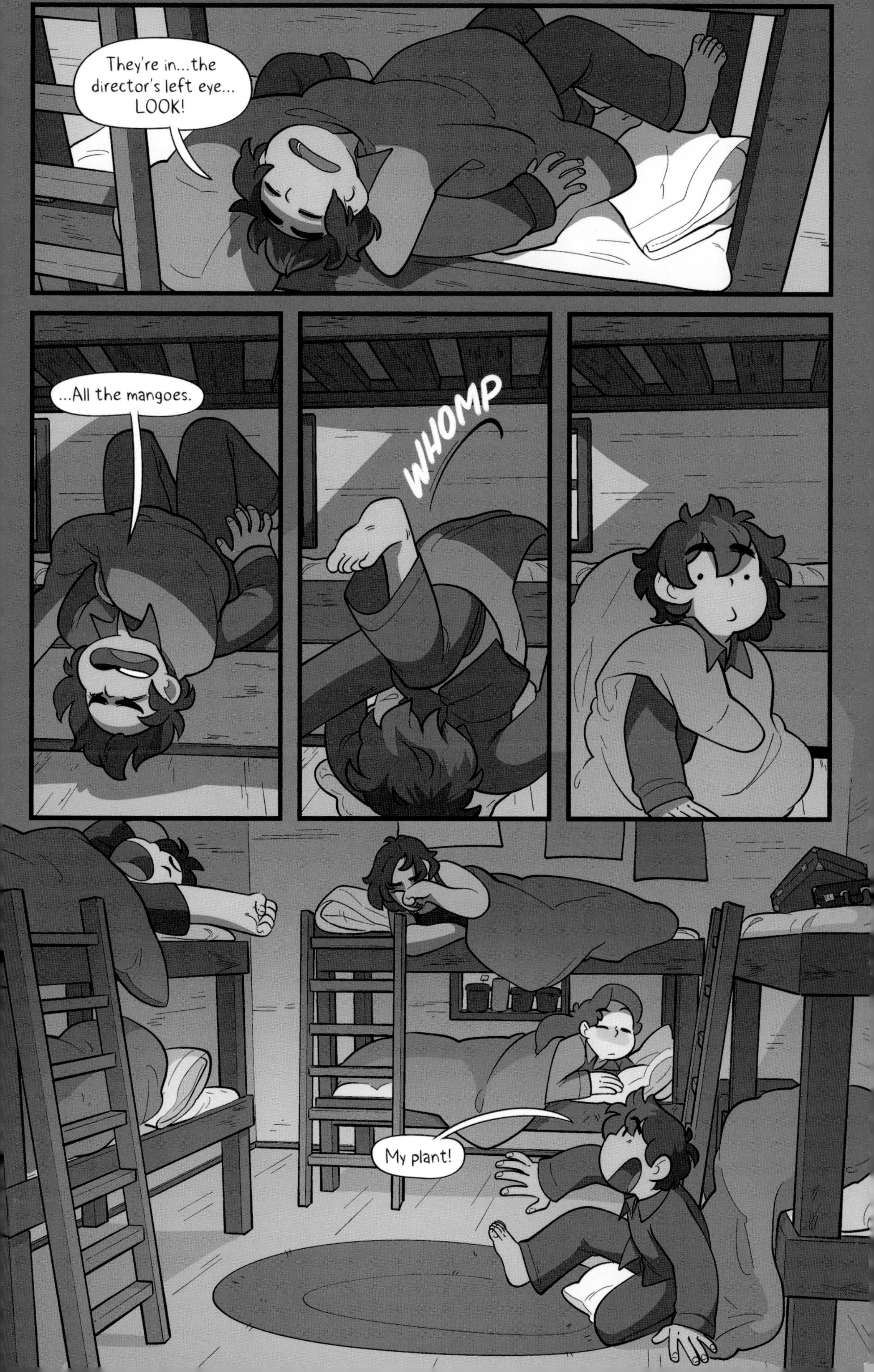
They're in...the director's left eye... LOOK!
...All the mangoes.
WHOMP
My plant!

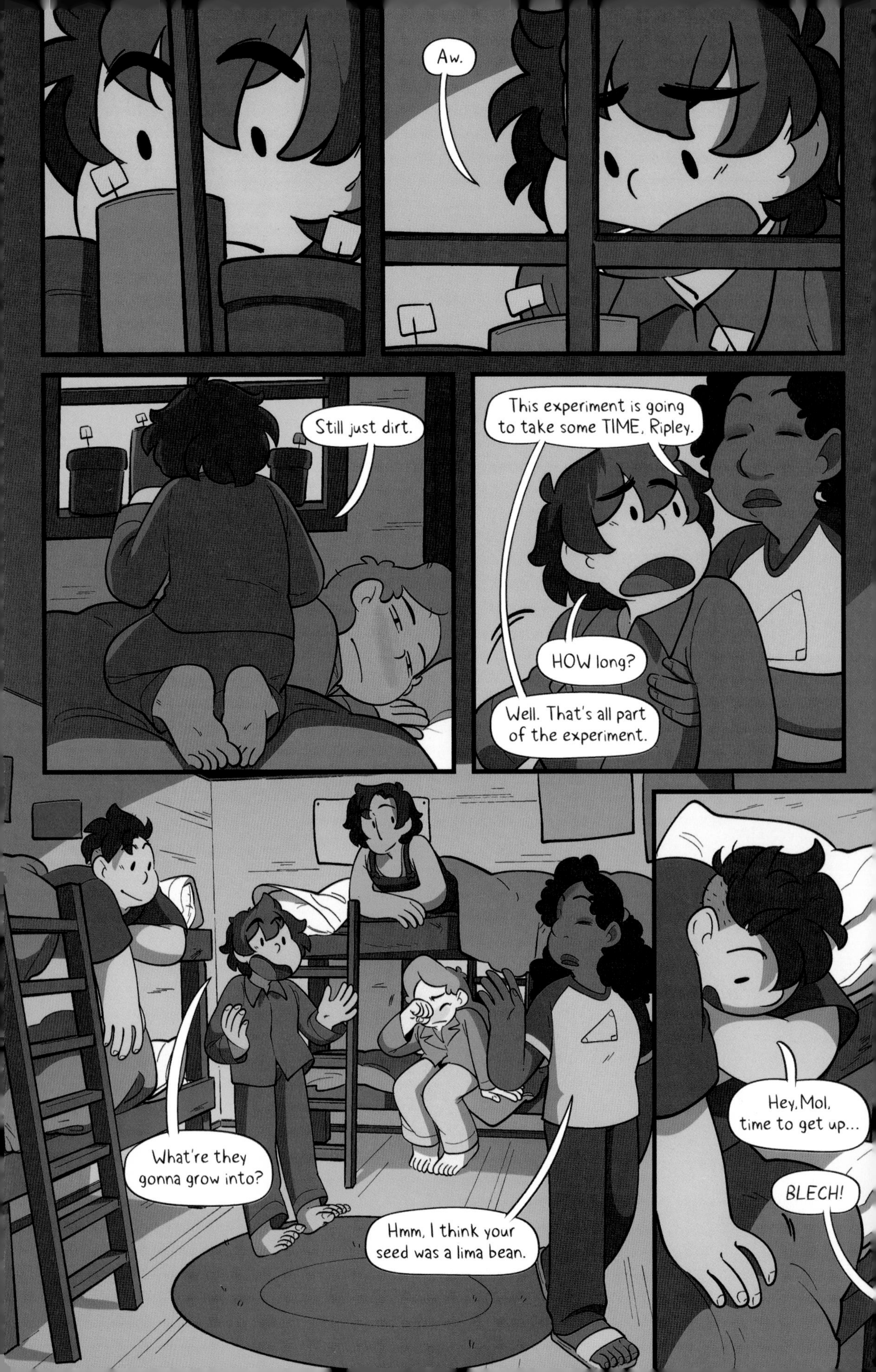
Aw.
Still just dirt.
This experiment is going to take some TIME, Ripley.
HOW long?
Well. That's all part of the experiment.
What're they gonna grow into?
Hmm, I think your seed was a lima bean.
Hey, Mol, time to get up...
BLECH!

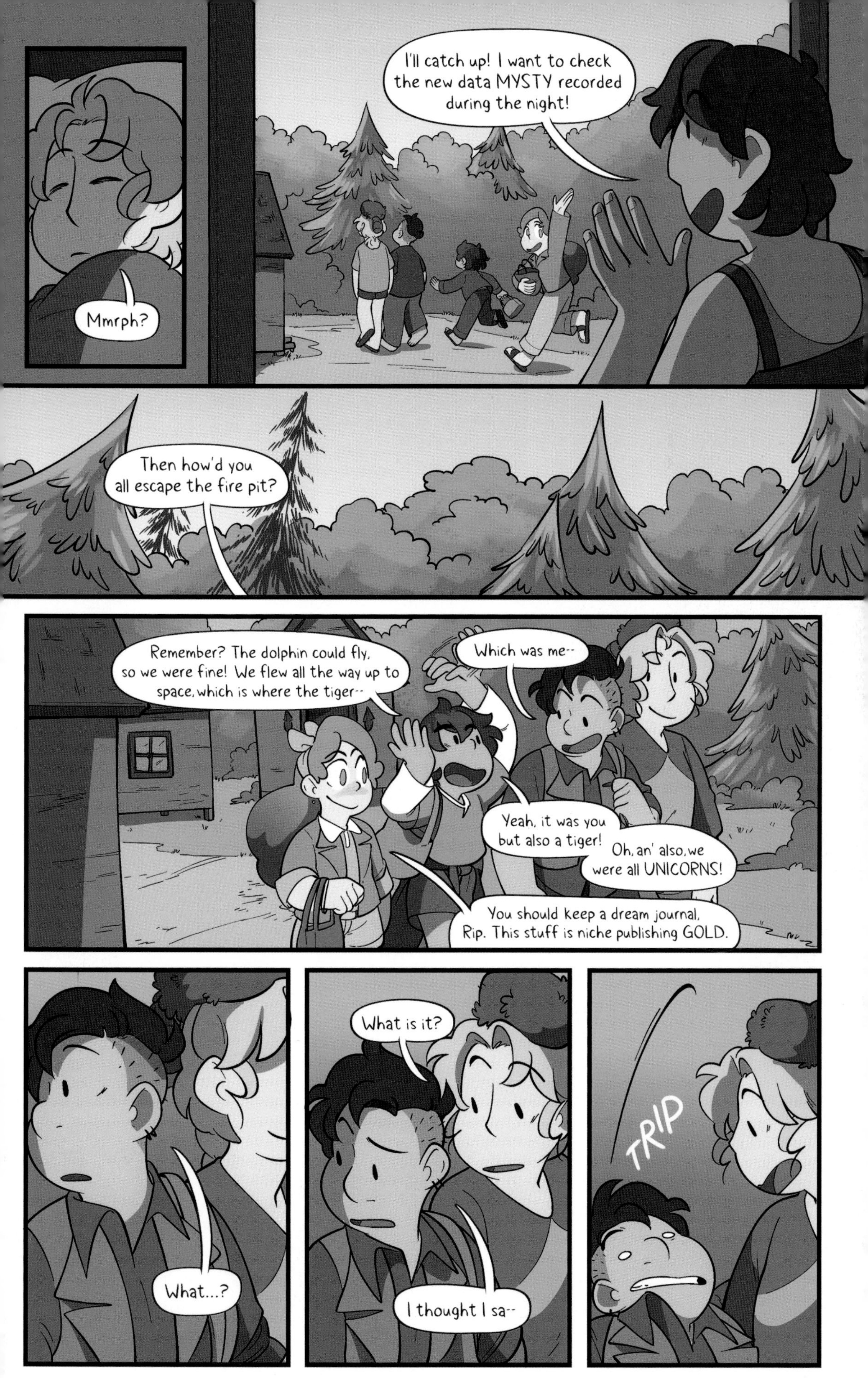
Mmrph?
I'll catch up! I want to check the new data MYSTY recorded during the night!
Then how'd you all escape the fire pit?
Remember? The dolphin could fly, so we were fine! We flew all the way up to space, which is where the tiger--
Which was me--
Yeah, it was you but also a tiger!
Oh, an' also, we were all UNICORNS!
You should keep a dream journal, Rip. This stuff is niche publishing GOLD.
What...?
What is it?
I thought I sa--
TRIP

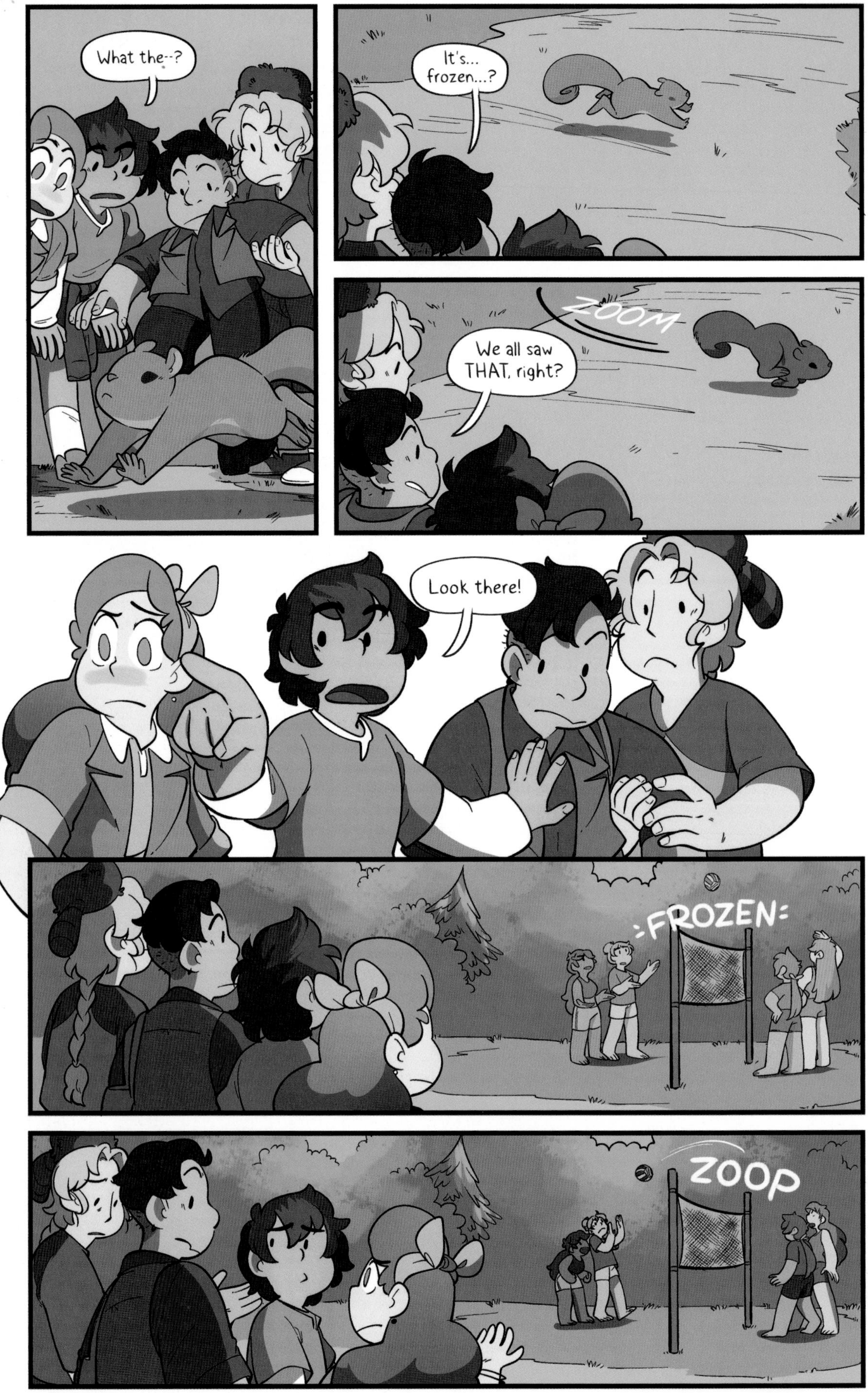
What the--?
It's... frozen...?
ZOOM
We all saw THAT, right?
Look there!
FROZEN
ZOOP

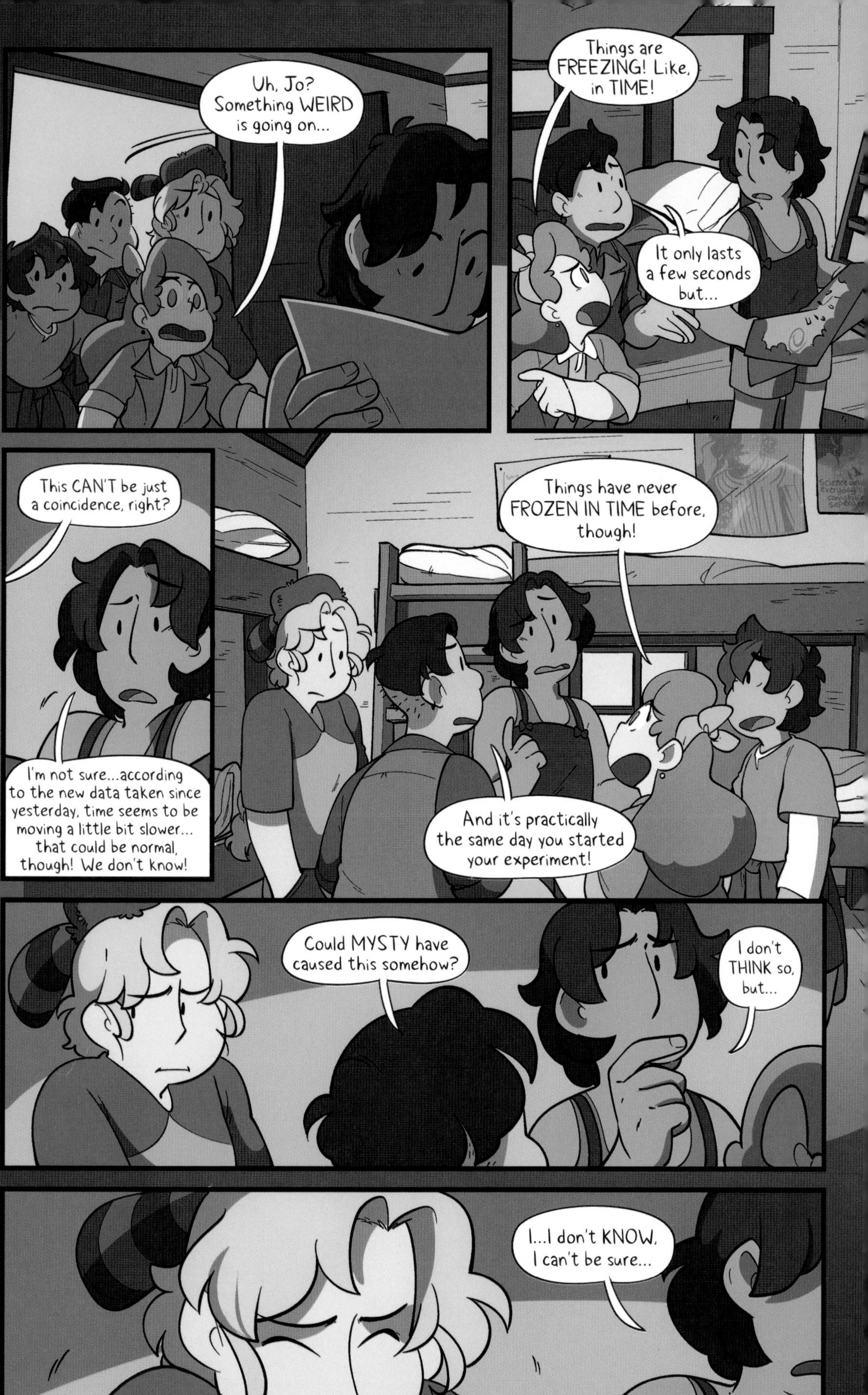
Uh, Jo? Something WEIRD is going on...
Things are FREEZING! Like, in TIME!
It only lasts a few seconds but...
This CAN'T be just a coincidence, right?
I'm not sure...according to the new data taken since yesterday, time seems to be moving a little bit slower... that could be normal, though! We don't know!
Things have never FROZEN IN TIME before, though!
And it's practically the same day you started your experiment!
Could MYSTY have caused this somehow?
I don't THINK so, but...
I...I don't KNOW, I can't be sure...

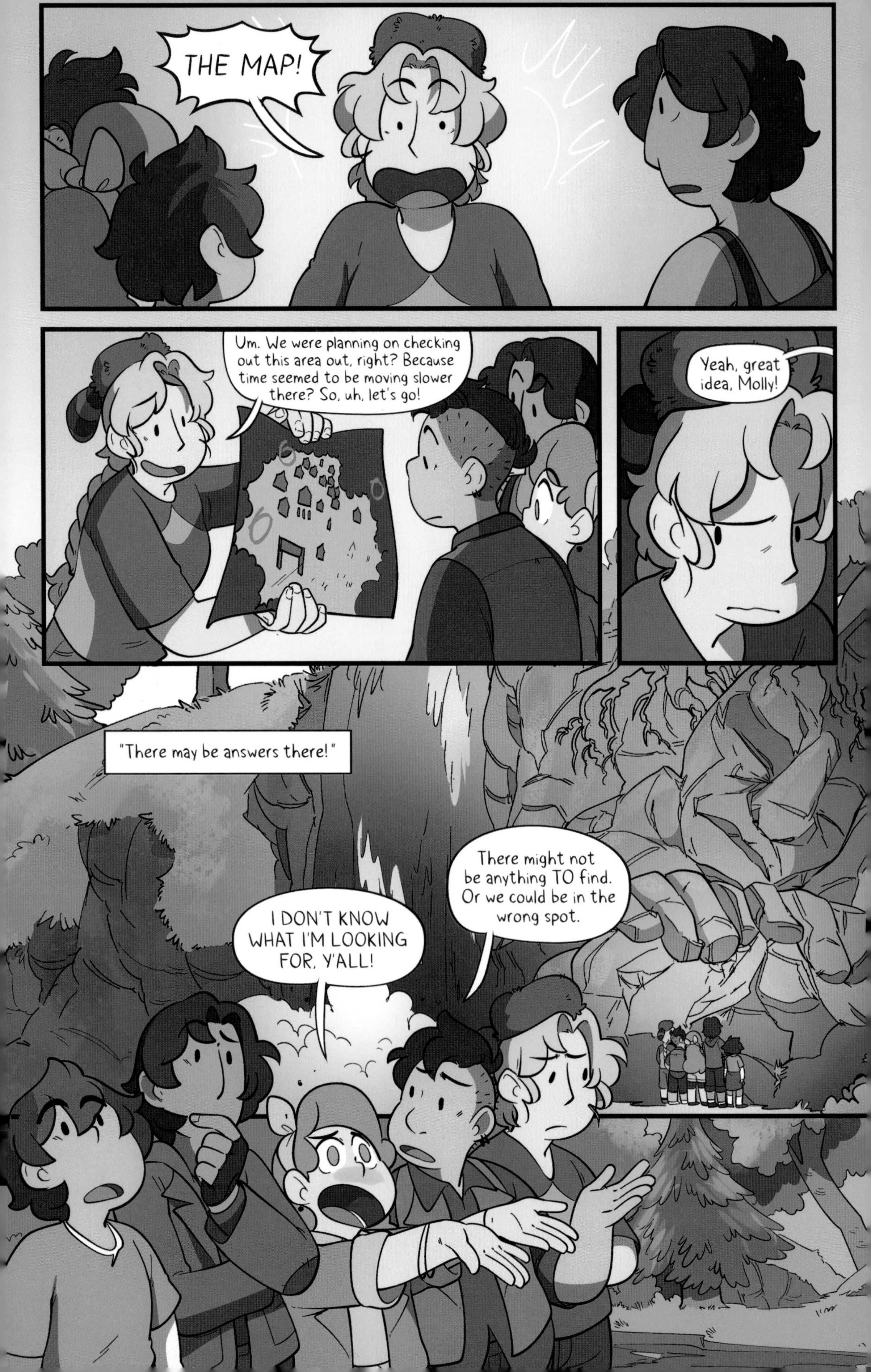
THE MAP!
Um. We were planning on checking out this area out, right? Because time seemed to be moving slower there? So, uh, let's go!
Yeah, great idea, Molly!
"There may be answers there!"
I DON'T KNOW WHAT I'M LOOKING FOR, Y'ALL!
There might not be anything TO find. Or we could be in the wrong spot.

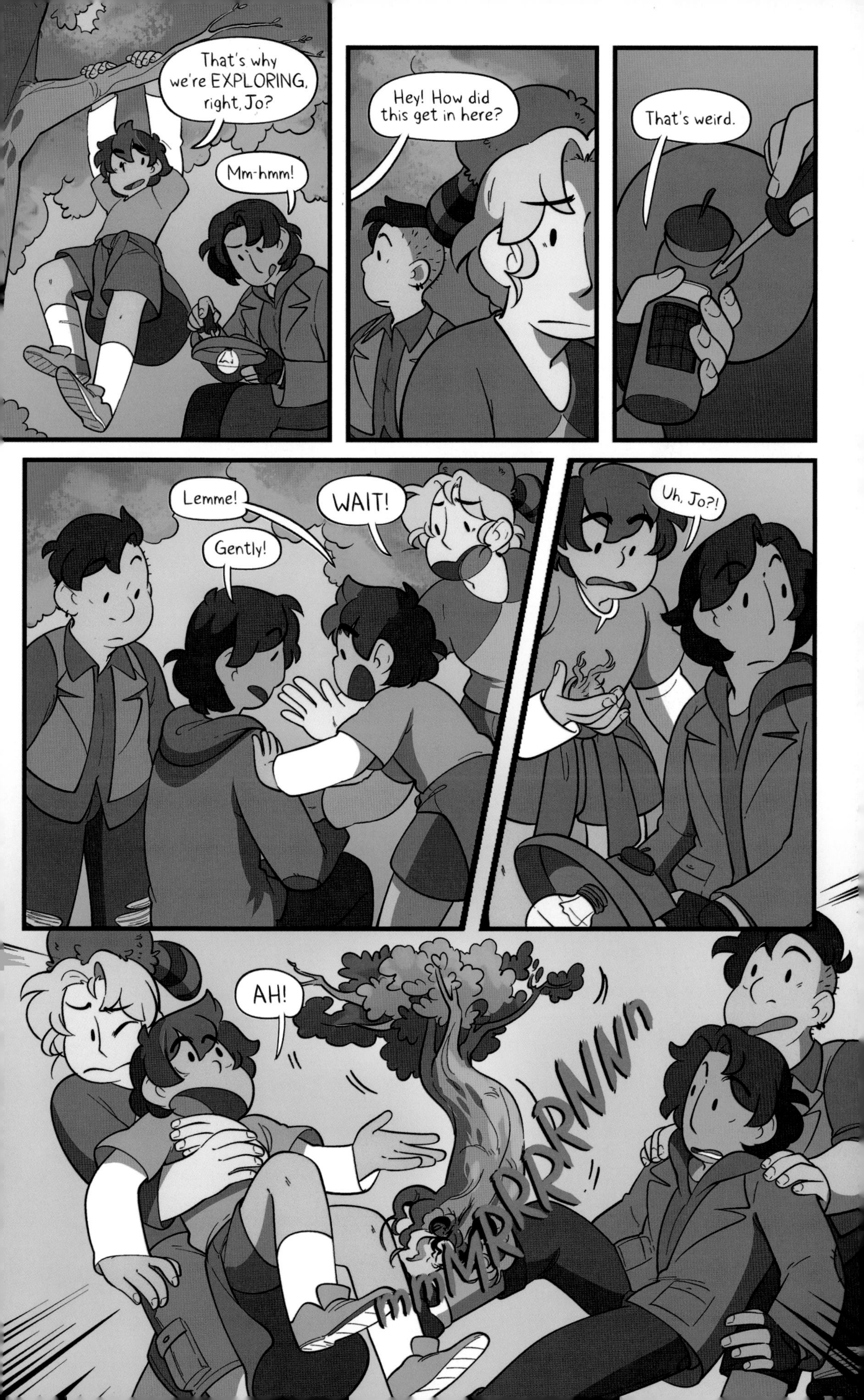
That's why we're EXPLORING, right, Jo?
Mm-hmm!
Hey! How did this get in here?
That's weird.
Lemme!
Gently!
WAIT!
Uh, Jo?!
AH!
mmMRRRRNNNn

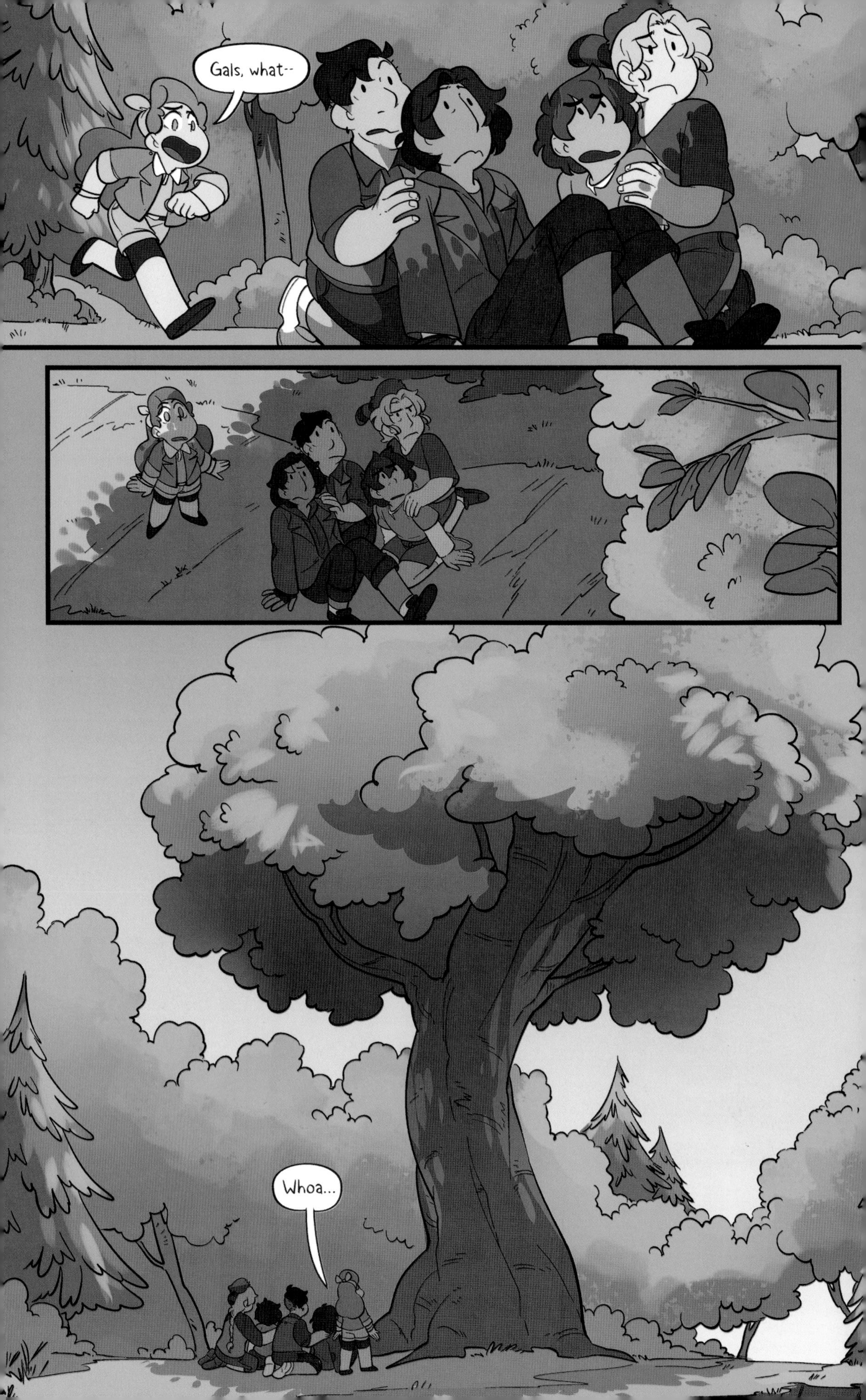
Gals, what--
Whoa...

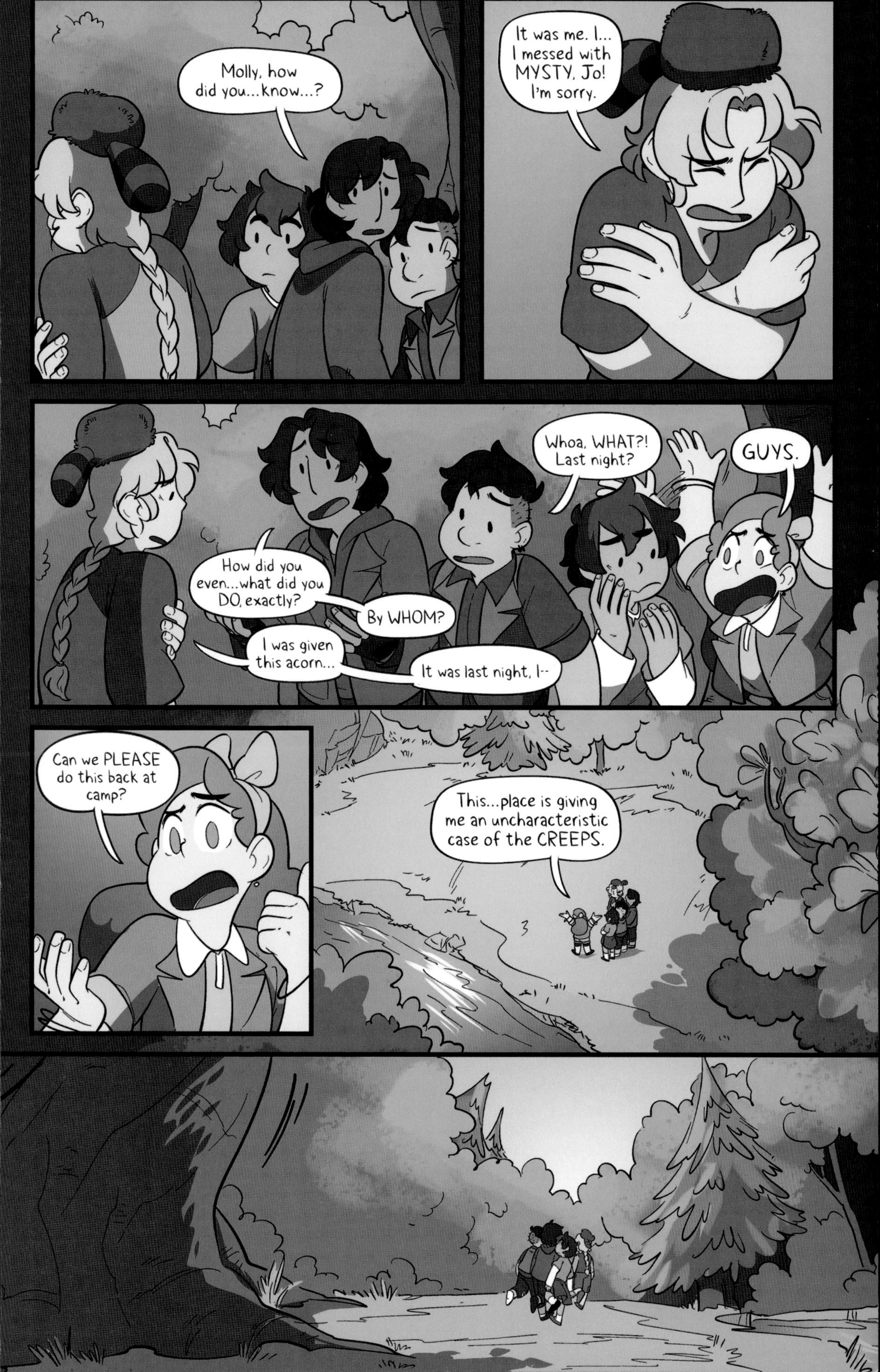
Molly, how did you...know...?
It was me. I... I messed with MYSTY, Jo! I'm sorry.
Whoa, WHAT?! Last night?
GUYS.
How did you even...what did you DO, exactly?
By WHOM?
I was given this acorn...
It was last night, I--
Can we PLEASE do this back at camp?
This...place is giving me an uncharacteristic case of the CREEPS.

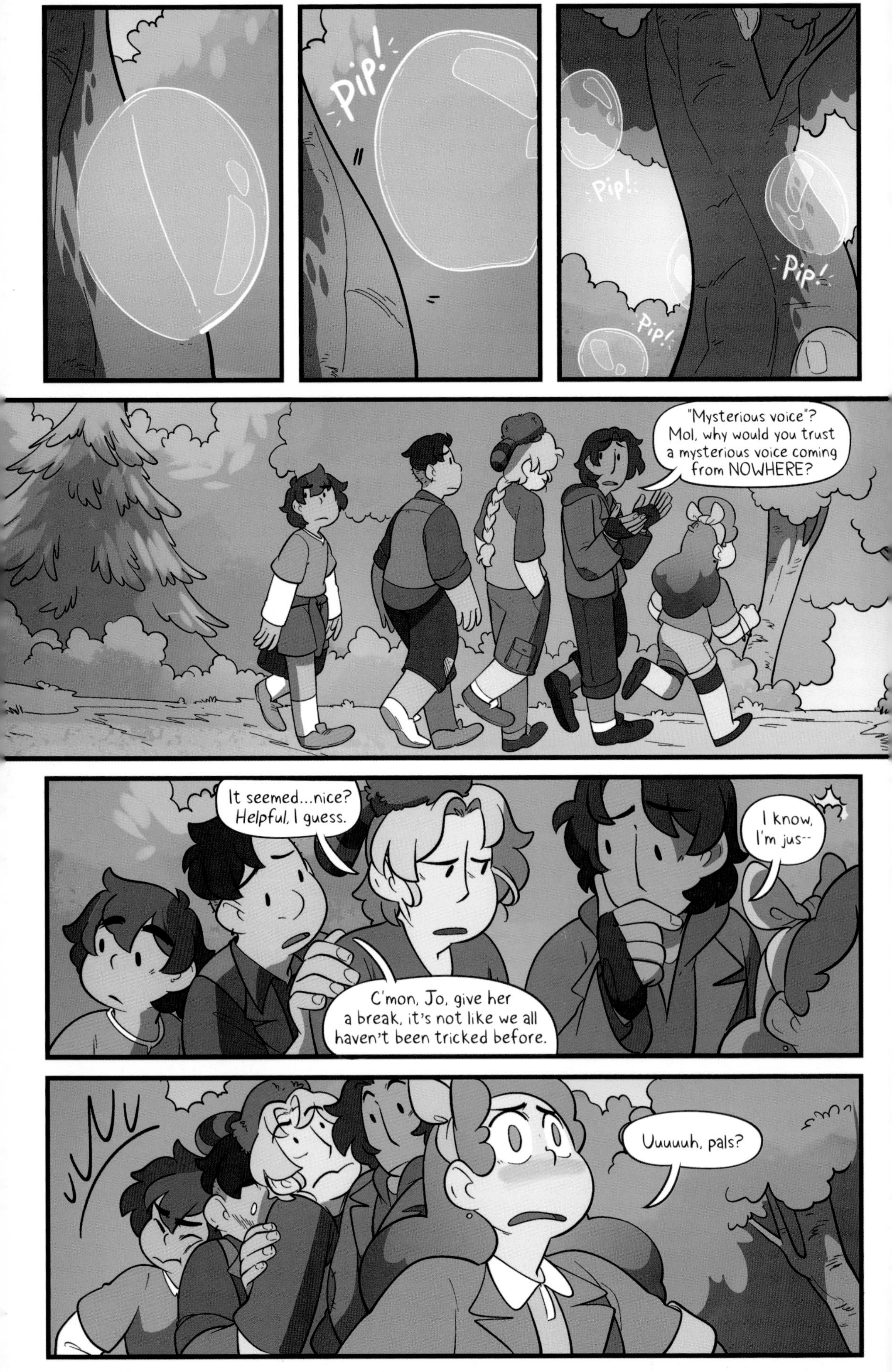
PIP!
PIP!
PIP!
PIP!
"Mysterious voice"? Mol, why would you trust a mysterious voice coming from NOWHERE?
It seemed...nice? Helpful, I guess.
C'mon, Jo, give her a break, it's not like we all haven't been tricked before.
I know, I'm jus--
Uuuuuh, pals?

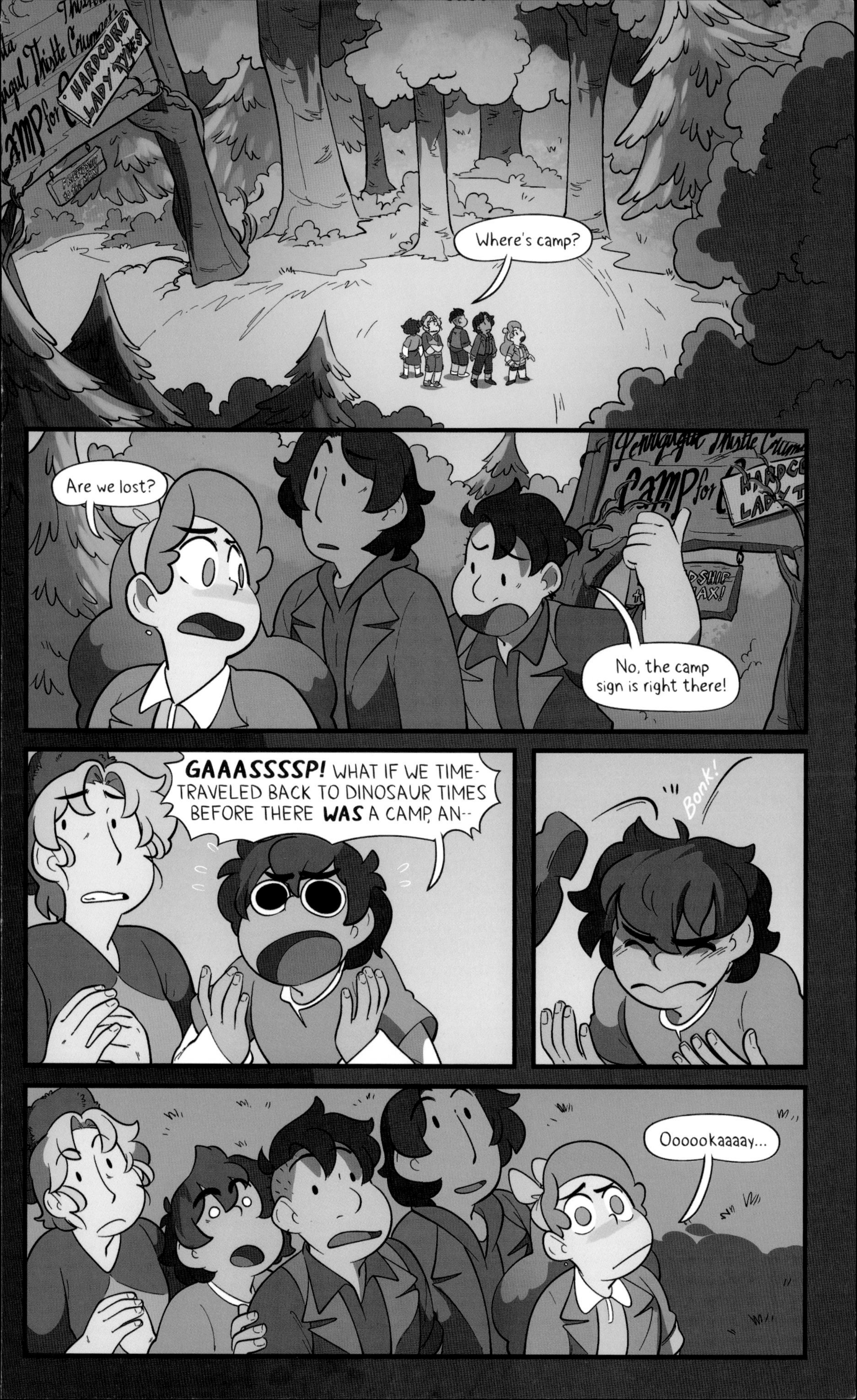
Where's camp?
Are we lost?
No, the camp sign is right there!
GAAASSSSP! WHAT IF WE TIME-TRAVELED BACK TO DINOSAUR TIMES BEFORE THERE WAS A CAMP, AN--
Bonk!
Oooookaaaay...

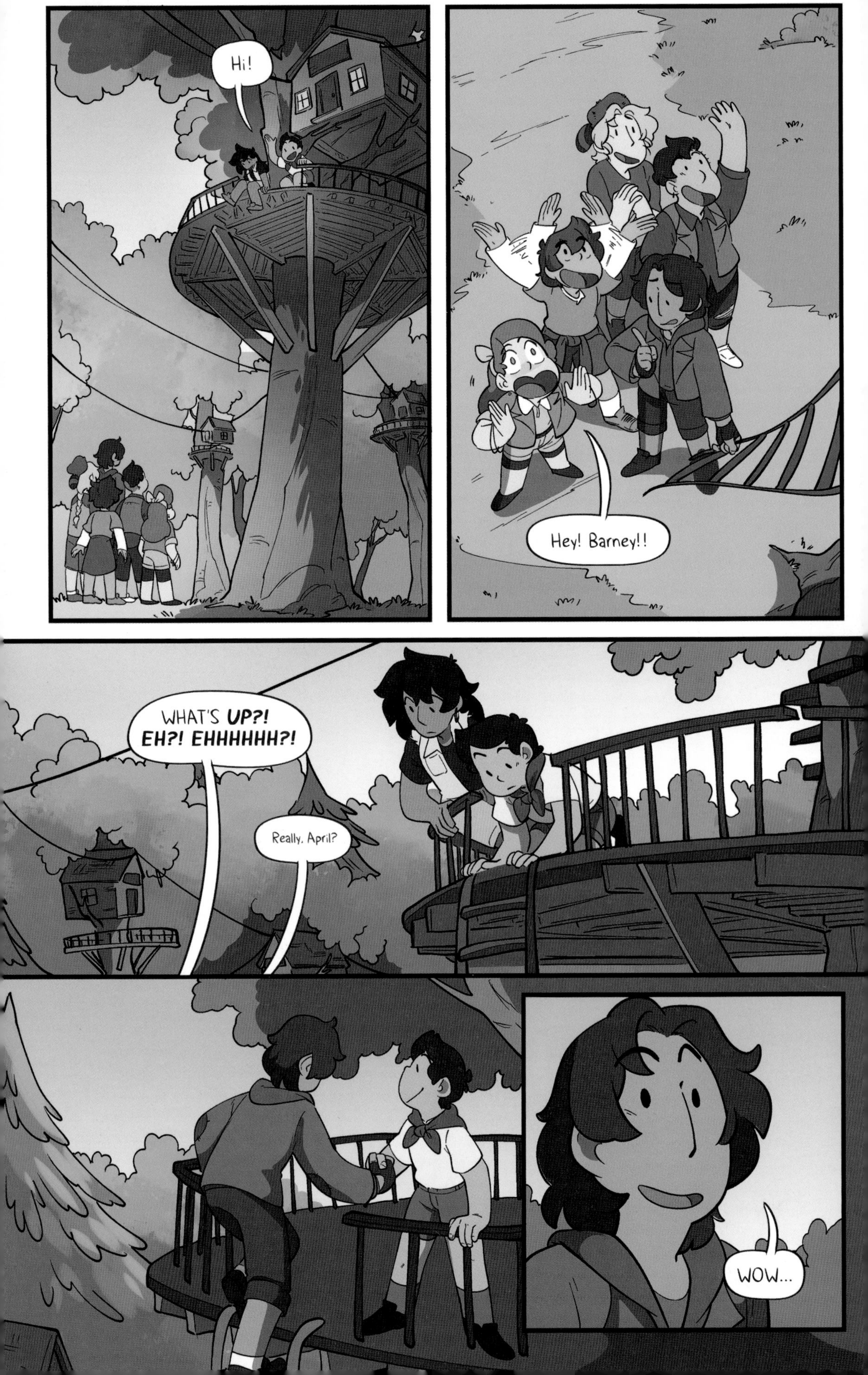
Hi!
Hey! Barney!!
WHAT'S UP?! EH?! EHHHHHH?!
Really, April?
WOW...

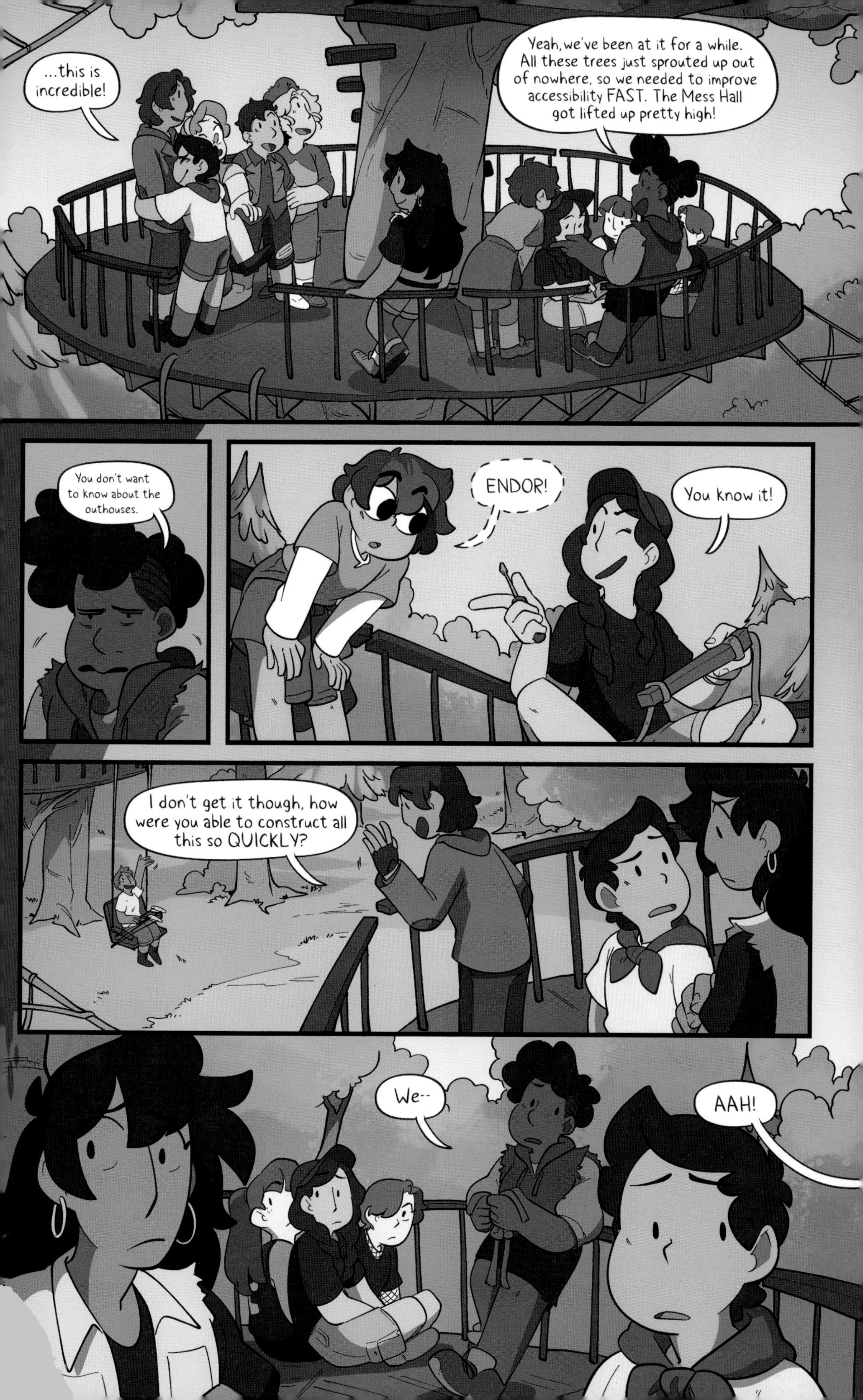
...this is incredible!
Yeah, we've been at it for a while. All these trees just sprouted up out of nowhere, so we needed to improve accessibility FAST. The Mess Hall got lifted up pretty high!
You don't want to know about the outhouses.
ENDOR!
You know it!
I don't get it though, how were you able to construct all this so QUICKLY?
We--
AAH!

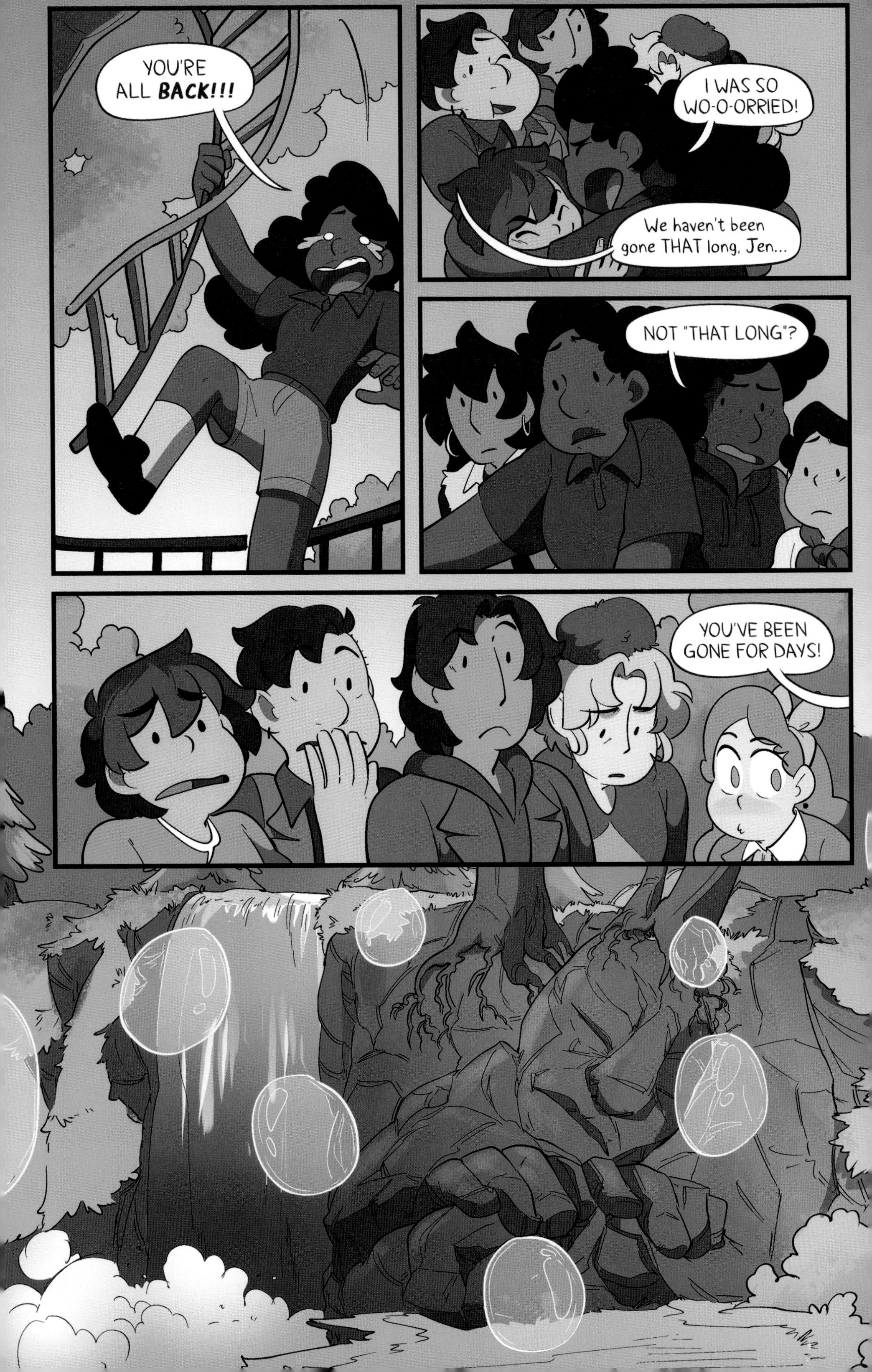
YOU'RE ALL **BACK!!!**
I WAS SO WO-O-ORRIED!
We haven't been gone THAT long, Jen...
NOT "THAT LONG"?
YOU'VE BEEN GONE FOR DAYS!

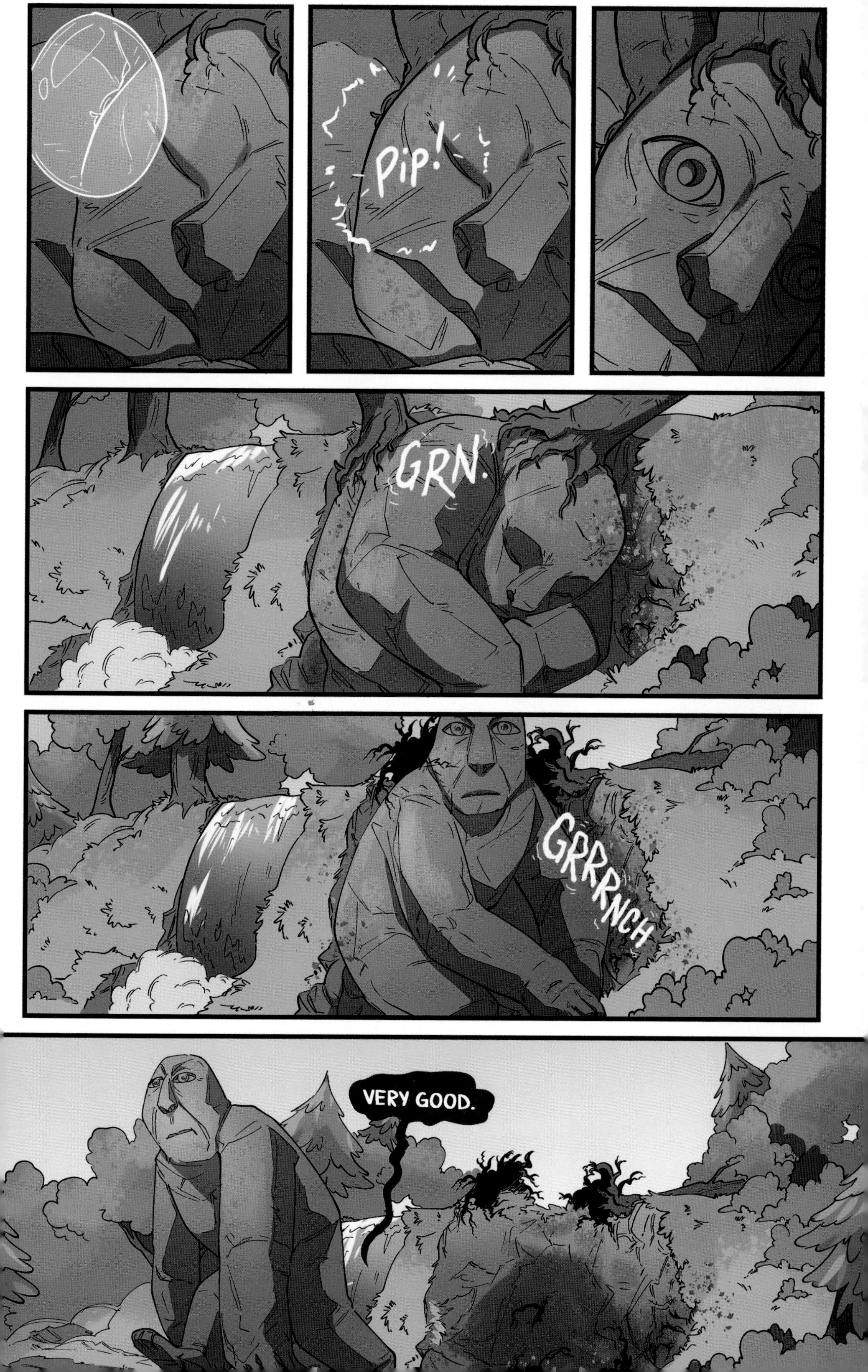
Pip!
GRN.
GRRRNCH
VERY GOOD.

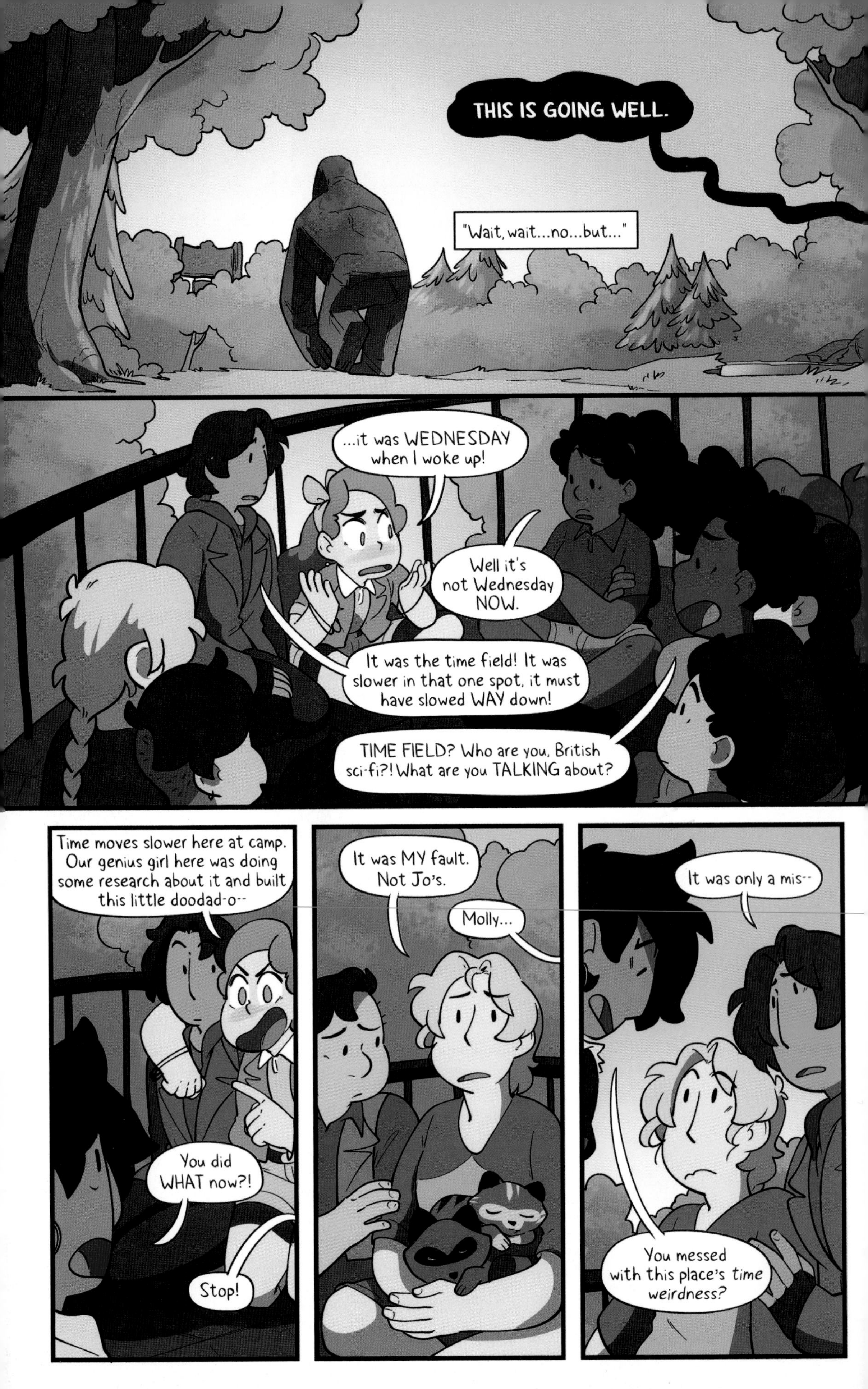
THIS IS GOING WELL.
"Wait, wait...no...but..."
...it was WEDNESDAY when I woke up!
Well it's not Wednesday NOW.
It was the time field! It was slower in that one spot, it must have slowed WAY down!
TIME FIELD? Who are you, British sci-fi?! What are you TALKING about?
Time moves slower here at camp. Our genius girl here was doing some research about it and built this little doodad-o--
You did WHAT now?!
Stop!
It was MY fault. Not Jo's.
Molly...
It was only a mis--
You messed with this place's time weirdness?

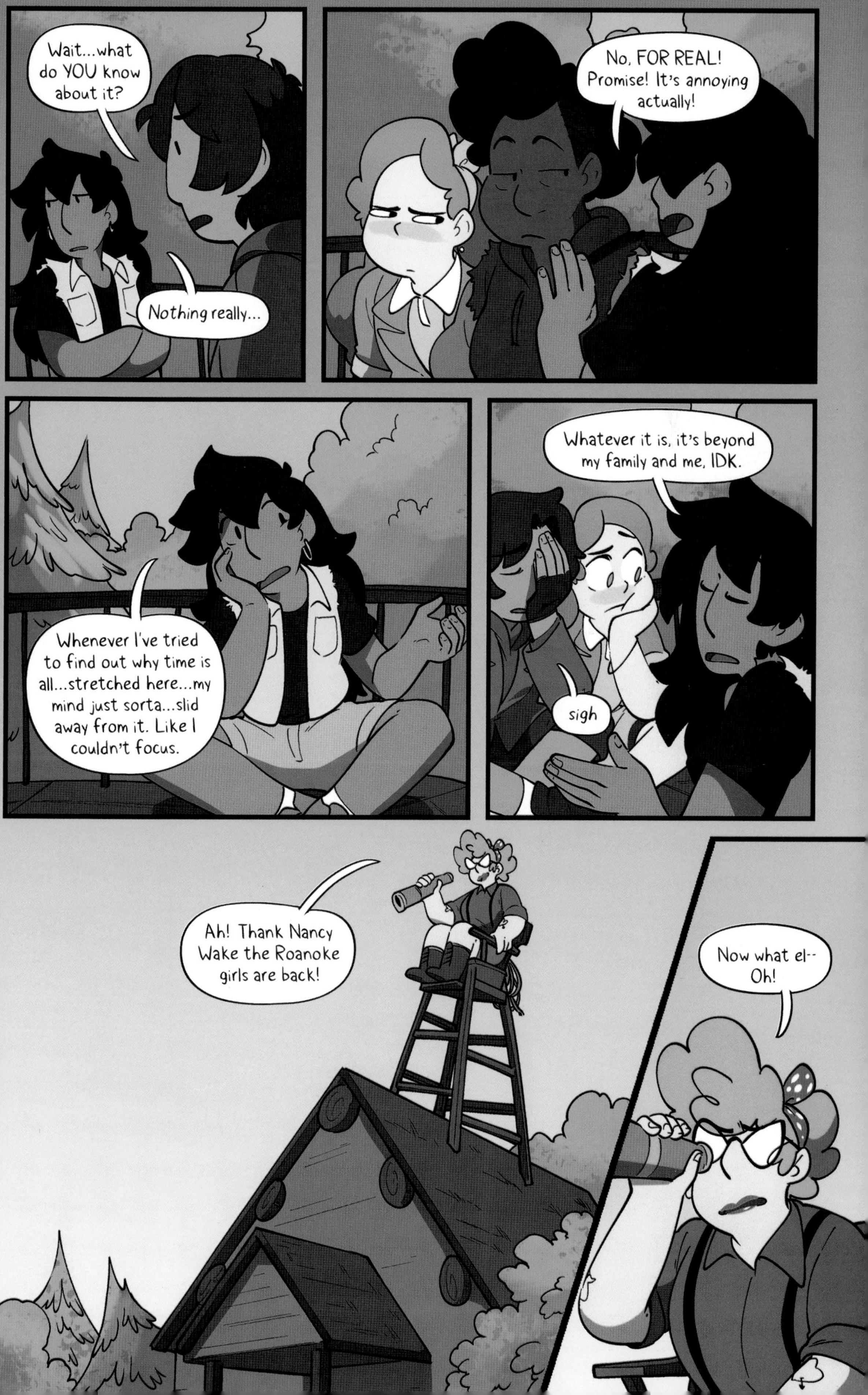
Wait...what do YOU know about it?
Nothing really...
No, FOR REAL! Promise! It's annoying actually!
Whenever I've tried to find out why time is all...stretched here...my mind just sorta...slid away from it. Like I couldn't focus.
Whatever it is, it's beyond my family and me, IDK.
sigh
Ah! Thank Nancy Wake the Roanoke girls are back!
Now what el-- Oh!

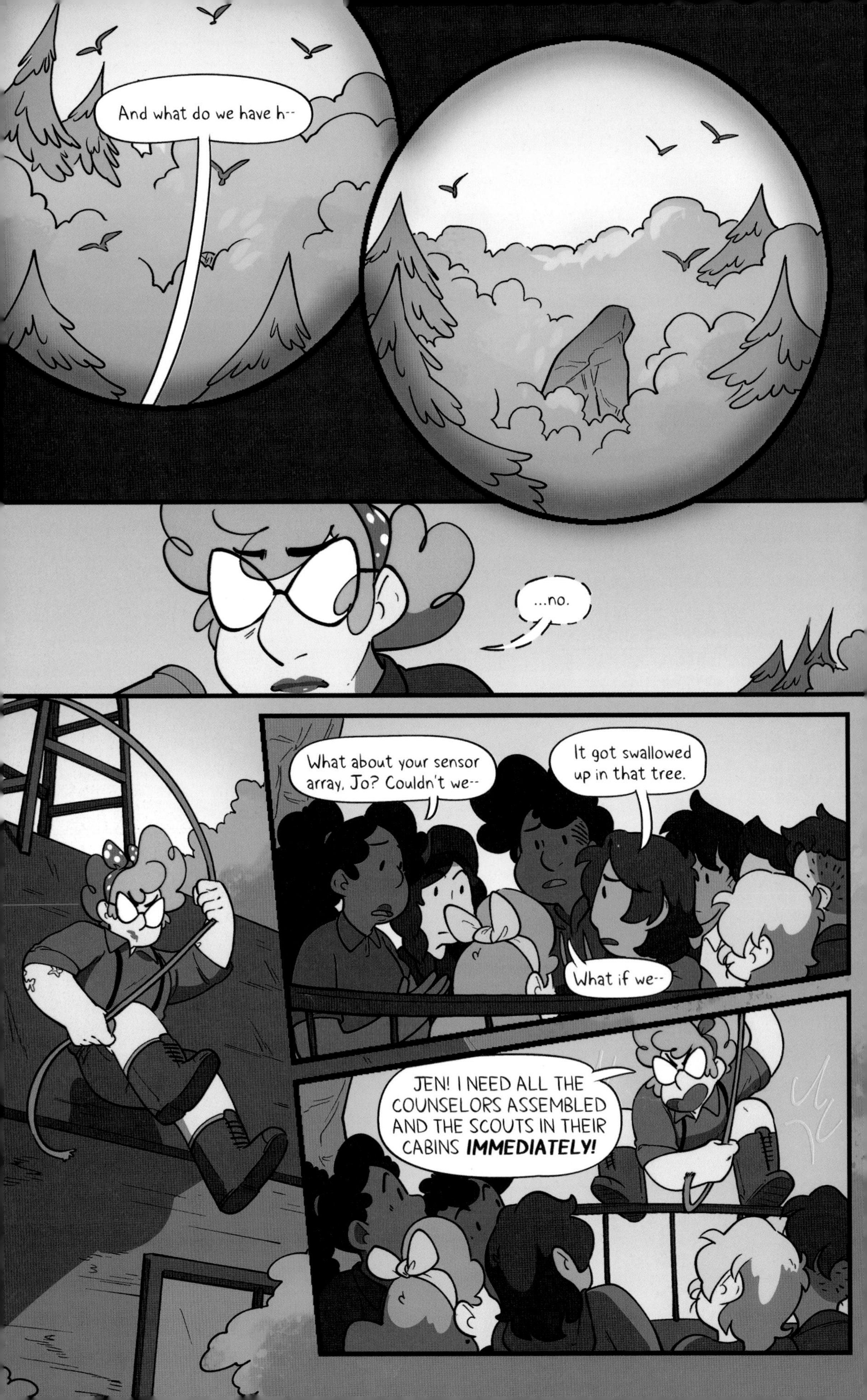
And what do we have h--
...no.
What about your sensor array, Jo? Couldn't we--
It got swallowed up in that tree.
What if we--
JEN! I NEED ALL THE COUNSELORS ASSEMBLED AND THE SCOUTS IN THEIR CABINS **IMMEDIATELY!**

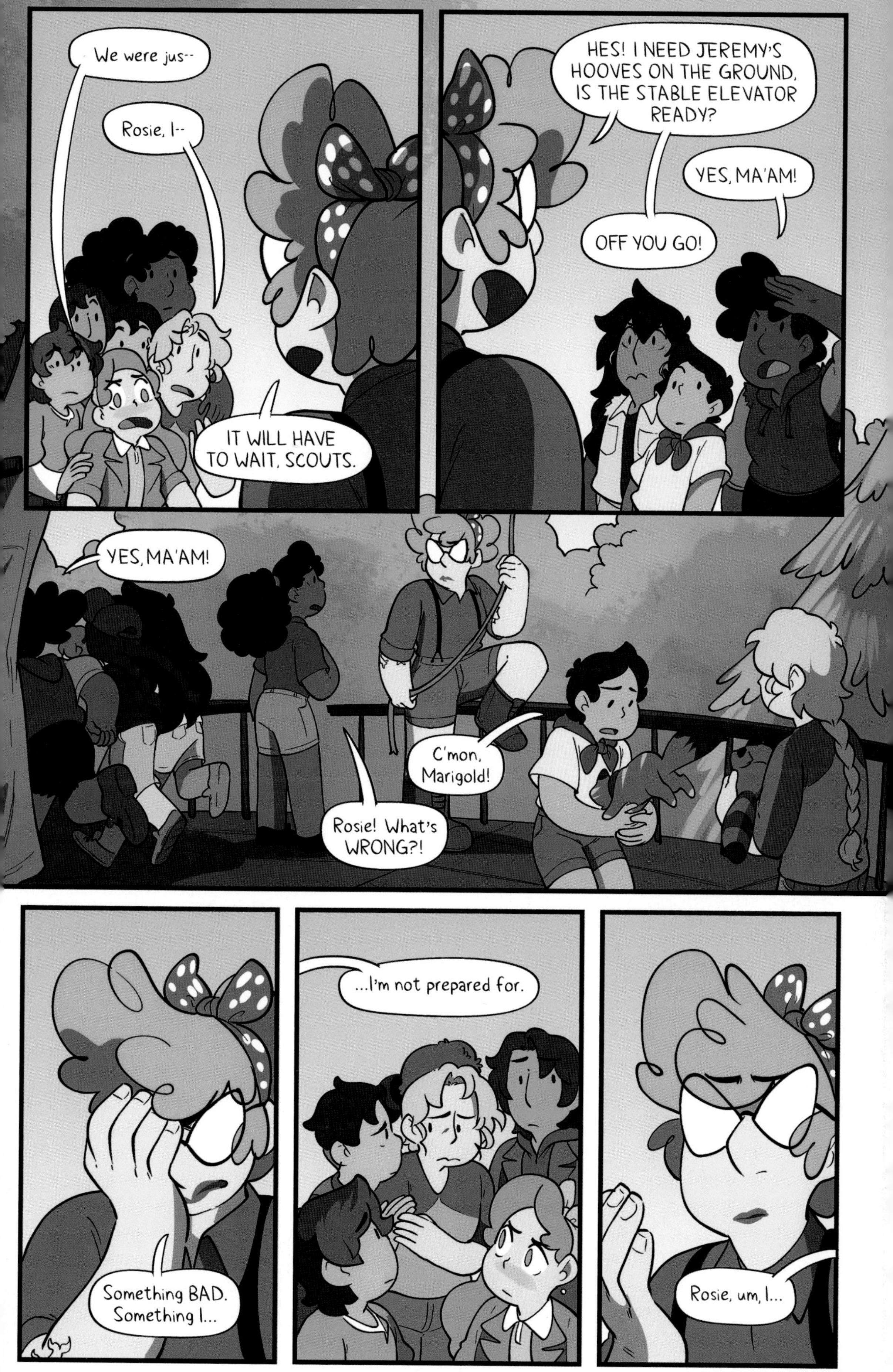
We were jus--
Rosie, I--
IT WILL HAVE TO WAIT, SCOUTS.
HES! I NEED JEREMY'S HOOVES ON THE GROUND, IS THE STABLE ELEVATOR READY?
YES, MA'AM!
OFF YOU GO!
YES, MA'AM!
Rosie! What's WRONG?!
C'mon, Marigold!
Something BAD. Something I...
...I'm not prepared for.
Rosie, um, I...

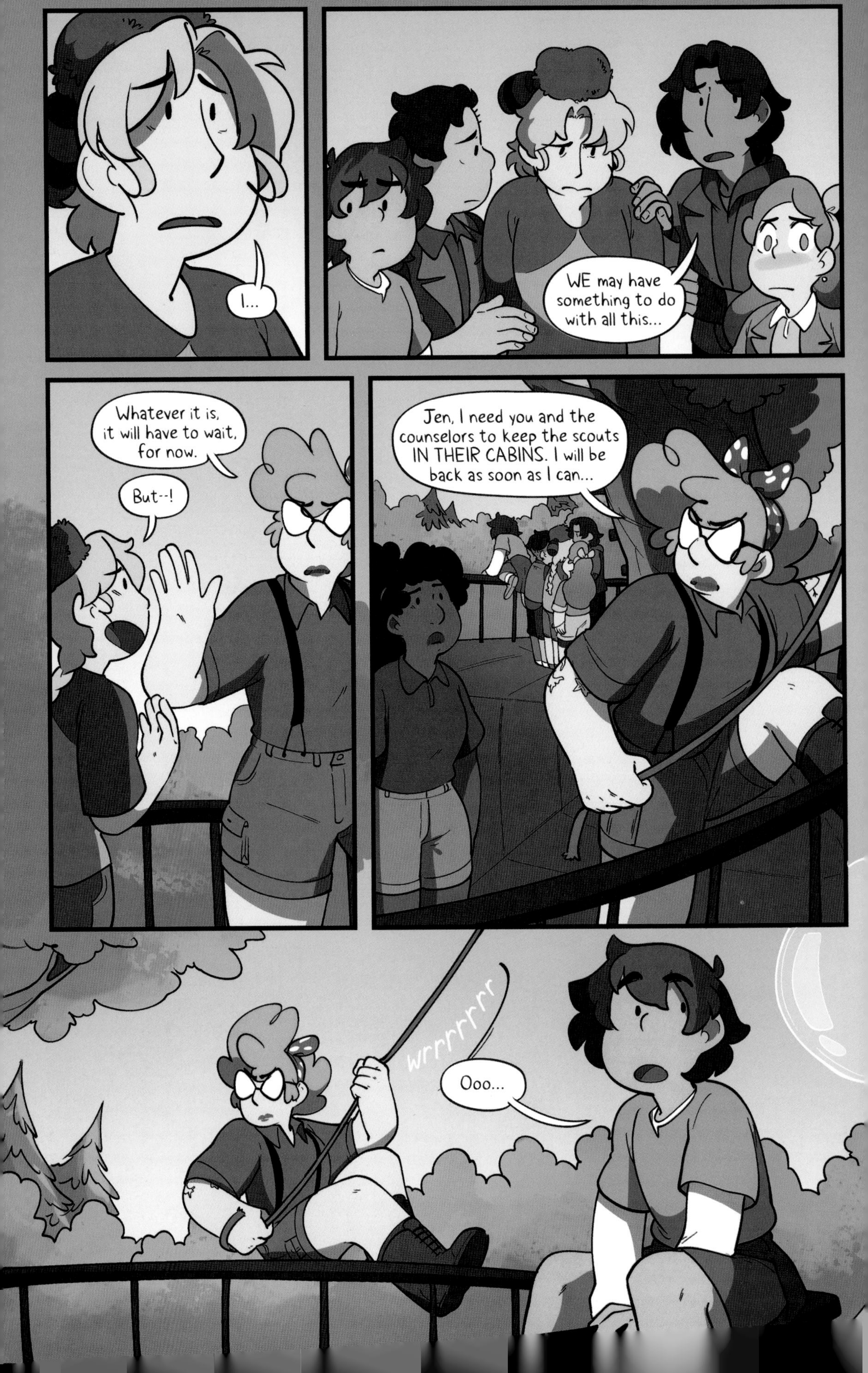
I...
WE may have something to do with all this...
Whatever it is, it will have to wait, for now.
But--!
Jen, I need you and the counselors to keep the scouts IN THEIR CABINS. I will be back as soon as I can...
wrrrrrr
Ooo...

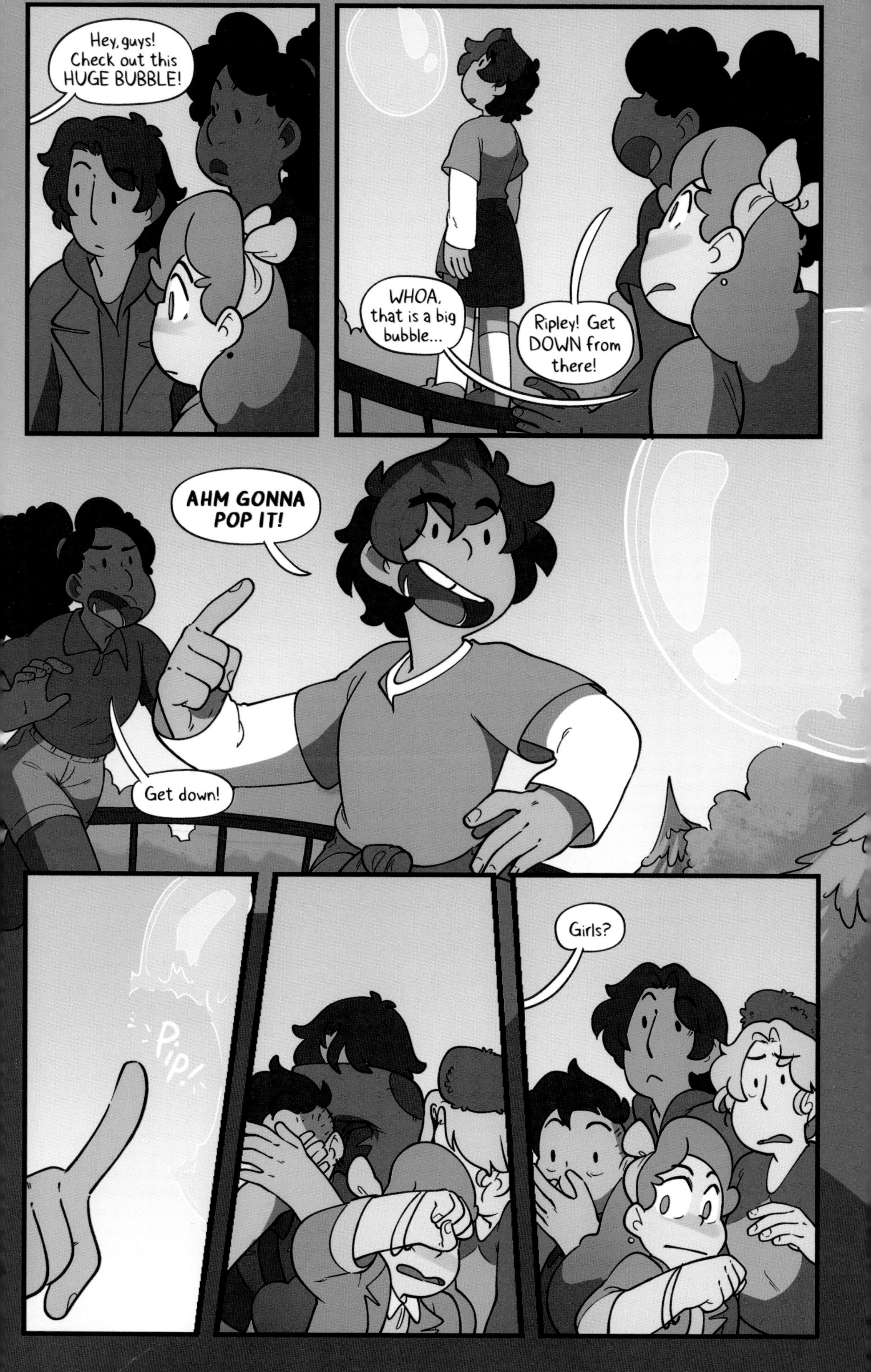
Hey, guys! Check out this HUGE BUBBLE!
WHOA, that is a big bubble...
Ripley! Get DOWN from there!
AHM GONNA POP IT!
Get down!
Pip!
Girls?

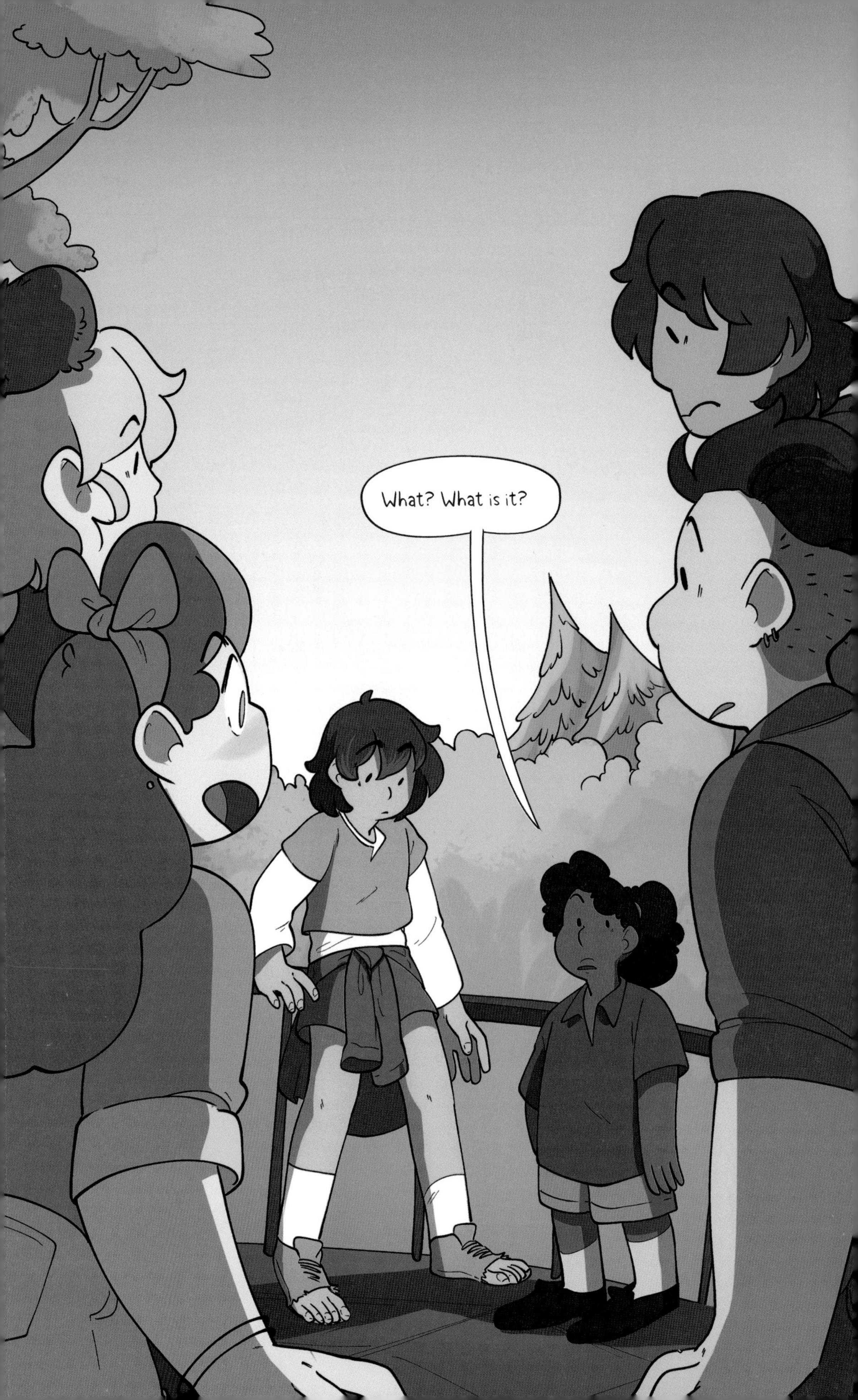
What? What is it?

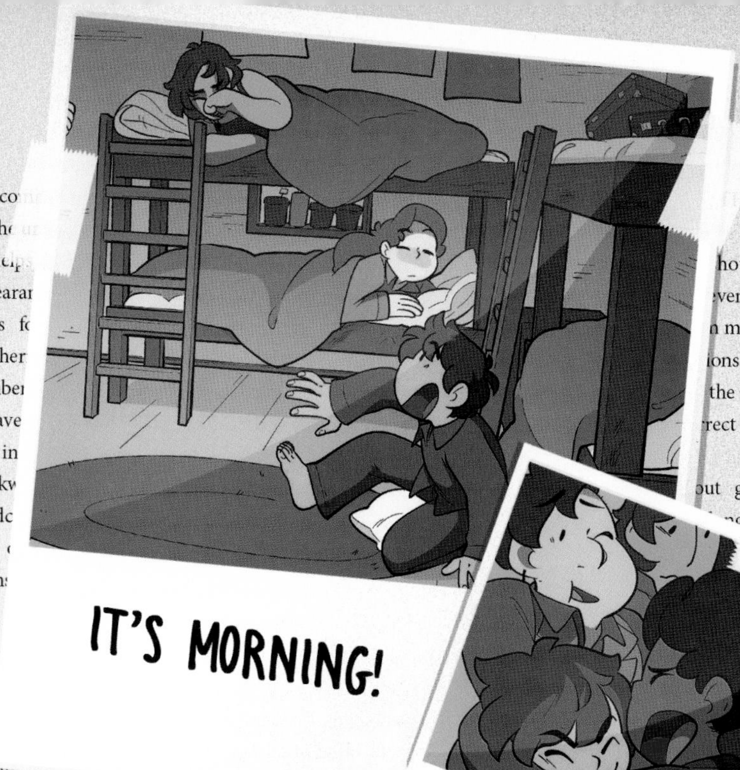
IT'S MORNING!

will co...

The u... It hel... appearan... dress fo... Further... Lumbe... to have... part in... Thiskw... Hardc... have ... thems...

The ... yellow, ... emb... the w... choose ... slacks, ... made o... out-of-do... green bere... the colla... Shoes ma... heels, rou... ...ings or socks shou... ...with the shoes or wit... the uniform. Ne... ...ces, bracelets, or other jewelry do ... belong with a Lumberjane uniform.

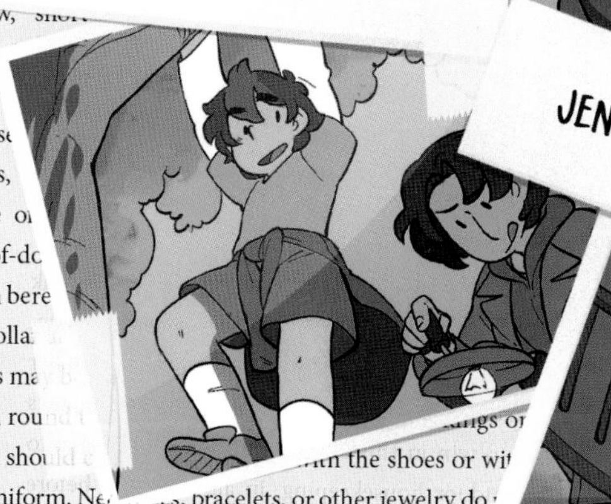

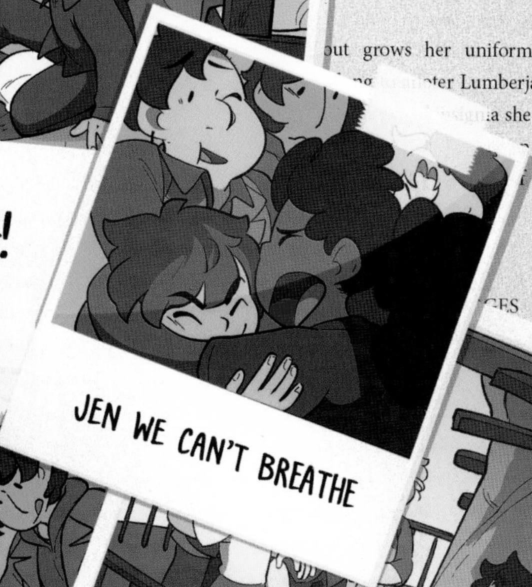
JEN WE CAN'T BREATHE

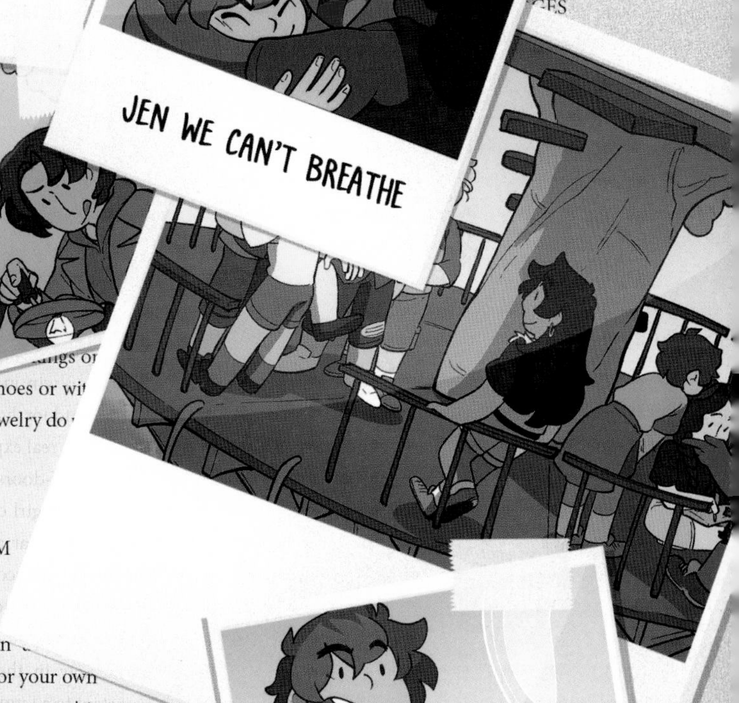

HOW TO WEAR THE UNIFORM

To look well in a uniform demands first of ... uniform be kept in good condition—clean ... pressed. See that the skirt is the right length for your own height and build, that the belt is adjusted to your waist, that your shoes and stockings are in keeping with the uniform, that you watch your posture and carry yourself with dignity and grace. If the beret is removed indoors, be sure that your hair is neat and kept in place with an insonspicuous clip or ribbon. When you wear a Lumberjane uniform you are identified as a member of this organization and you should be doubly careful to conduct yourself in a way that will show everyone that courtesy and thoughtfullness are part of being a Lumberjane. People are likely to judge a whole nation by the selfishness of a few individuals, to criticize a whole family because of the misconduct of one member, and to feel unkindly toward and organization because of the

...HE UNIFORM

...hould be worn at camp ...events when Lumberjanes ...n may also be worn at other ...ions. It should be worn as a ... the uniform dress with ...rrect shoes, and stocking or

...out grows her uniform or ...ng ...ter Lumberjane. ...a she has ... her ... her

...GES

The unifor... helps to cre... in a group. ... active life th... another bond... future, and pr... in order to b... Lumberjane pr... Penniquiqul Thi... ...ore Lady Types, but m... ...es will wish to have one. They can either bu... ...uniform, or make it themselves from materials available at the trading post.

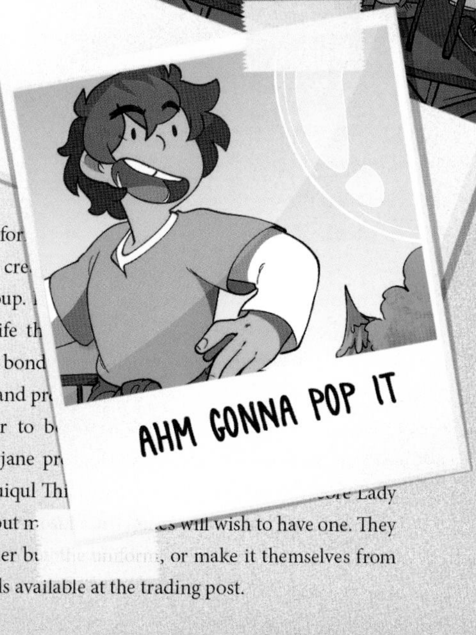
AHM GONNA POP IT

LUMBERJANES FIELD MANUAL

CHAPTER
FORTY-THREE

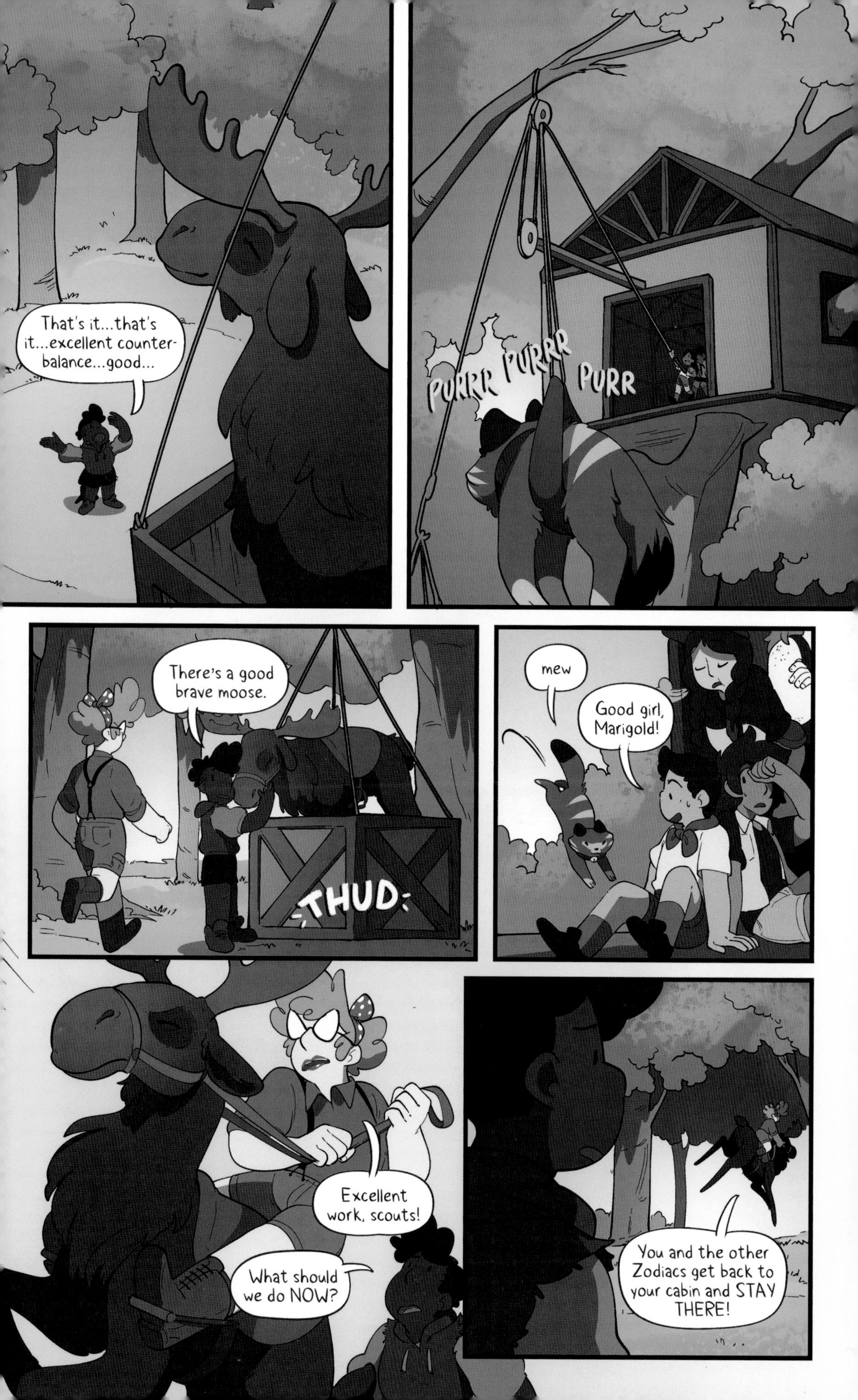
That's it...that's it...excellent counter-balance...good...
PURRR PURRR PURR
There's a good brave moose.
THUD
mew
Good girl, Marigold!
Excellent work, scouts!
What should we do NOW?
You and the other Zodiacs get back to your cabin and STAY THERE!

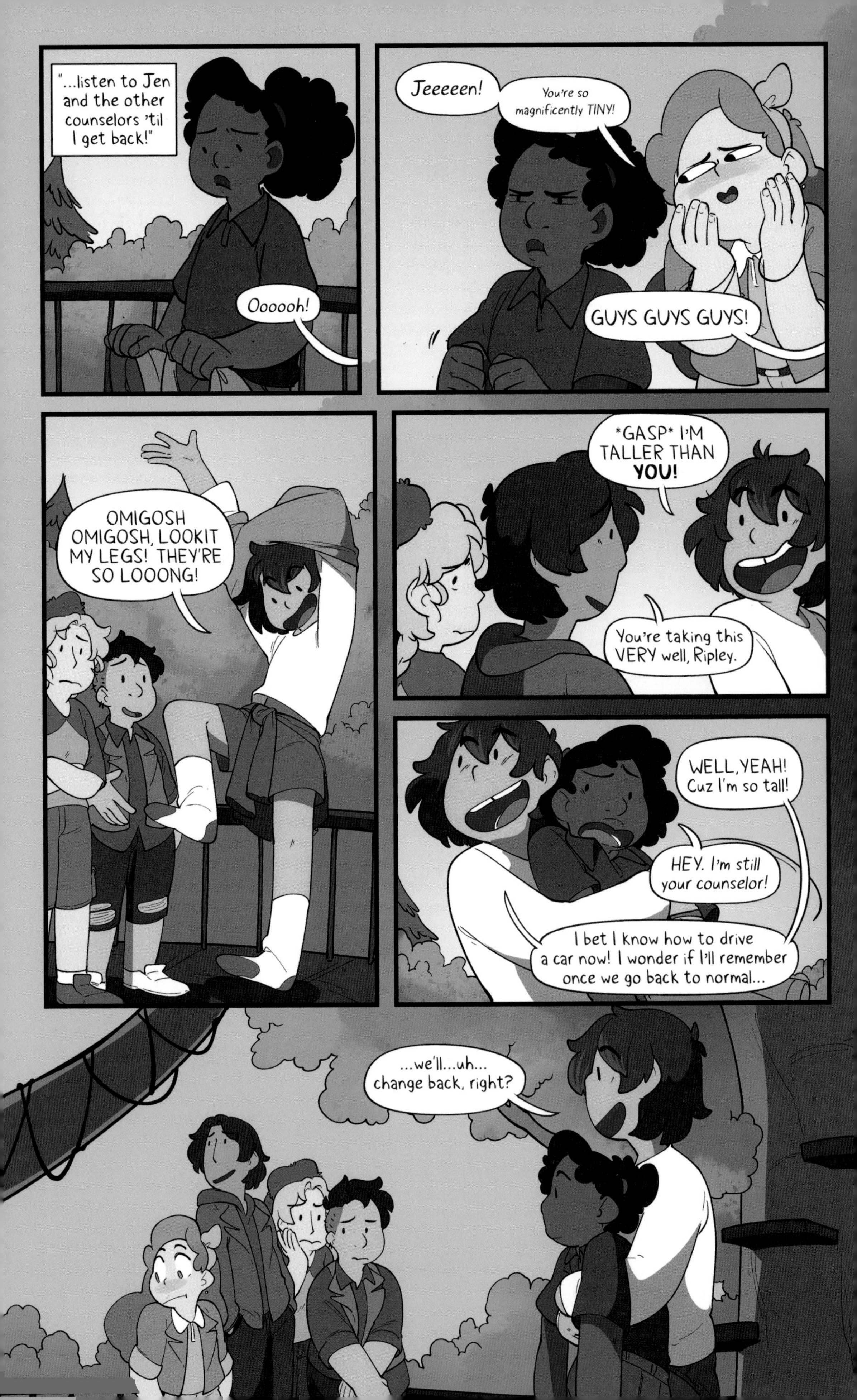
"...listen to Jen and the other counselors 'til I get back!"
Oooooh!
Jeeeeen!
You're so magnificently TINY!
GUYS GUYS GUYS!
OMIGOSH OMIGOSH, LOOKIT MY LEGS! THEY'RE SO LOOONG!
GASP I'M TALLER THAN YOU!
You're taking this VERY well, Ripley.
WELL, YEAH! Cuz I'm so tall!
HEY. I'm still your counselor!
I bet I know how to drive a car now! I wonder if I'll remember once we go back to normal...
...we'll...uh... change back, right?

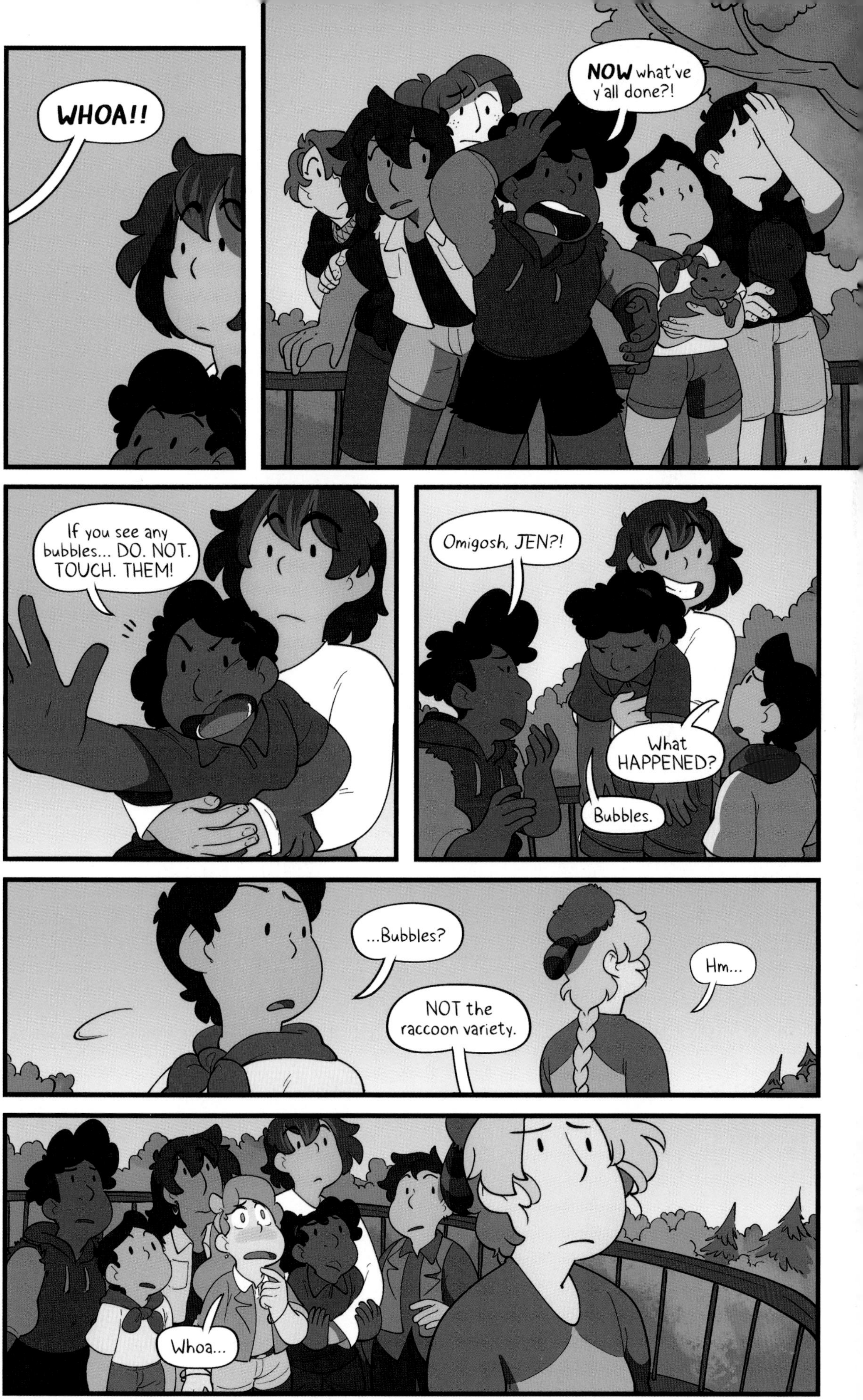
WHOA!!
NOW what've y'all done?!
If you see any bubbles... DO. NOT. TOUCH. THEM!
Omigosh, JEN?!
What HAPPENED?
Bubbles.
...Bubbles?
NOT the raccoon variety.
Hm...
Whoa...

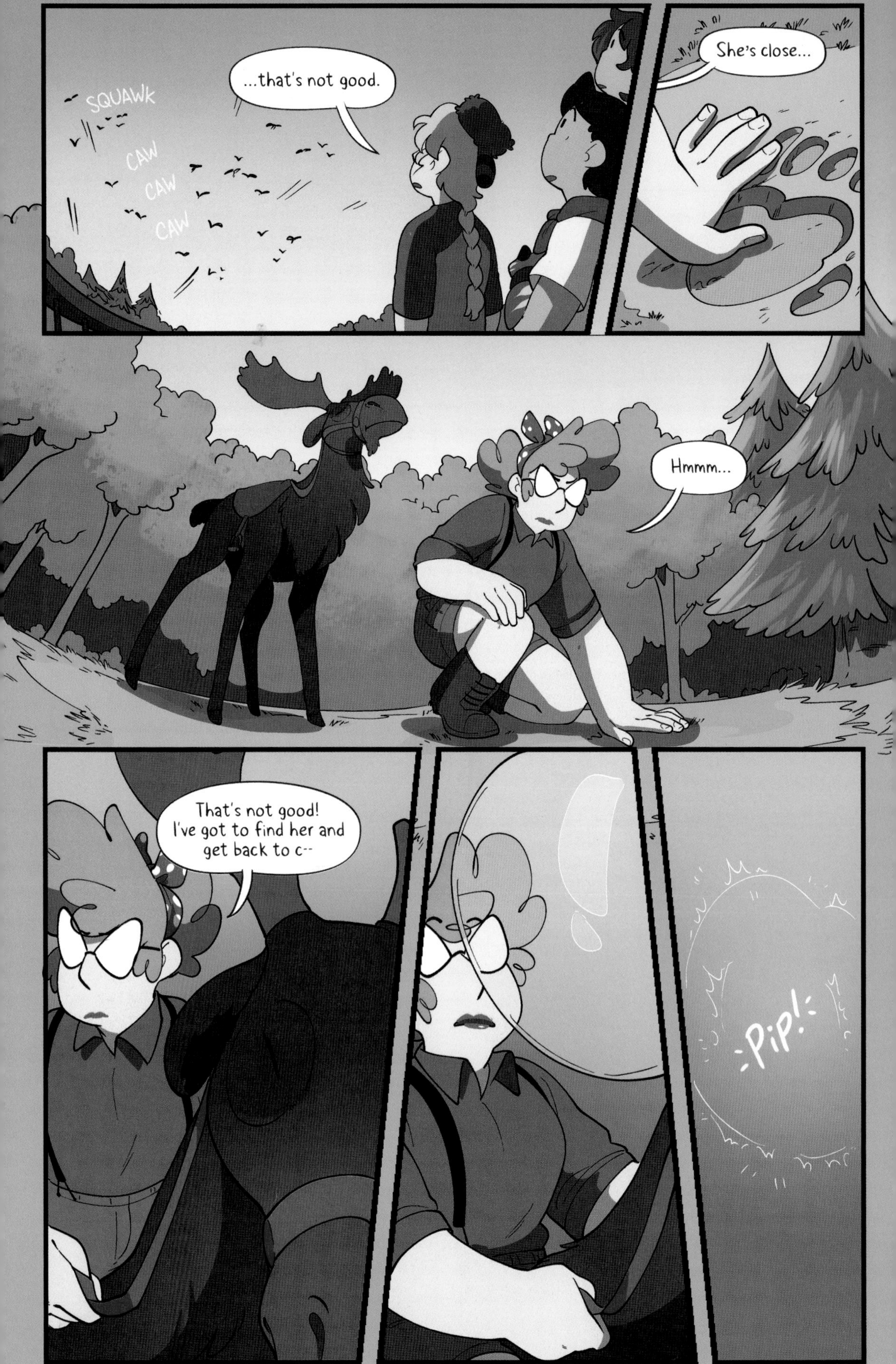
SQUAWK
CAW
CAW
CAW
...that's not good.
She's close...
Hmmm...
That's not good! I've got to find her and get back to c--
PIP!

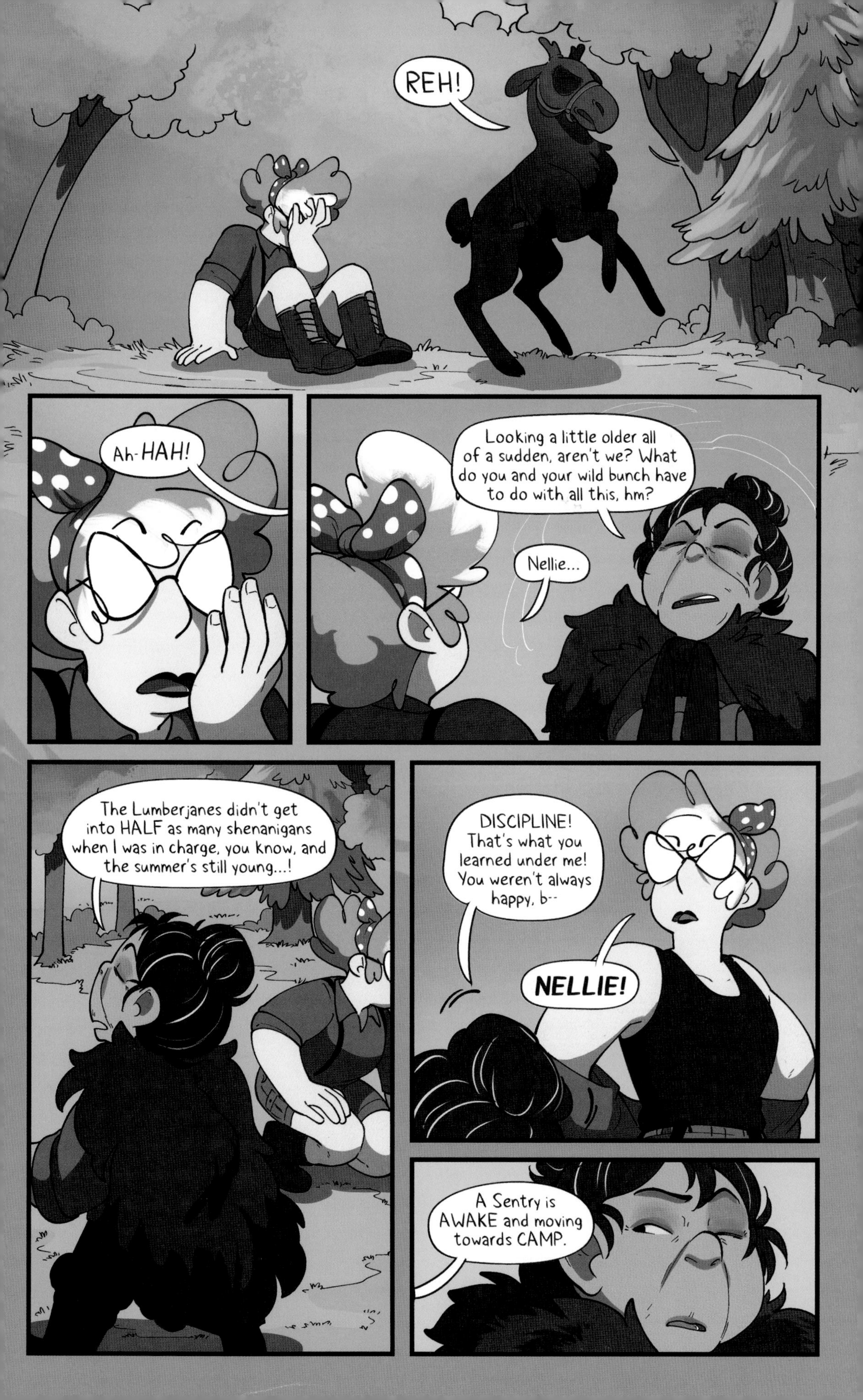
REH!
Ah-HAH!
Looking a little older all of a sudden, aren't we? What do you and your wild bunch have to do with all this, hm?
Nellie...
The Lumberjanes didn't get into HALF as many shenanigans when I was in charge, you know, and the summer's still young...!
DISCIPLINE! That's what you learned under me! You weren't always happy, b--
NELLIE!
A Sentry is AWAKE and moving towards CAMP.

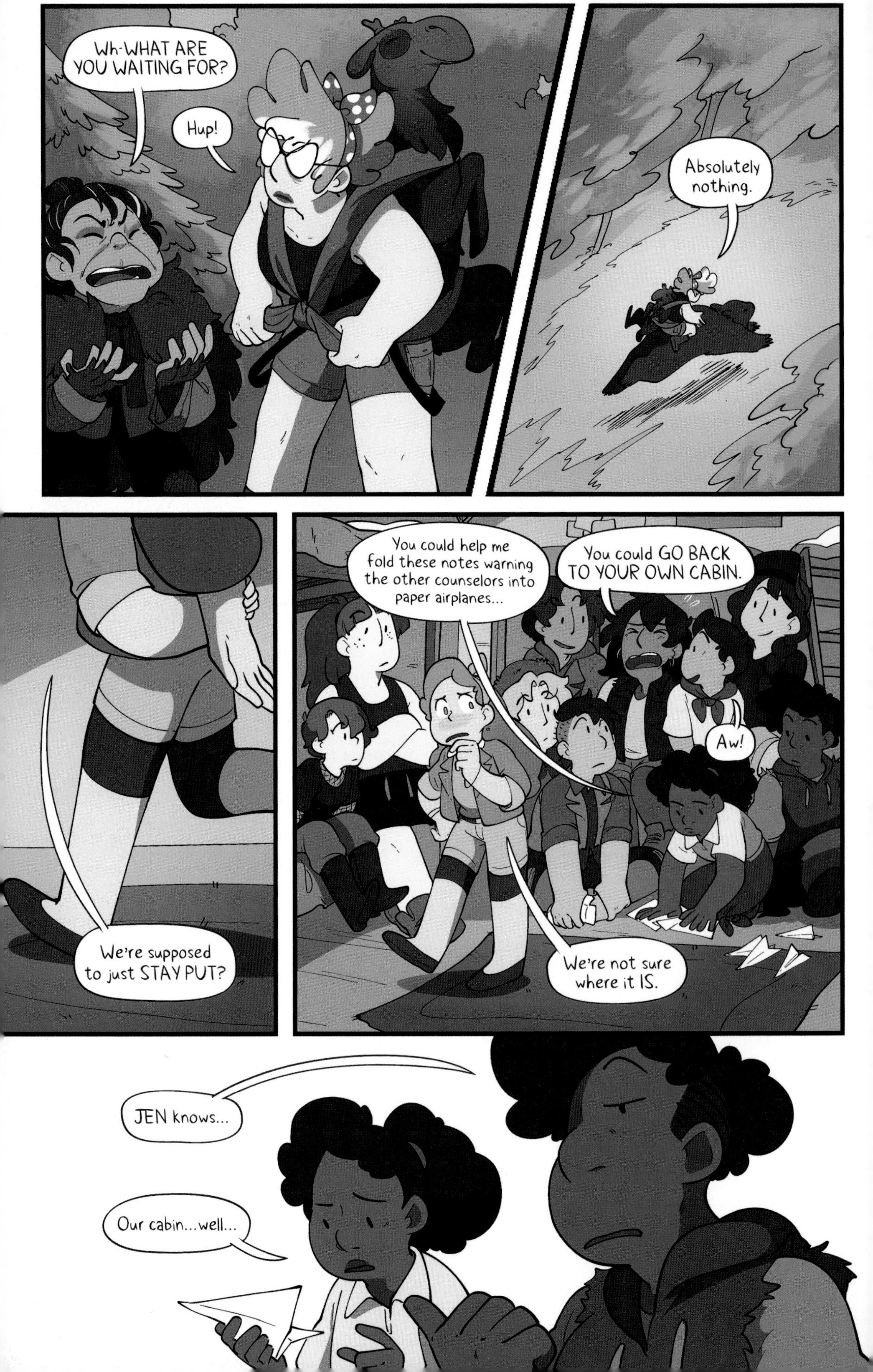
Wh-WHAT ARE YOU WAITING FOR?
Hup!
Absolutely nothing.
We're supposed to just STAY PUT?
You could help me fold these notes warning the other counselors into paper airplanes...
You could GO BACK TO YOUR OWN CABIN.
Aw!
We're not sure where it IS.
JEN knows...
Our cabin...well...

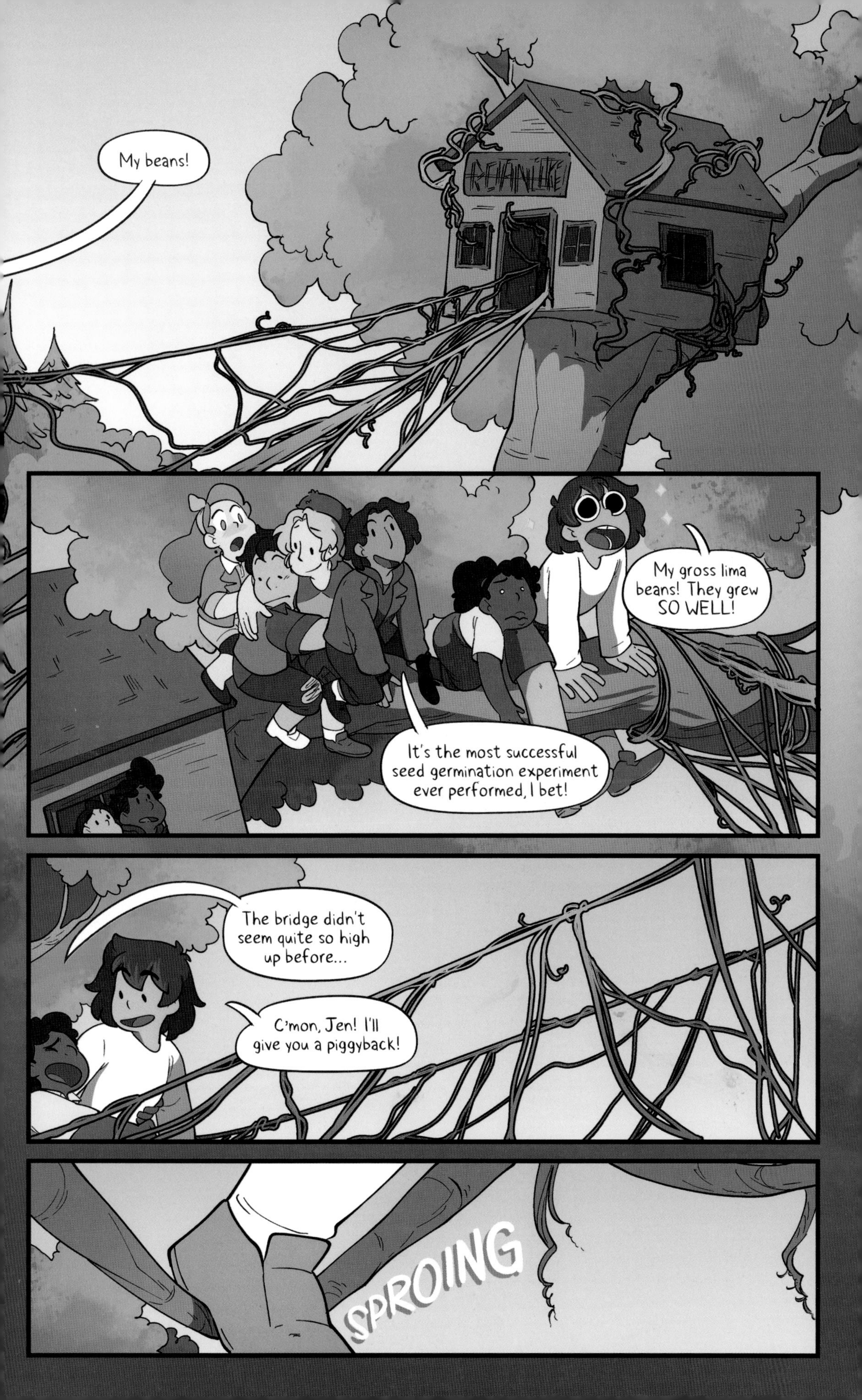
My beans!
My gross lima beans! They grew SO WELL!
It's the most successful seed germination experiment ever performed, I bet!
The bridge didn't seem quite so high up before...
C'mon, Jen! I'll give you a piggyback!
SPROING

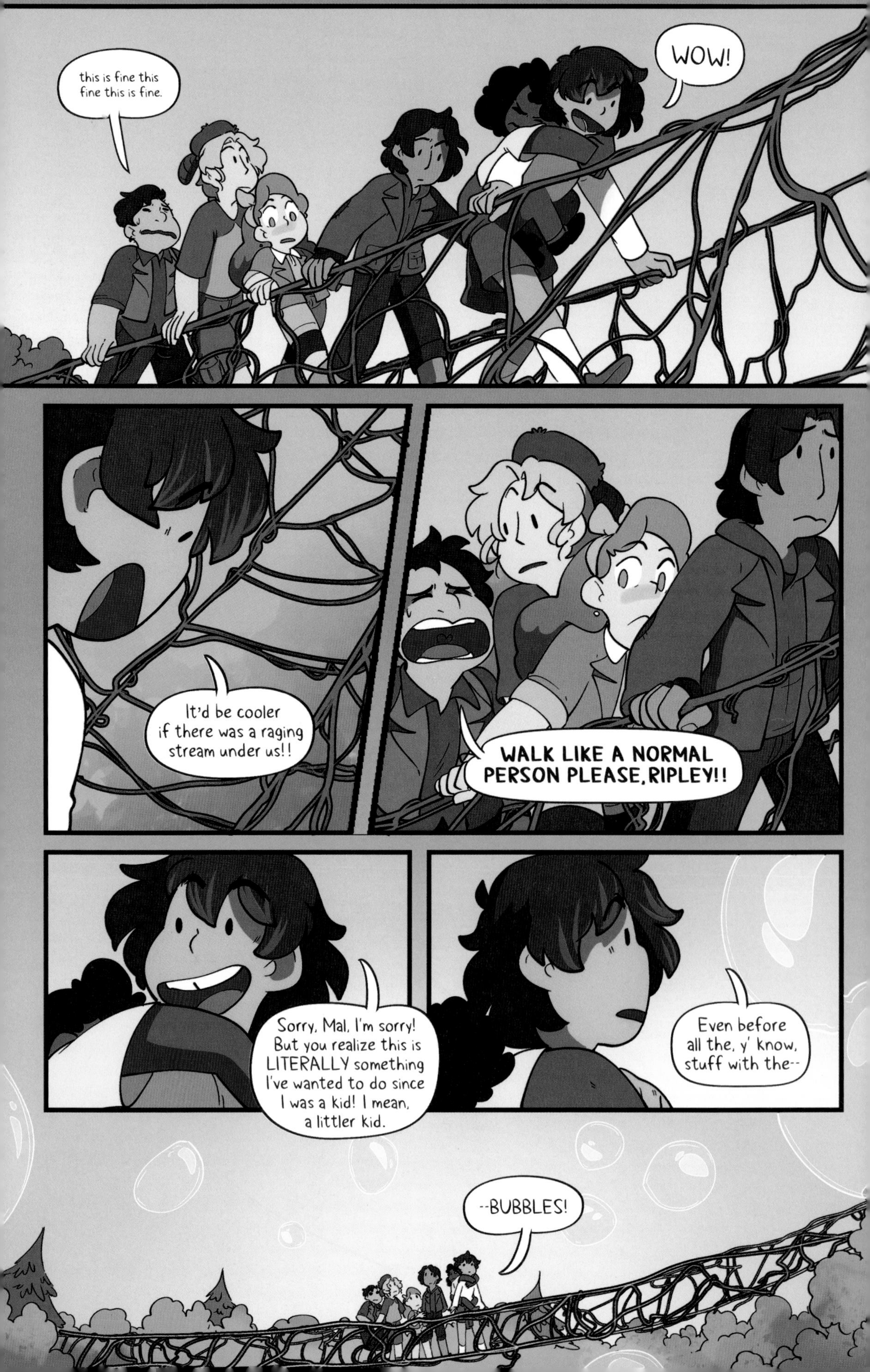
this is fine this fine this is fine.
WOW!
It'd be cooler if there was a raging stream under us!!
WALK LIKE A NORMAL PERSON PLEASE, RIPLEY!!
Sorry, Mal, I'm sorry! But you realize this is LITERALLY something I've wanted to do since I was a kid! I mean, a littler kid.
Even before all the, y' know, stuff with the--
--BUBBLES!

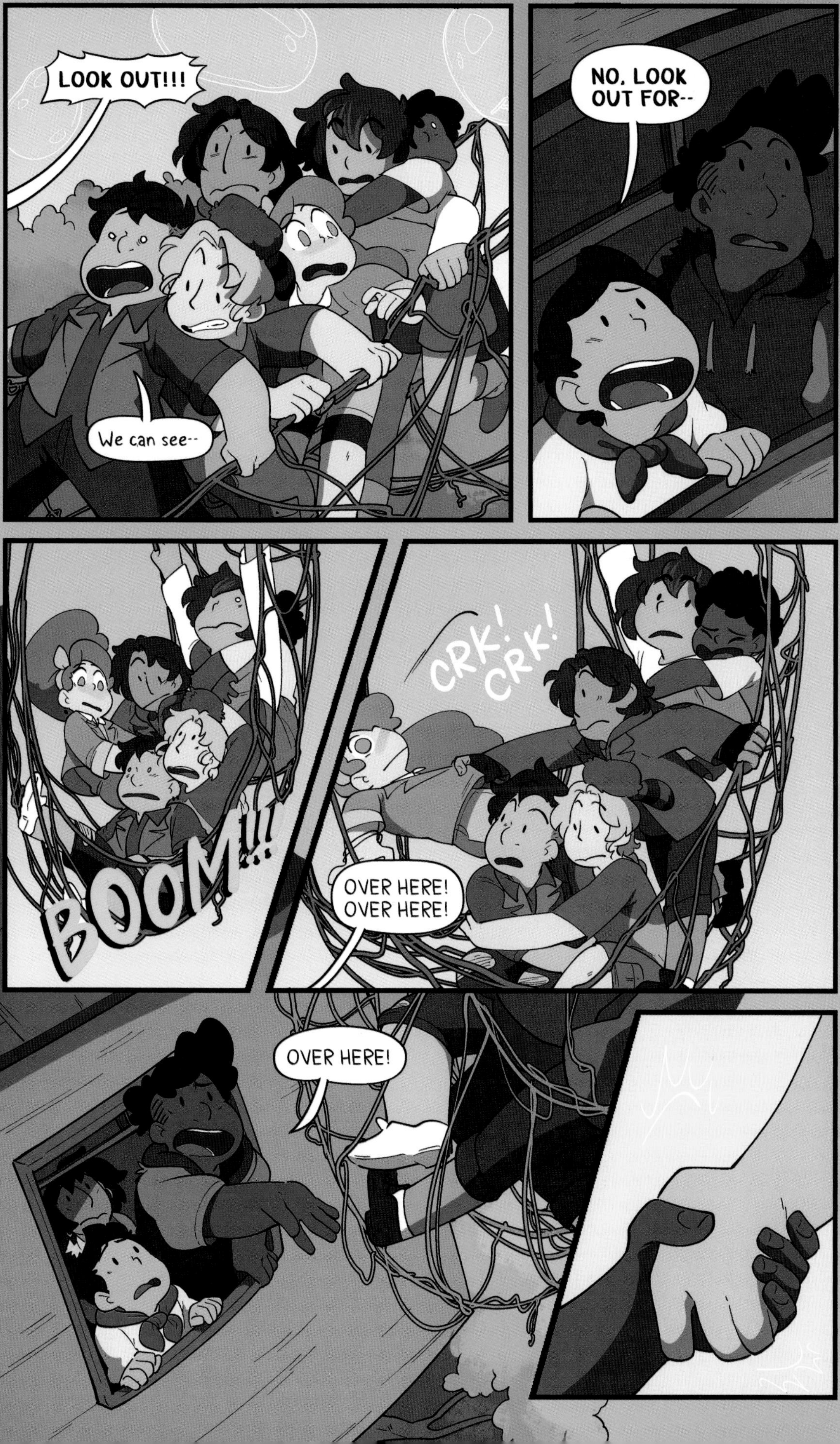
LOOK OUT!!!
We can see--
NO. LOOK OUT FOR--
BOOM!!!
CRK! CRK!
OVER HERE! OVER HERE!
OVER HERE!

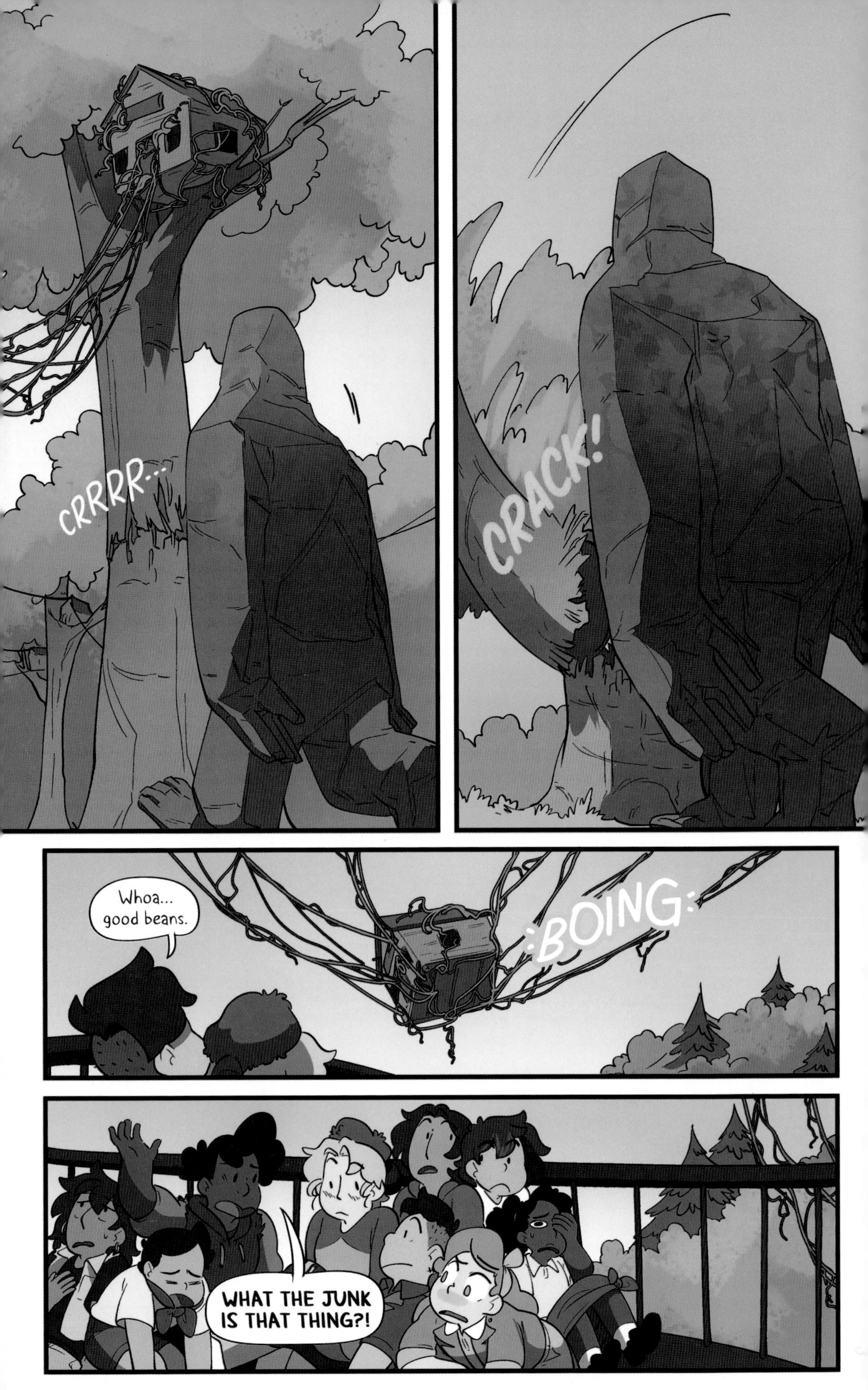
CRRRR...
CRACK!
Whoa... good beans.
BOING
WHAT THE JUNK IS THAT THING?!

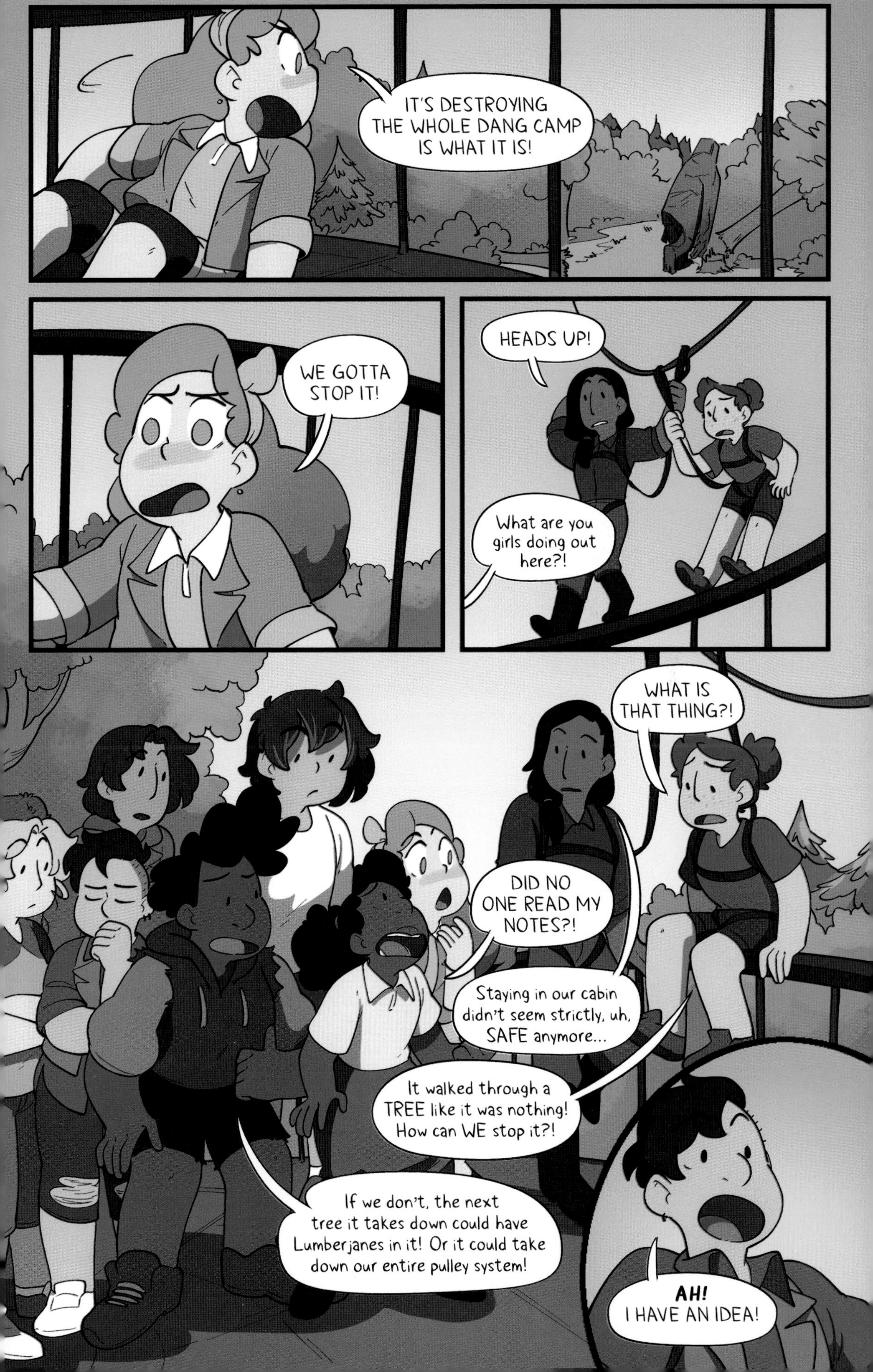
IT'S DESTROYING THE WHOLE DANG CAMP IS WHAT IT IS!
WE GOTTA STOP IT!
HEADS UP!
What are you girls doing out here?!
WHAT IS THAT THING?!
DID NO ONE READ MY NOTES?!
Staying in our cabin didn't seem strictly, uh, SAFE anymore...
It walked through a TREE like it was nothing! How can WE stop it?!
If we don't, the next tree it takes down could have Lumberjanes in it! Or it could take down our entire pulley system!
AH! I HAVE AN IDEA!

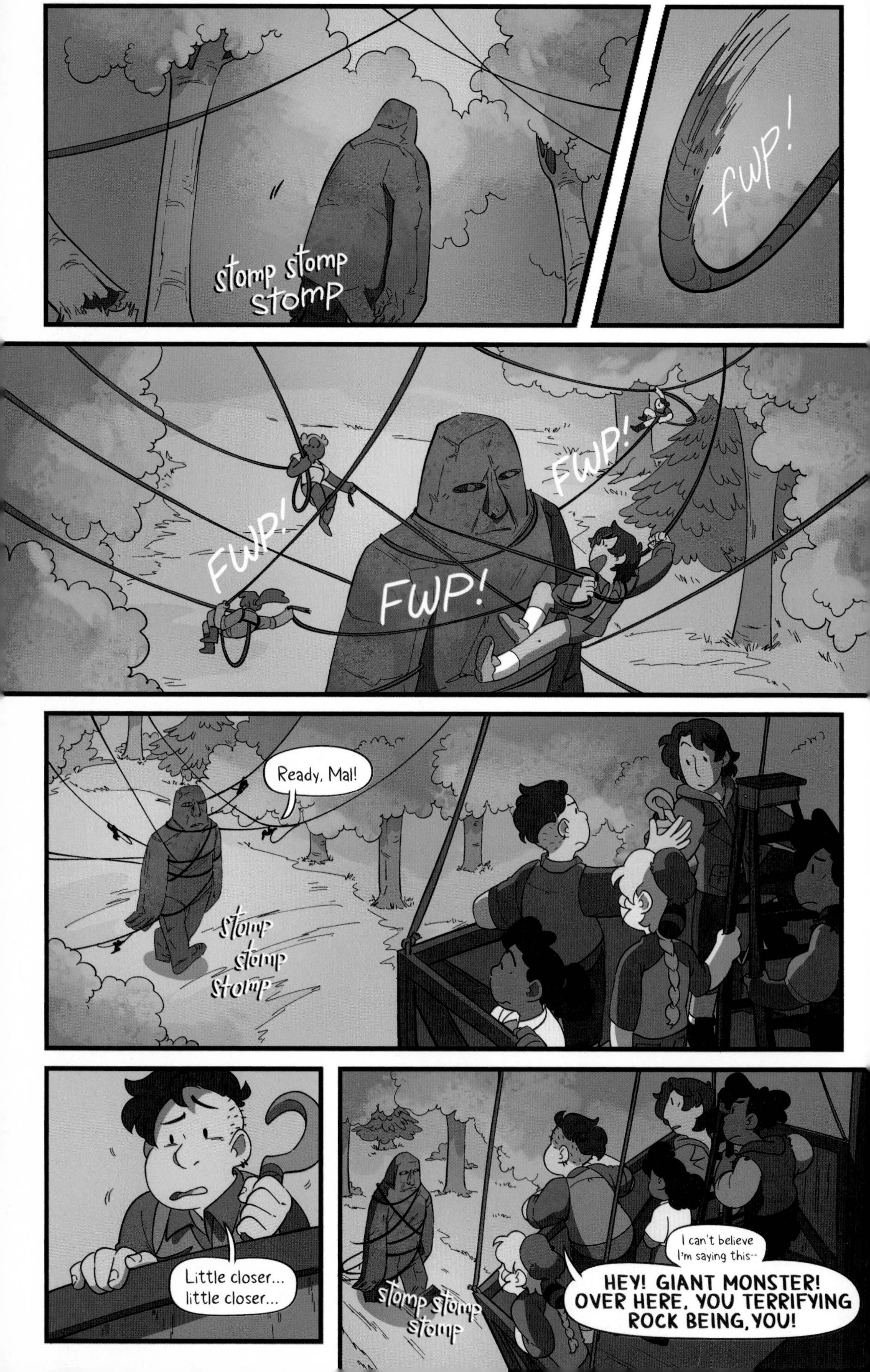
stomp stomp stomp
fwp!
FWP!
FWP!
FWP!
Ready, Mal!
stomp stomp stomp
Little closer... little closer...
stomp stomp stomp
I can't believe I'm saying this--
HEY! GIANT MONSTER! OVER HERE, YOU TERRIFYING ROCK BEING, YOU!

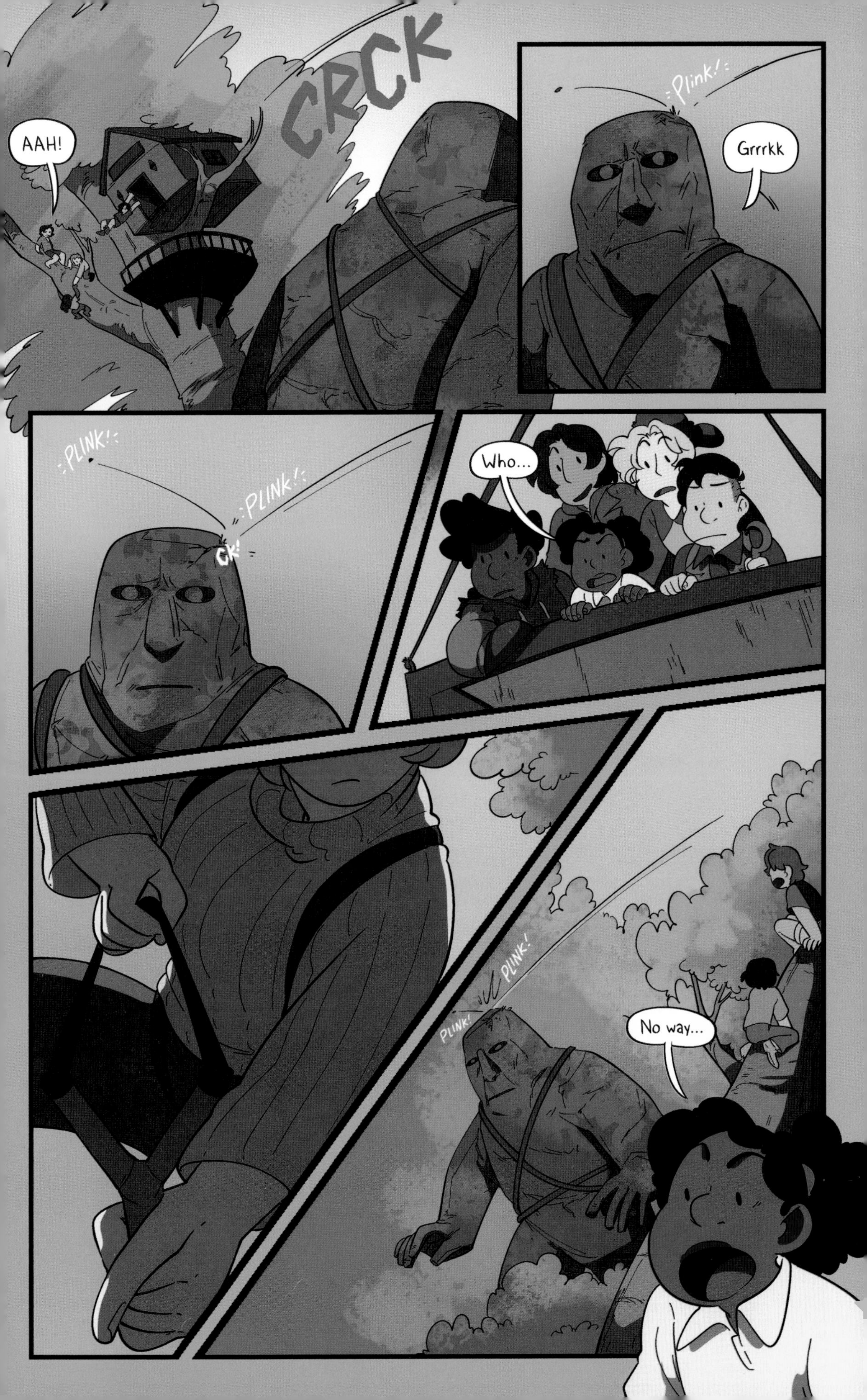
CRCK
AAH!
PLINK!
Grrrkk
PLINK!
PLINK!
CK!
Who...
PLINK!
PLINK!
No way...

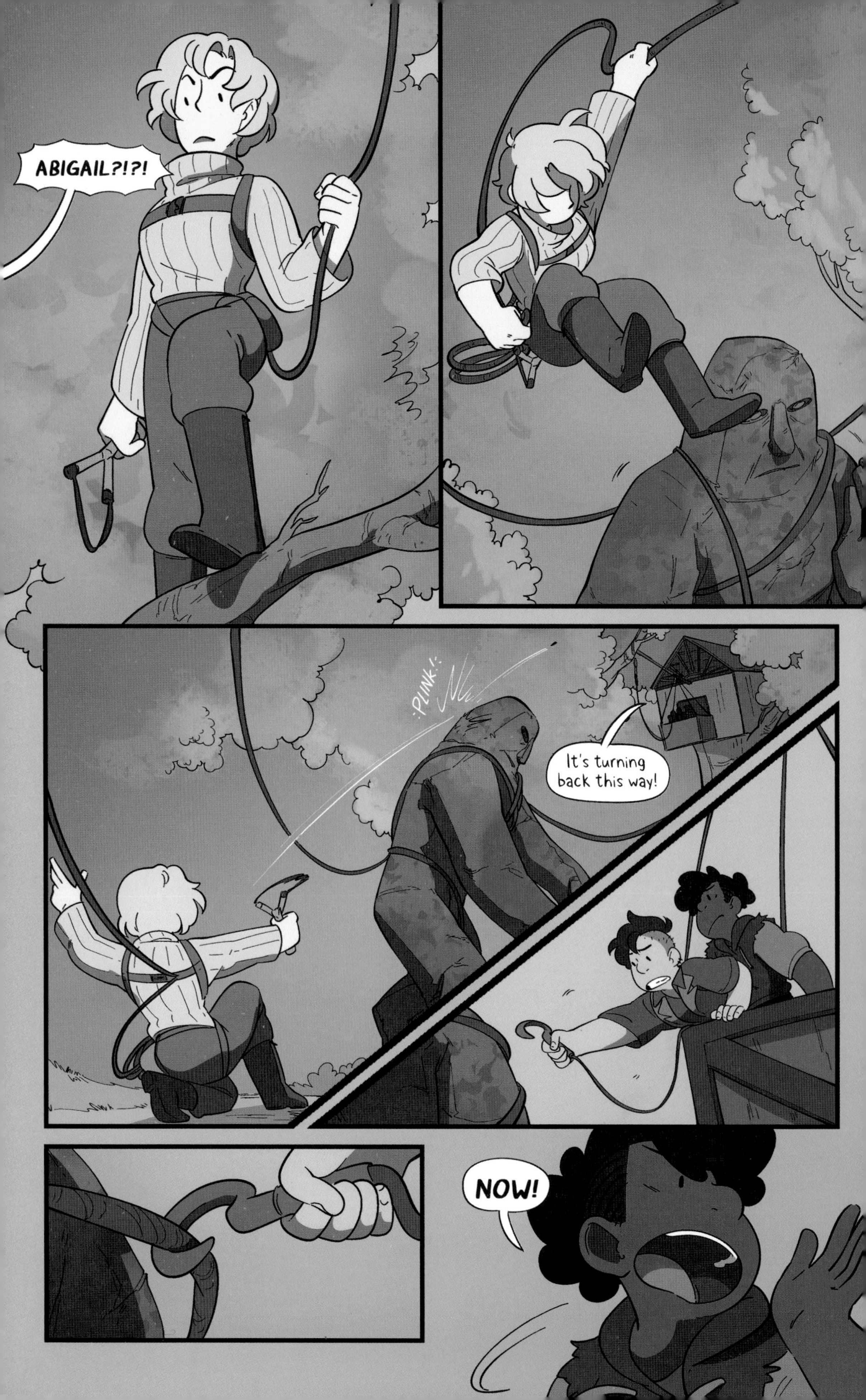
ABIGAIL?!?!
PLINK!
It's turning back this way!
NOW!

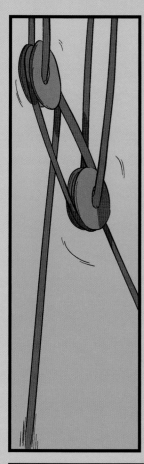

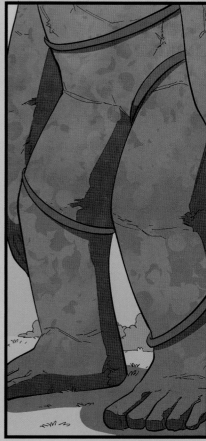

Make like Sarah Robles and PULL! Use your legs!

ptoo!

SWOOP

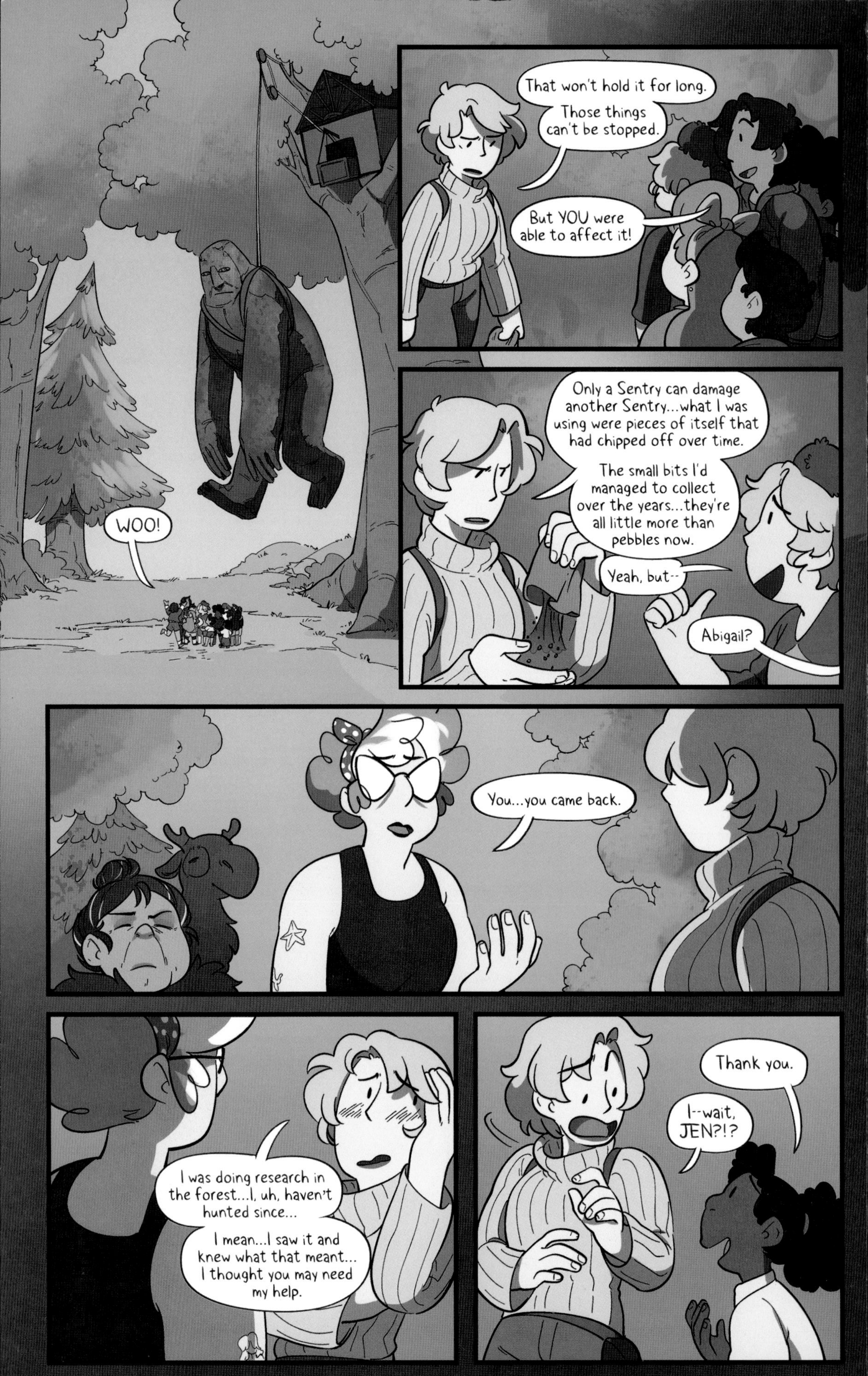
WOO!
That won't hold it for long.
Those things can't be stopped.
But YOU were able to affect it!
Only a Sentry can damage another Sentry...what I was using were pieces of itself that had chipped off over time.
The small bits I'd managed to collect over the years...they're all little more than pebbles now.
Yeah, but--
Abigail?
You...you came back.
I was doing research in the forest...I, uh, haven't hunted since...
I mean...I saw it and knew what that meant... I thought you may need my help.
Thank you.
I--wait, JEN?!?

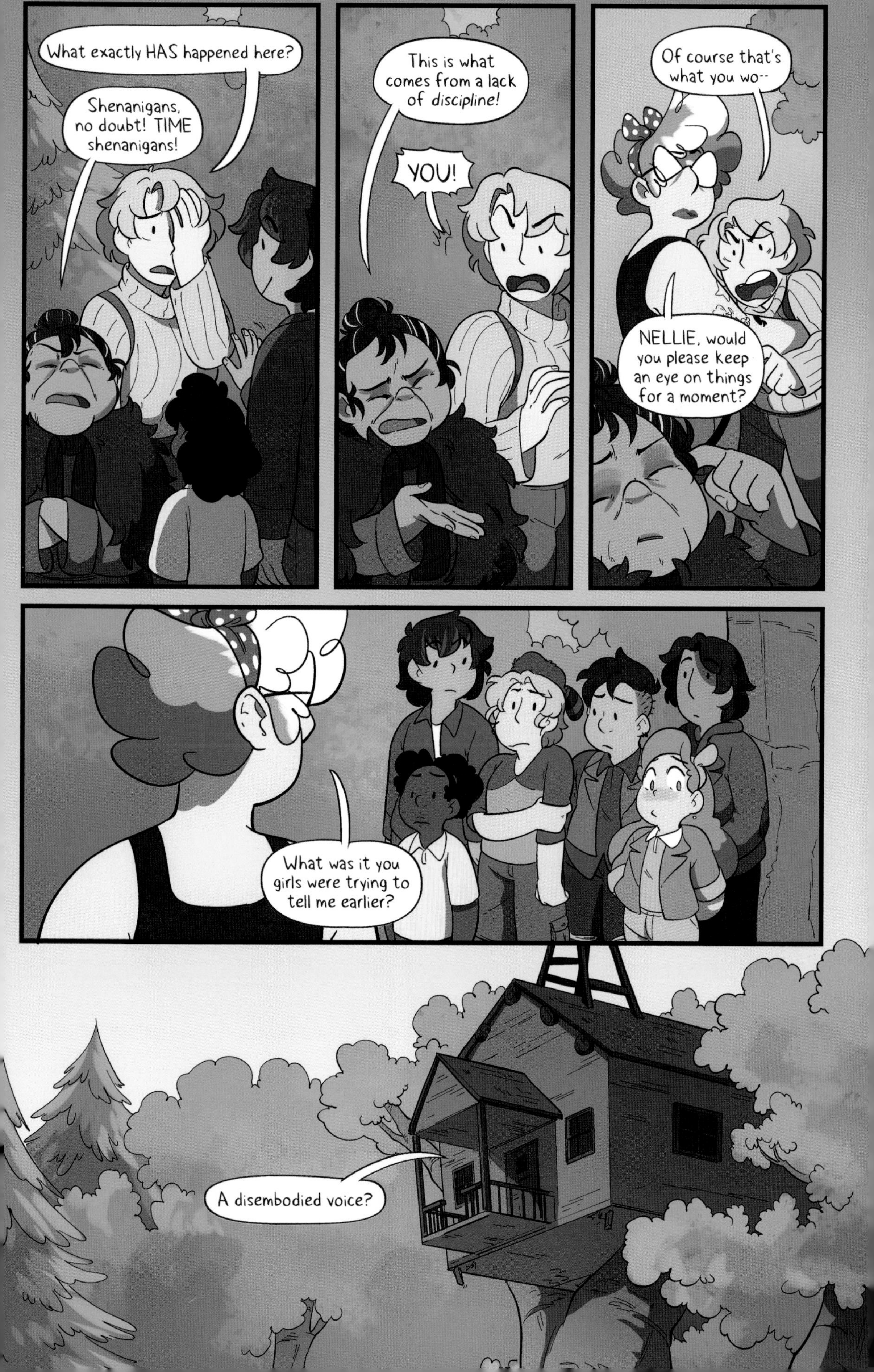
What exactly HAS happened here?
Shenanigans, no doubt! TIME shenanigans!
This is what comes from a lack of *discipline*!
YOU!
Of course that's what you wo--
NELLIE, would you please keep an eye on things for a moment?
What was it you girls were trying to tell me earlier?
A disembodied voice?

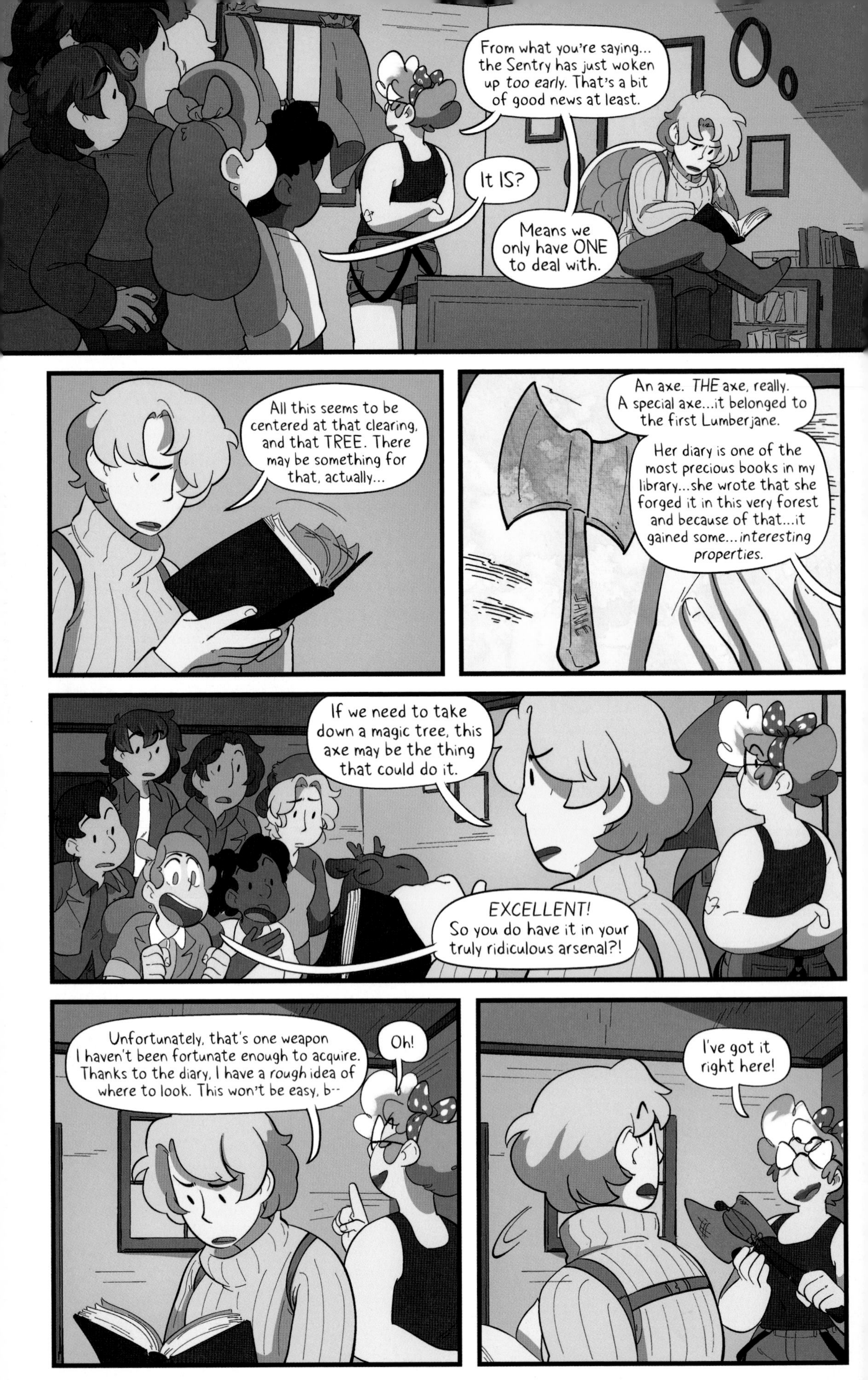
From what you're saying... the Sentry has just woken up *too early*. That's a bit of good news at least.
It IS?
Means we only have ONE to deal with.
All this seems to be centered at that clearing, and that TREE. There may be something for that, actually...
An axe. *THE* axe, really. A special axe...it belonged to the first Lumberjane.
Her diary is one of the most precious books in my library...she wrote that she forged it in this very forest and because of that...it gained some... *interesting properties.*
JANE
If we need to take down a magic tree, this axe may be the thing that could do it.
EXCELLENT! So you do have it in your truly ridiculous arsenal?!
Unfortunately, that's one weapon I haven't been fortunate enough to acquire. Thanks to the diary, I have a *rough* idea of where to look. This won't be easy, b--
Oh!
I've got it right here!

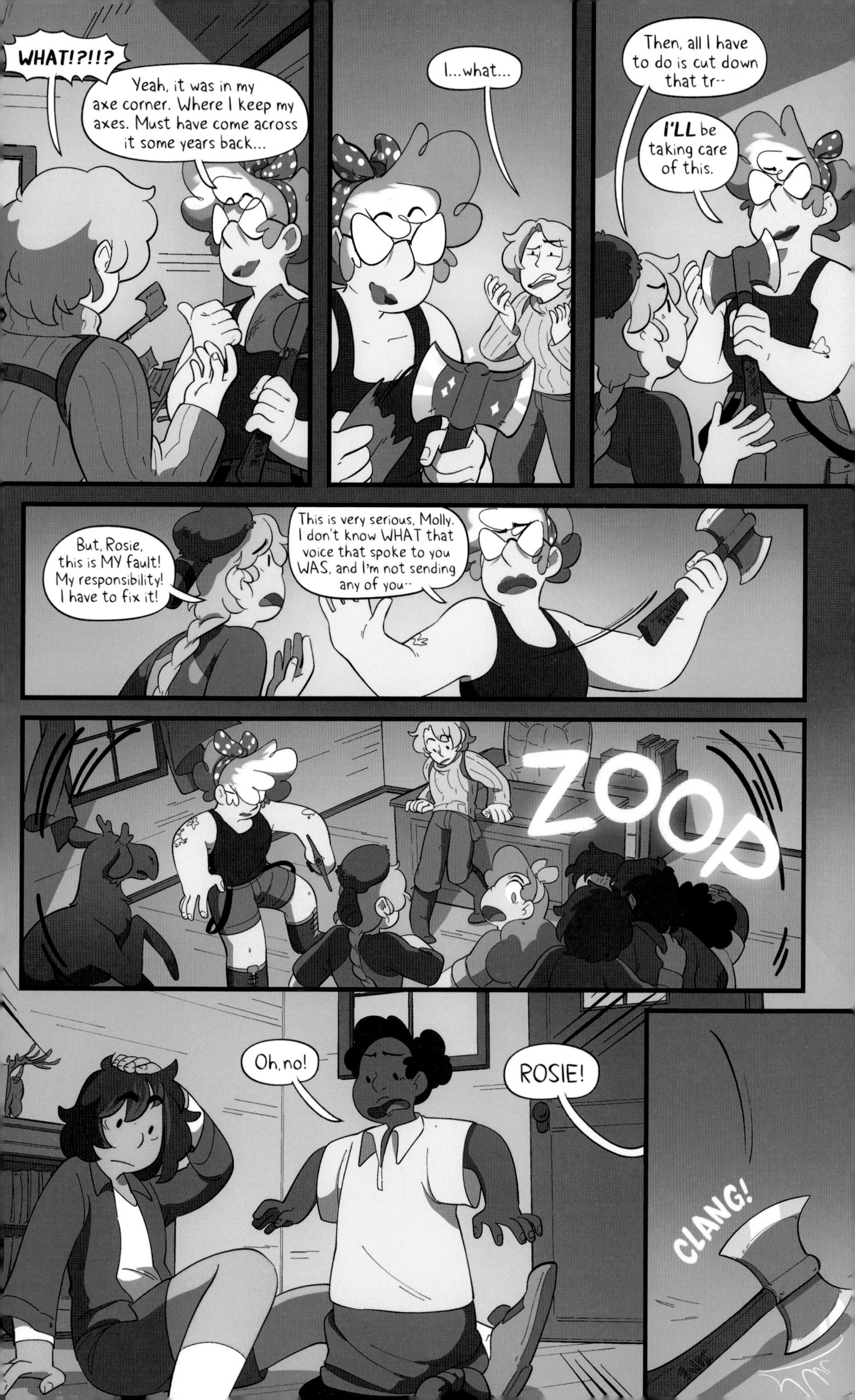
WHAT!?!!?
Yeah, it was in my axe corner. Where I keep my axes. Must have come across it some years back...
I...what...
Then, all I have to do is cut down that tr--
I'LL be taking care of this.
But, Rosie, this is MY fault! My responsibility! I have to fix it!
This is very serious, Molly. I don't know WHAT that voice that spoke to you WAS, and I'm not sending any of you--
ZOOP
Oh, no!
ROSIE!
CLANG!

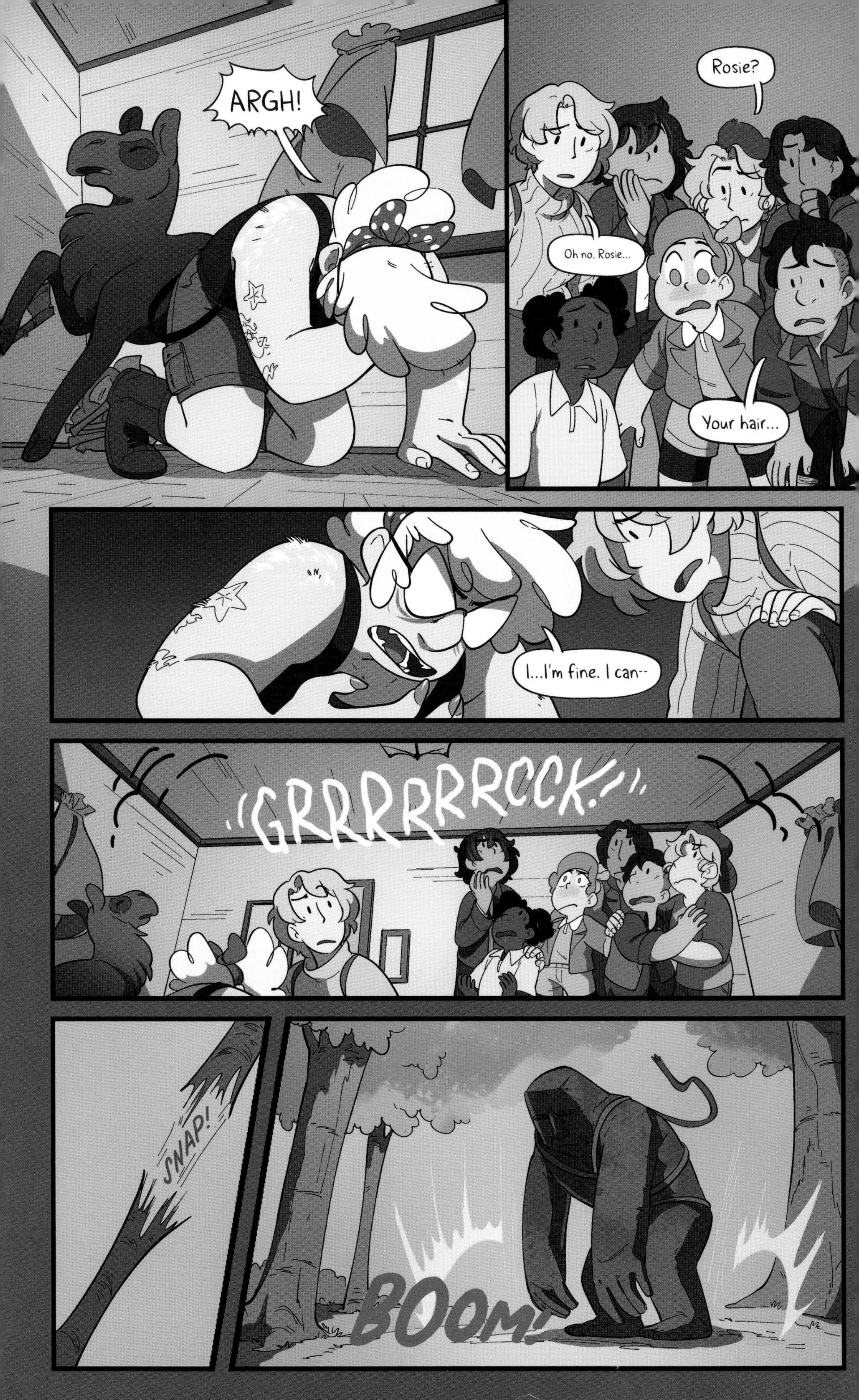
ARGH!
Rosie?
Oh no, Rosie...
Your hair...
I...I'm fine. I can--
GRRRRRRCCK!
SNAP!
BOOM!

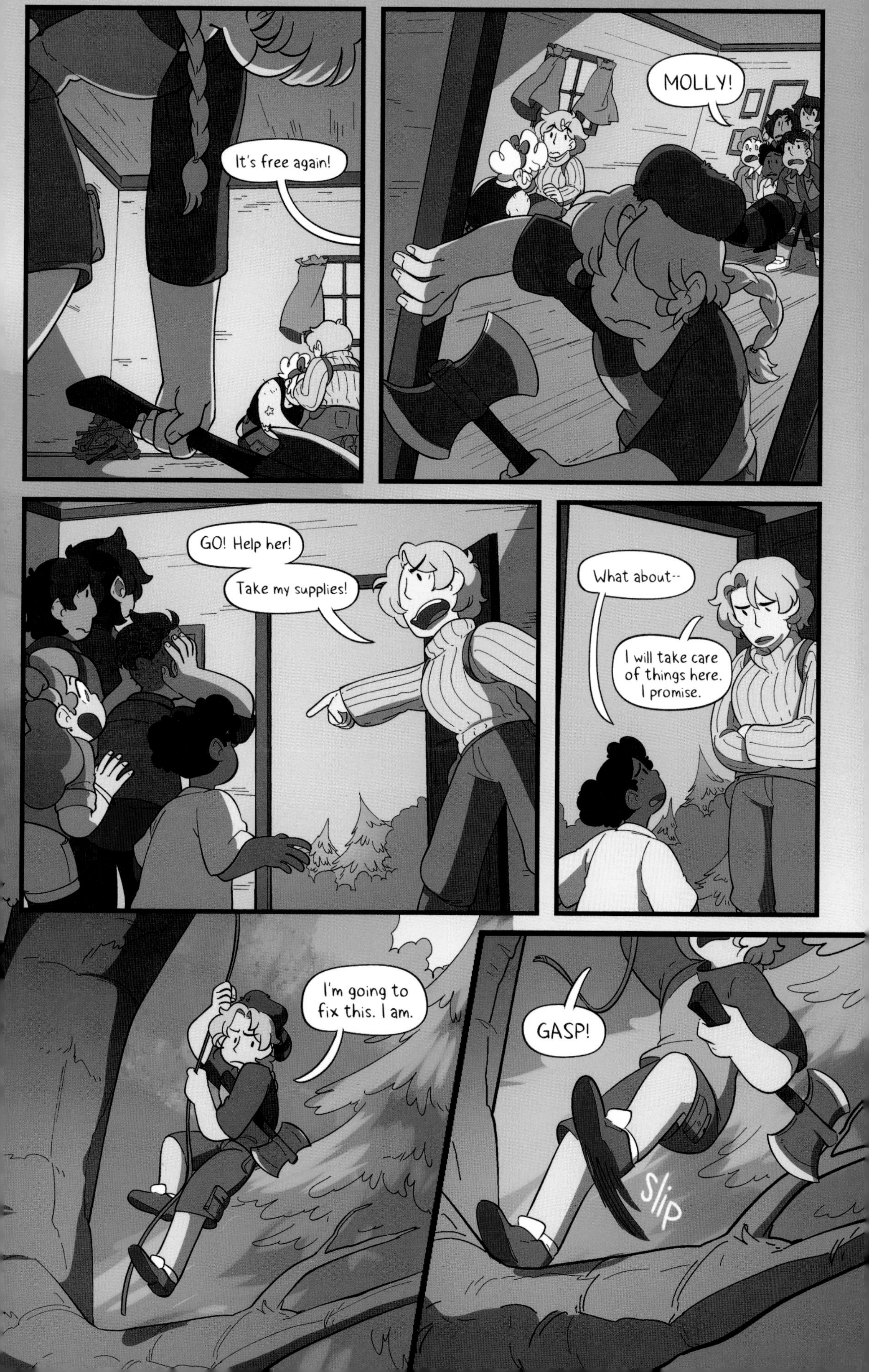
It's free again!
MOLLY!
GO! Help her!
Take my supplies!
What about--
I will take care of things here. I promise.
I'm going to fix this. I am.
GASP!
slip

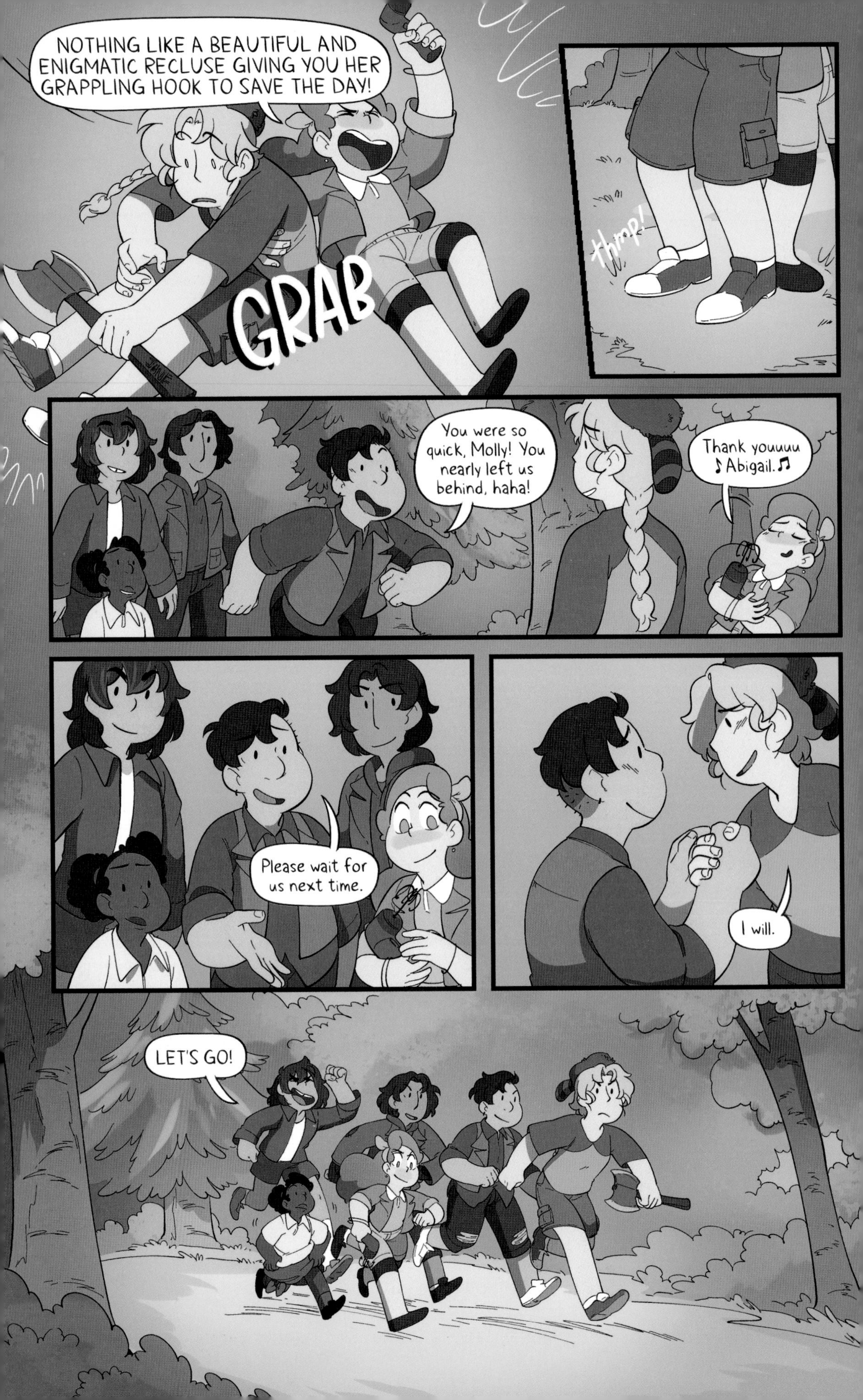
NOTHING LIKE A BEAUTIFUL AND ENIGMATIC RECLUSE GIVING YOU HER GRAPPLING HOOK TO SAVE THE DAY!
GRAB
thmp!
You were so quick, Molly! You nearly left us behind, haha!
Thank youuuu ♪ Abigail. ♫
Please wait for us next time.
I will.
LET'S GO!

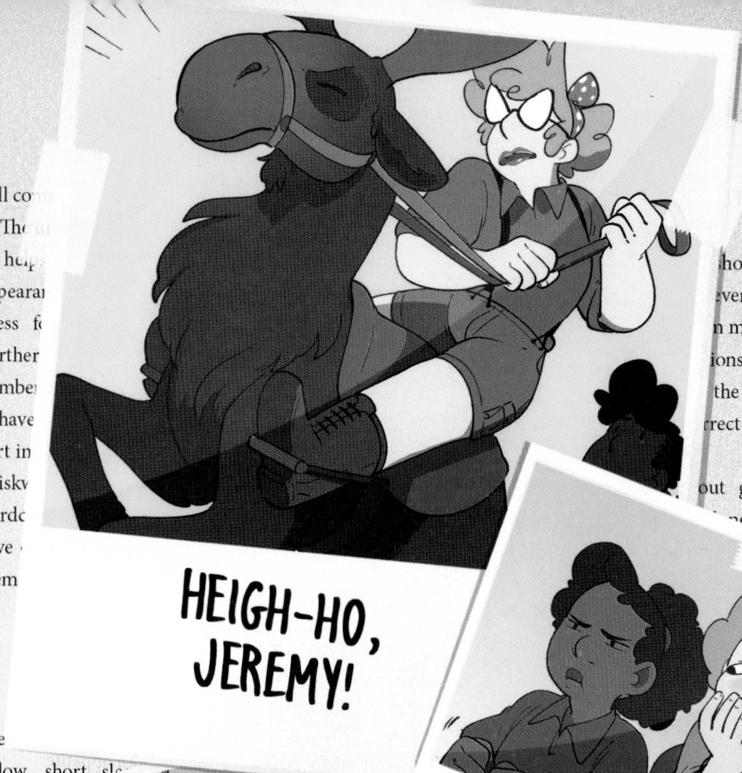
HEIGH-HO, JEREMY!

will co

The

It h

appearan

dress f

Further

Lumbe

to have

part in

Thiskv

Hardc

have

them

HE UNIFORM

hould be worn at camp
vents when Lumberjanes
n may also be worn at other
ions. It should be worn as a
the uniform dress with
rrect shoes, and stocking or

out grows her uniform or
to another Lumberjane.
a she has
her
her

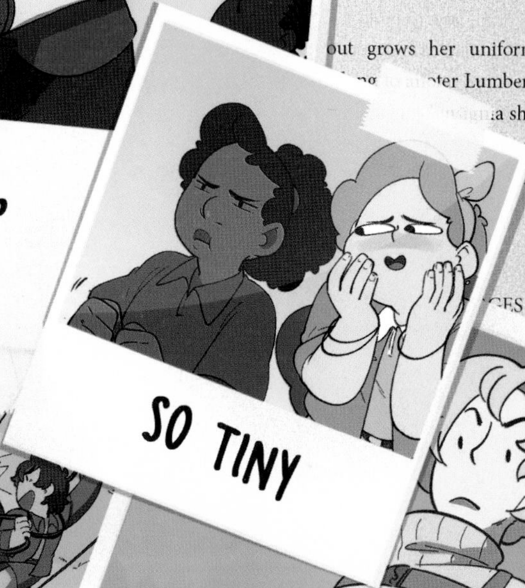
SO TINY

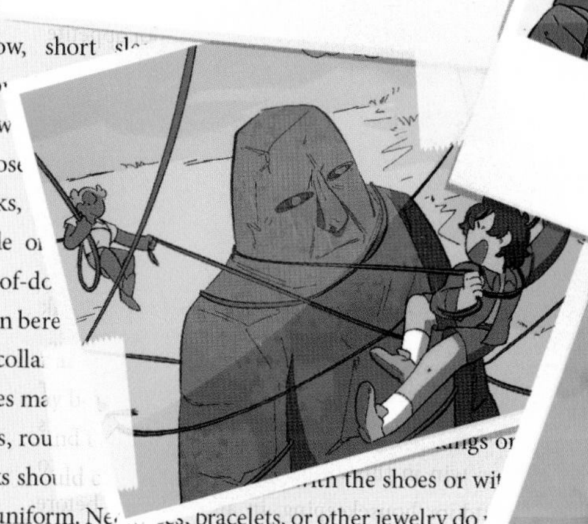

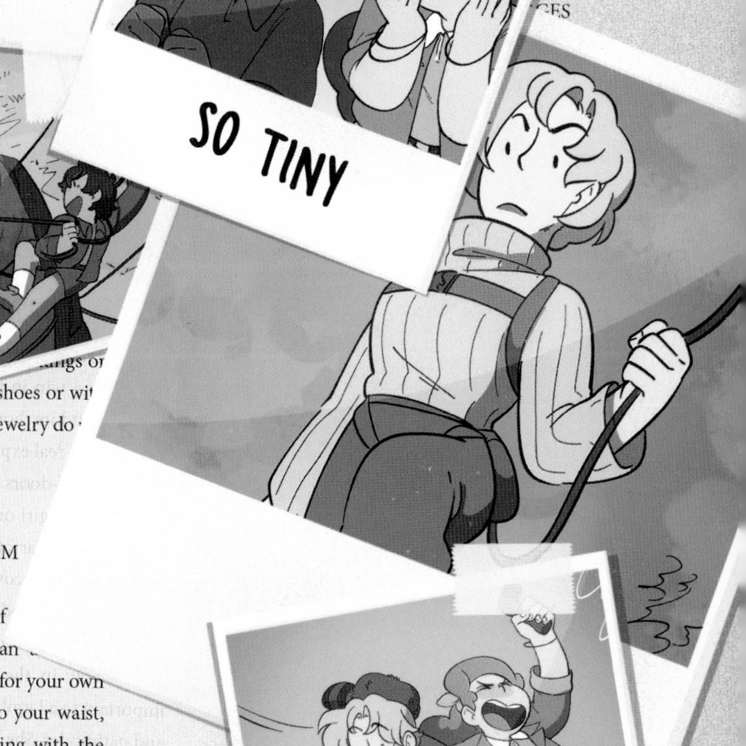

The
yellow, short sl
emb
the w
choos
slacks,
made o
out-of-d
green bere
the colla
Shoes ma
heels, rou ings or
socks shou with the shoes or wi
the uniform. Ne bracelets, or other jewelry do
belong with a Lumberjane uniform.

HOW TO WEAR THE UNIFORM

To look well in a uniform demands first of uniform be kept in good condition—clean pressed. See that the skirt is the right length for your own height and build, that the belt is adjusted to your waist, that your shoes and stockings are in keeping with the uniform, that you watch your posture and carry yourself with dignity and grace. If the beret is removed indoors, be sure that your hair is neat and kept in place with an insonspicuous clip or ribbon. When you wear a Lumberjane uniform you are identified as a member of this organization and you should be doubly careful to conduct yourself in a way that will show everyone that courtesy and thoughtfullness are part of being a Lumberjane. People are likely to judge a whole nation by the selfishness of a few individuals, to criticize a whole family because of the misconduct of one member, and to feel unkindly toward and organization because of the

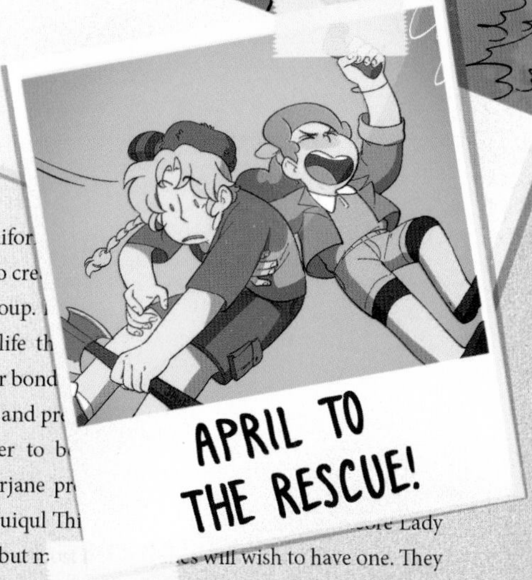
APRIL TO THE RESCUE!

The unifor
helps to cre
in a group.
active life th
another bond
future, and pr
in order to b
Lumberjane pr
Penniquiqul Thi ore Lady
Types, but m will wish to have one. They
can either bu the uniform, or make it themselves from
materials available at the trading post.

LUMBERJANES FIELD MANUAL

CHAPTER FORTY-FOUR

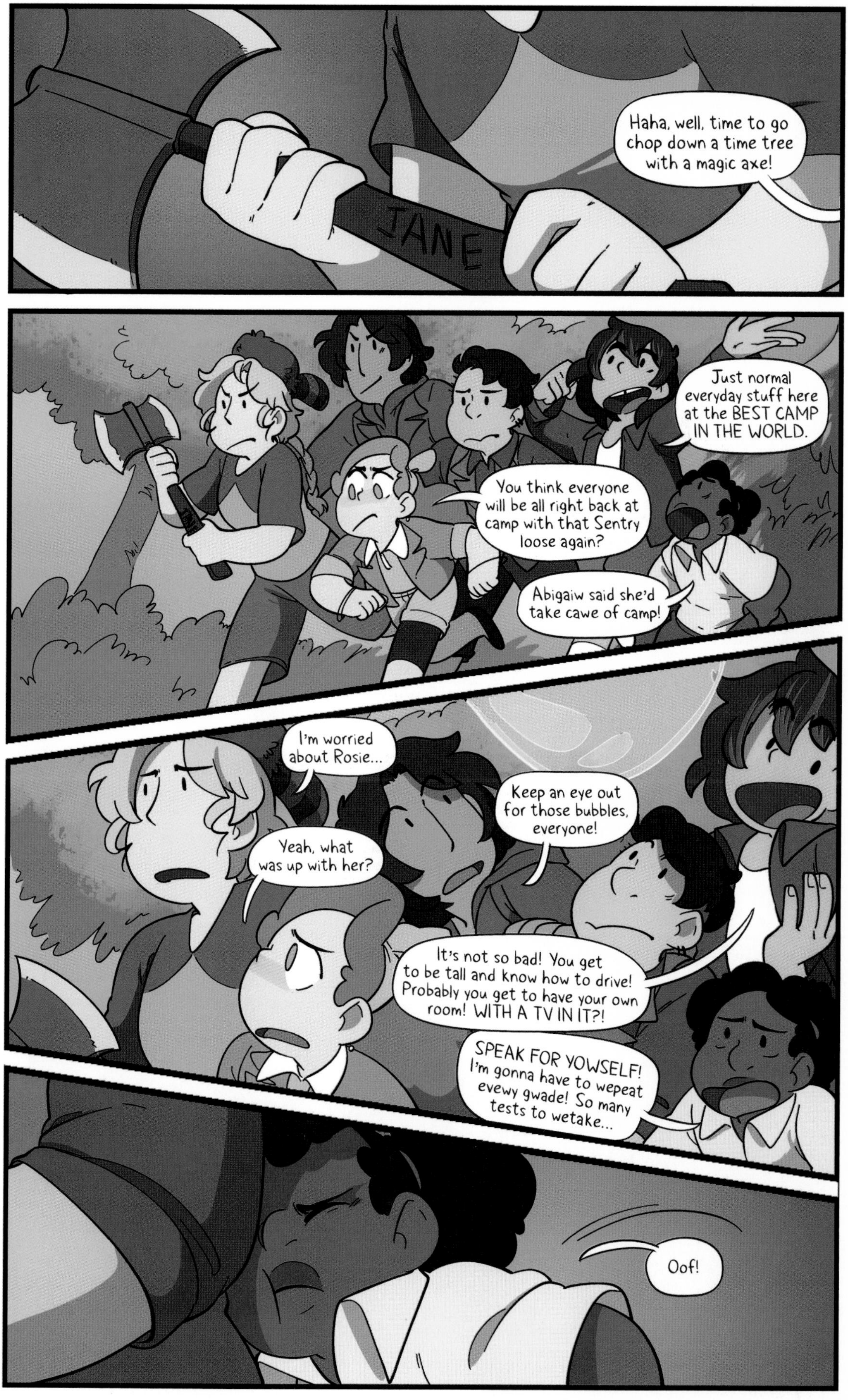
Haha, well, time to go chop down a time tree with a magic axe!
JANE
Just normal everyday stuff here at the BEST CAMP IN THE WORLD.
You think everyone will be all right back at camp with that Sentry loose again?
Abigaiw said she'd take cawe of camp!
I'm worried about Rosie...
Keep an eye out for those bubbles, everyone!
Yeah, what was up with her?
It's not so bad! You get to be tall and know how to drive! Probably you get to have your own room! WITH A TV IN IT?!
SPEAK FOR YOWSELF! I'm gonna have to wepeat evewy gwade! So many tests to wetake...
Oof!

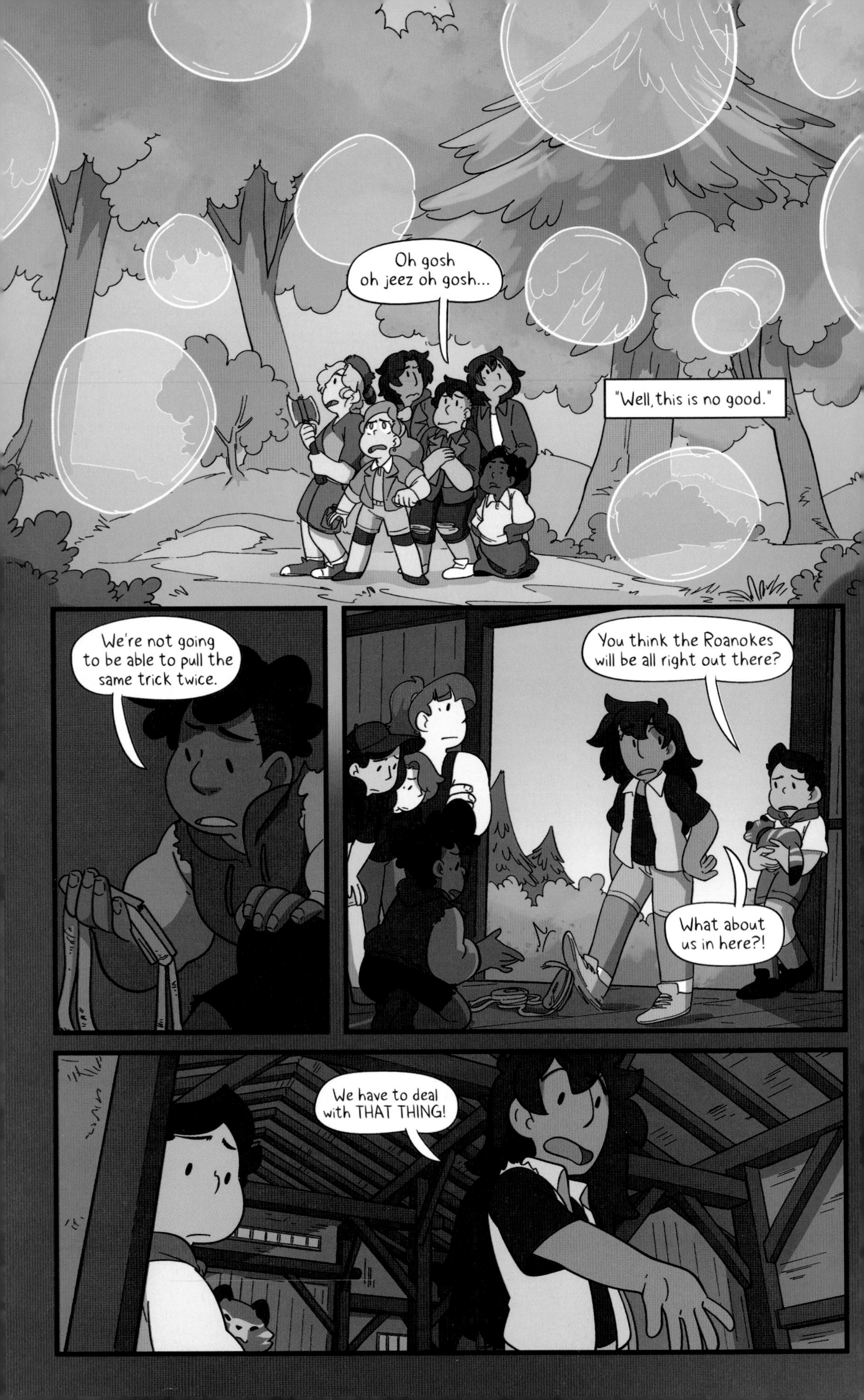
Oh gosh oh jeez oh gosh...
"Well, this is no good."
We're not going to be able to pull the same trick twice.
You think the Roanokes will be all right out there?
What about us in here?!
We have to deal with THAT THING!

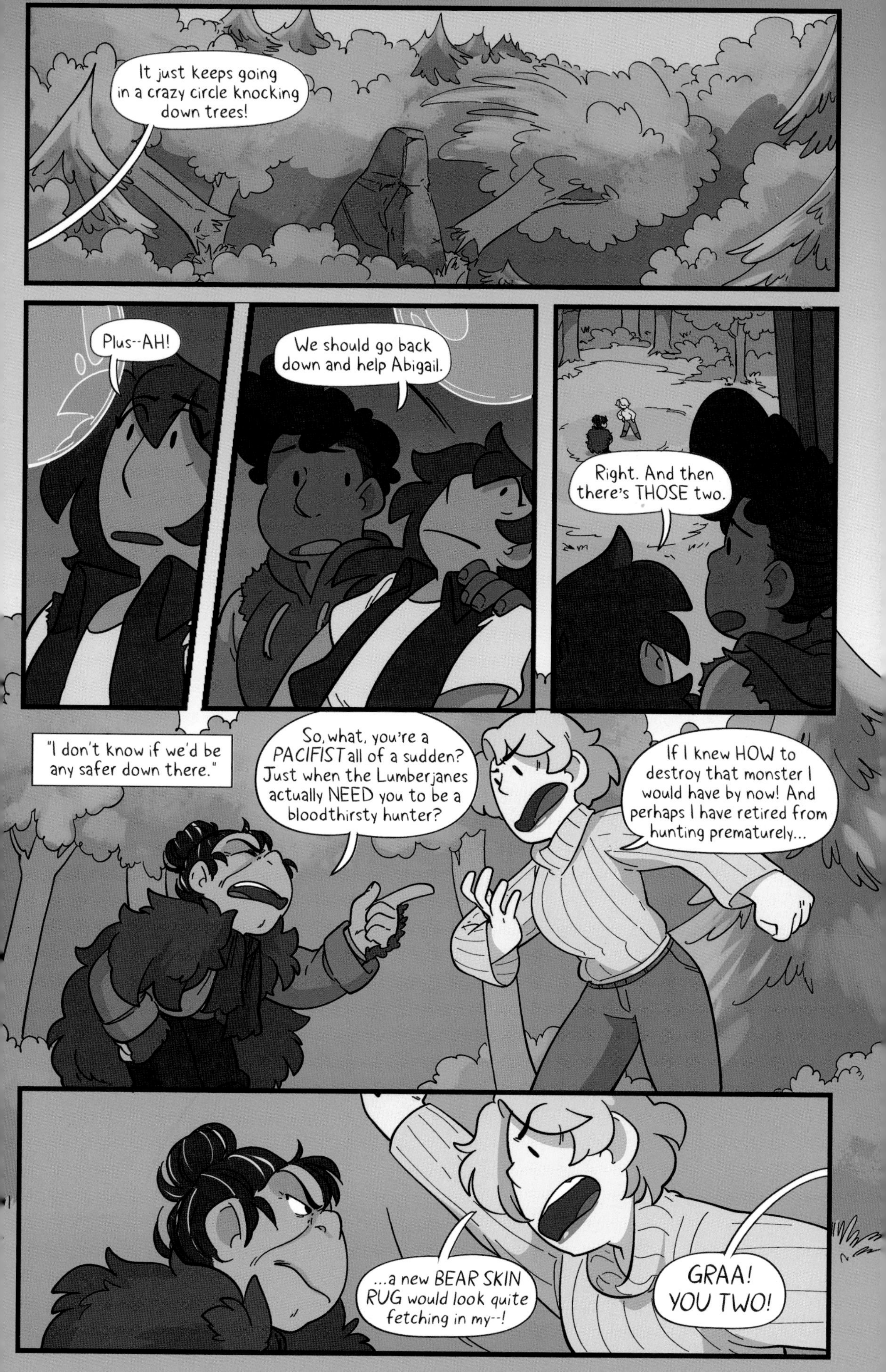
It just keeps going in a crazy circle knocking down trees!
Plus--AH!
We should go back down and help Abigail.
Right. And then there's THOSE two.
"I don't know if we'd be any safer down there."
So, what, you're a PACIFIST all of a sudden? Just when the Lumberjanes actually NEED you to be a bloodthirsty hunter?
If I knew HOW to destroy that monster I would have by now! And perhaps I have retired from hunting prematurely...
...a new BEAR SKIN RUG would look quite fetching in my--!
GRAA! YOU TWO!

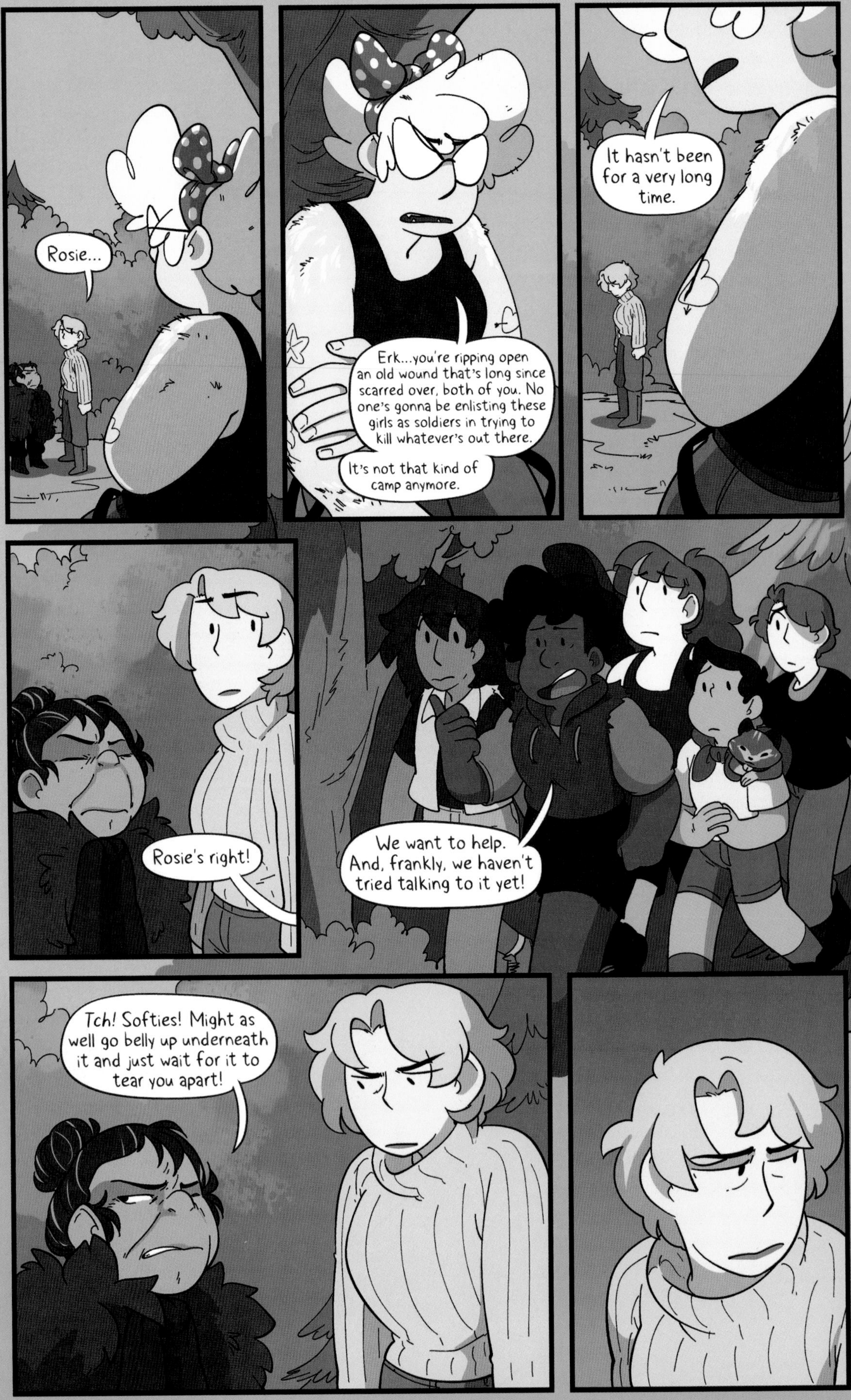
Rosie...
Erk...you're ripping open an old wound that's long since scarred over, both of you. No one's gonna be enlisting these girls as soldiers in trying to kill whatever's out there.
It's not that kind of camp anymore.
It hasn't been for a very long time.
Rosie's right!
We want to help. And, frankly, we haven't tried talking to it yet!
Tch! Softies! Might as well go belly up underneath it and just wait for it to tear you apart!

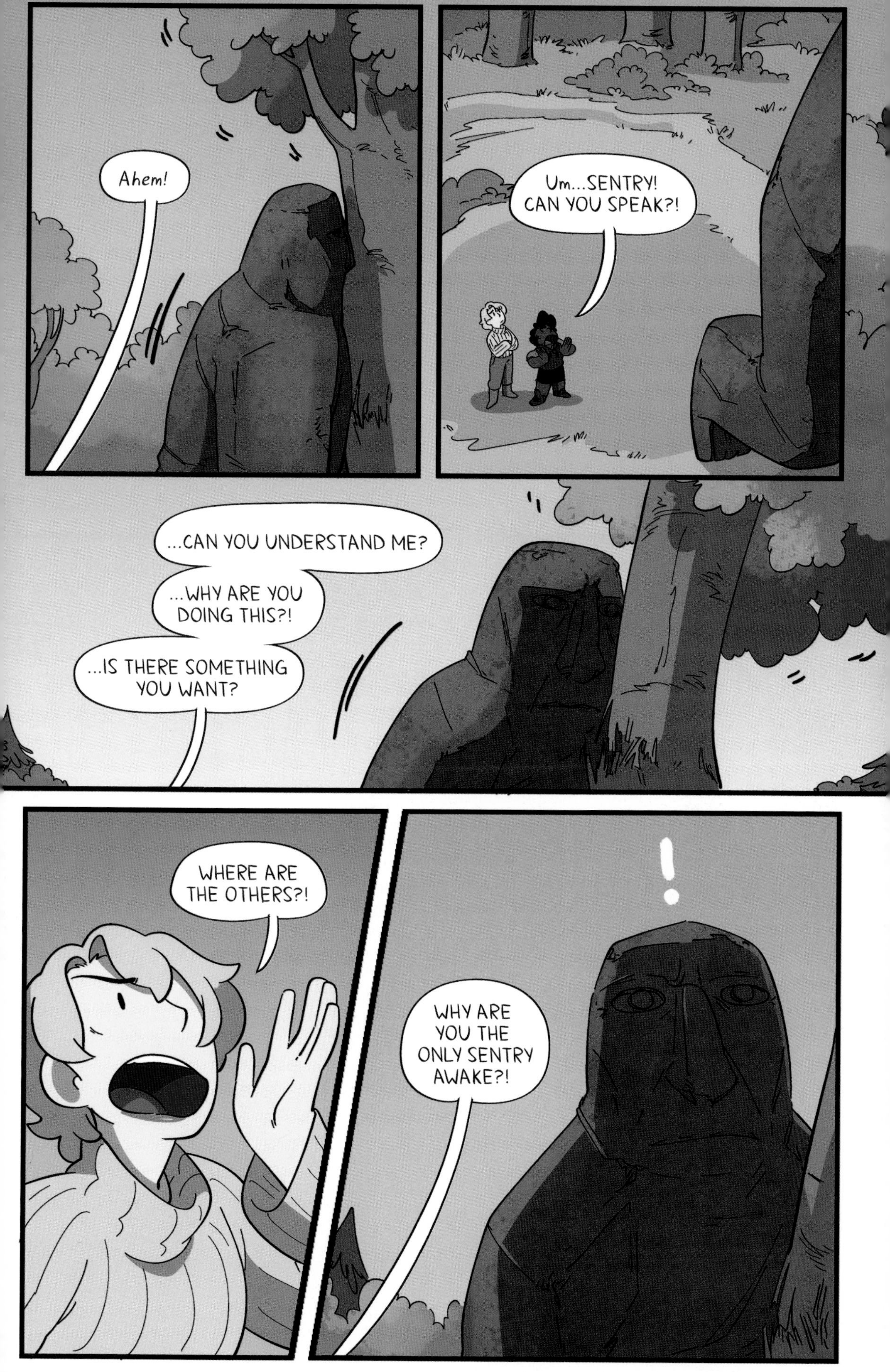
Ahem!
Um...SENTRY! CAN YOU SPEAK?!
...CAN YOU UNDERSTAND ME?
...WHY ARE YOU DOING THIS?!
...IS THERE SOMETHING YOU WANT?
WHERE ARE THE OTHERS?!
!
WHY ARE YOU THE ONLY SENTRY AWAKE?!

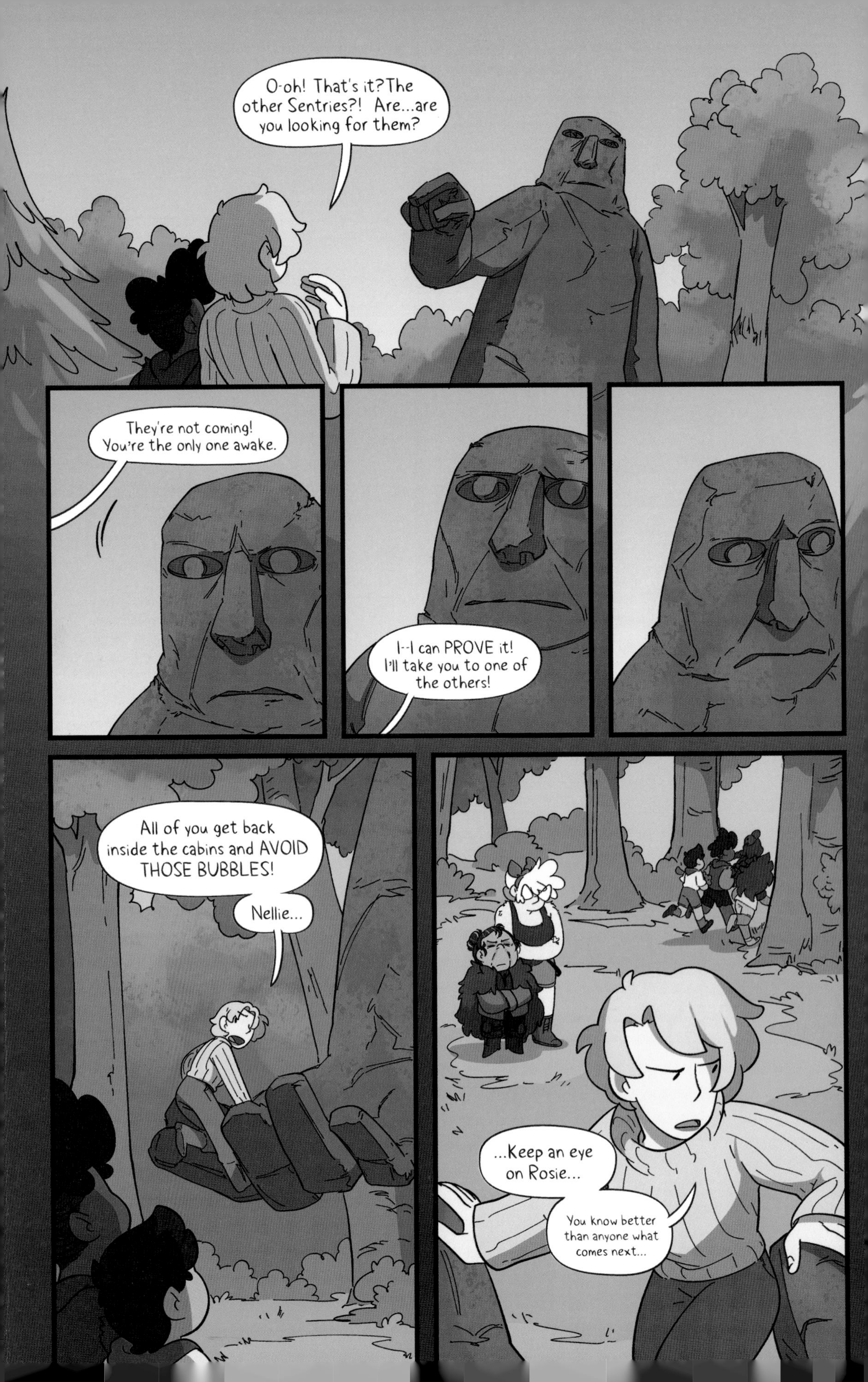
O-oh! That's it? The other Sentries?! Are...are you looking for them?
They're not coming! You're the only one awake.
I--I can PROVE it! I'll take you to one of the others!
All of you get back inside the cabins and AVOID THOSE BUBBLES!
Nellie...
...Keep an eye on Rosie...
You know better than anyone what comes next...

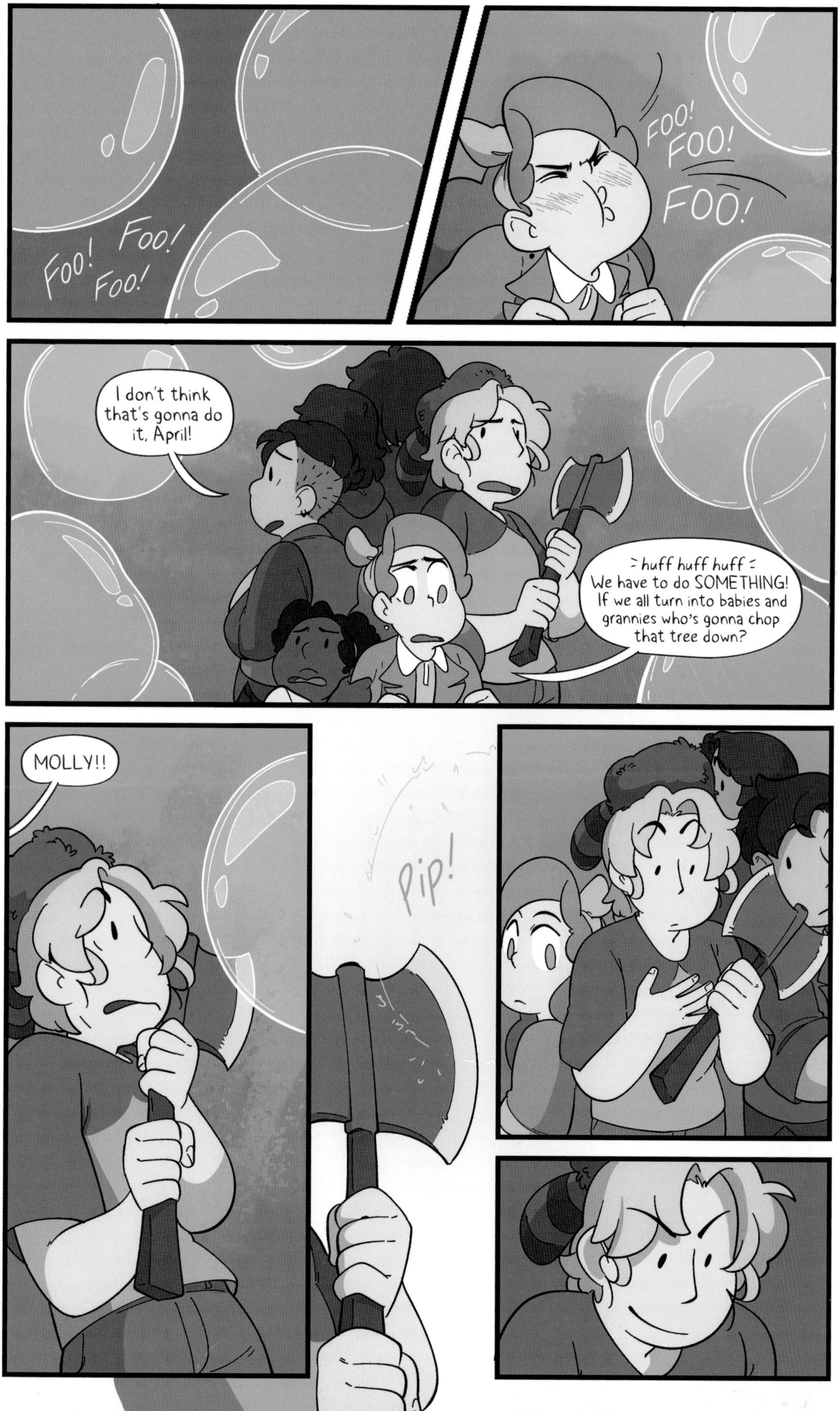

Foo! Foo! Foo!
FOO! FOO! FOO!
I don't think that's gonna do it, April!
huff huff huff
We have to do SOMETHING! If we all turn into babies and grannies who's gonna chop that tree down?
MOLLY!!
Pip!

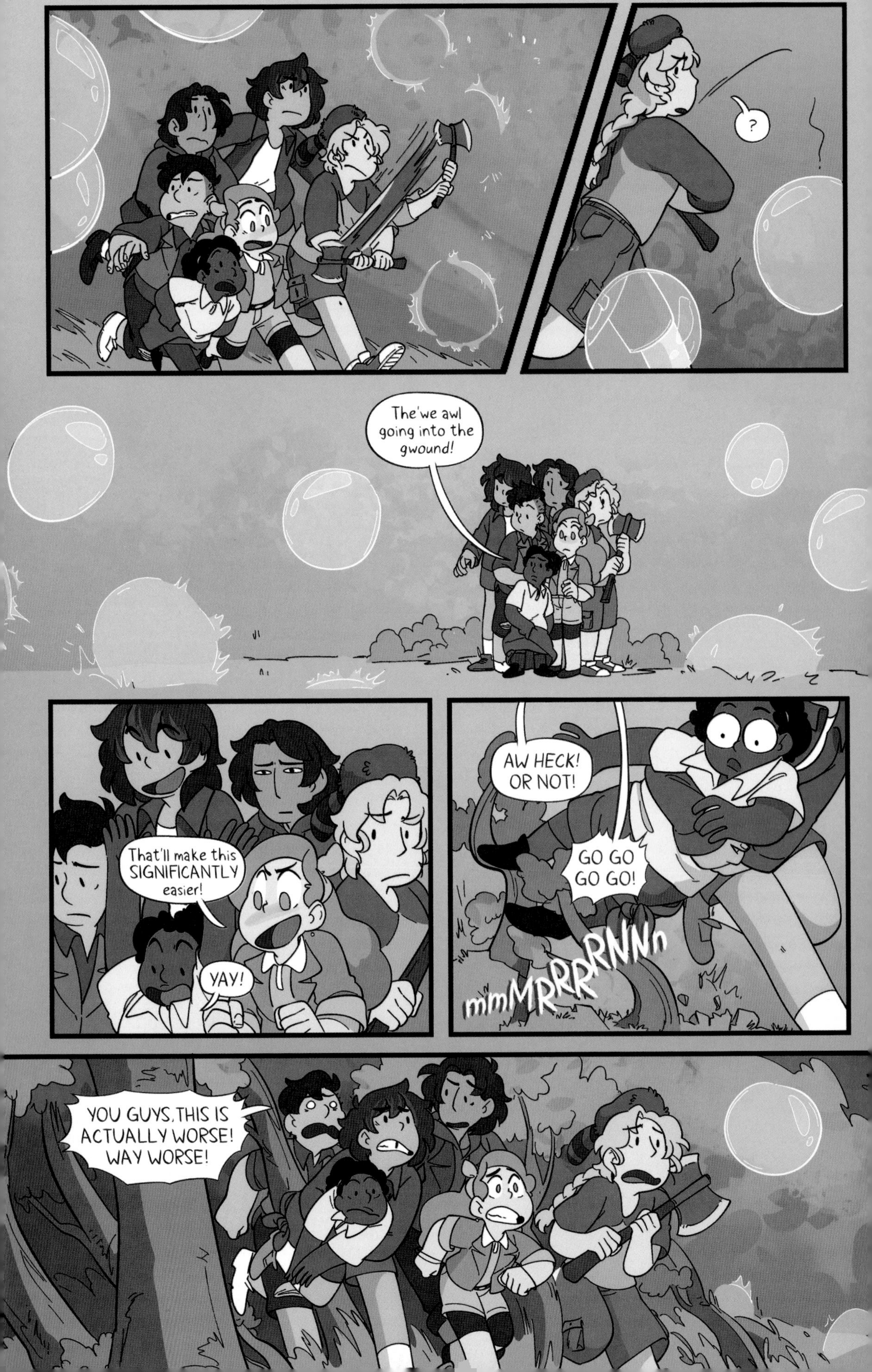
?
The'we awl going into the gwound!
That'll make this SIGNIFICANTLY easier!
YAY!
AW HECK! OR NOT!
GO GO GO GO!
mmMRRRRNNn
YOU GUYS, THIS IS ACTUALLY WORSE! WAY WORSE!

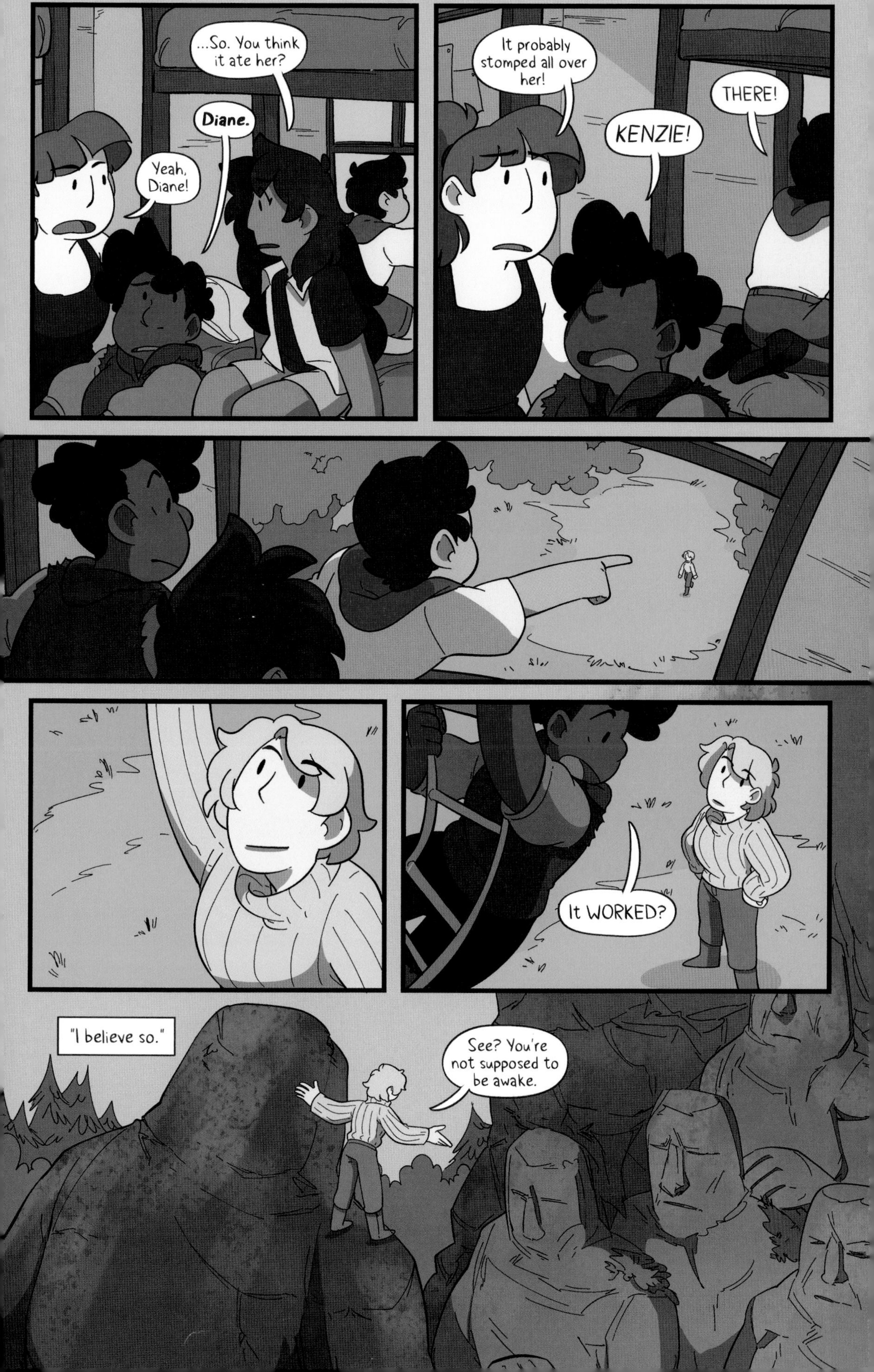
...So. You think it ate her?
Diane.
Yeah, Diane!
It probably stomped all over her!
KENZIE!
THERE!
It WORKED?
"I believe so."
See? You're not supposed to be awake.

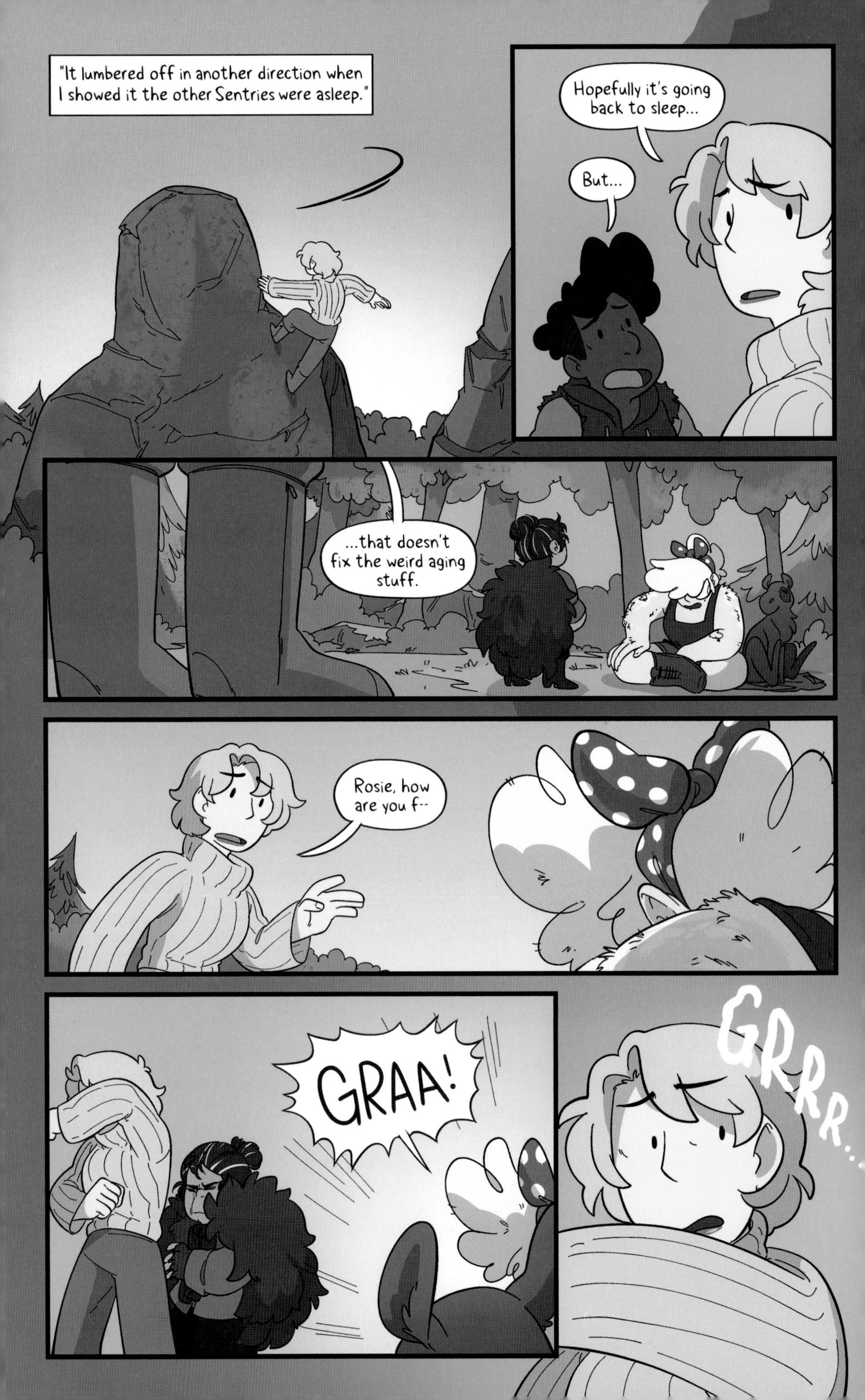
"It lumbered off in another direction when I showed it the other Sentries were asleep."
Hopefully it's going back to sleep...
But...
...that doesn't fix the weird aging stuff.
Rosie, how are you f--
GRAA!
GRRR...

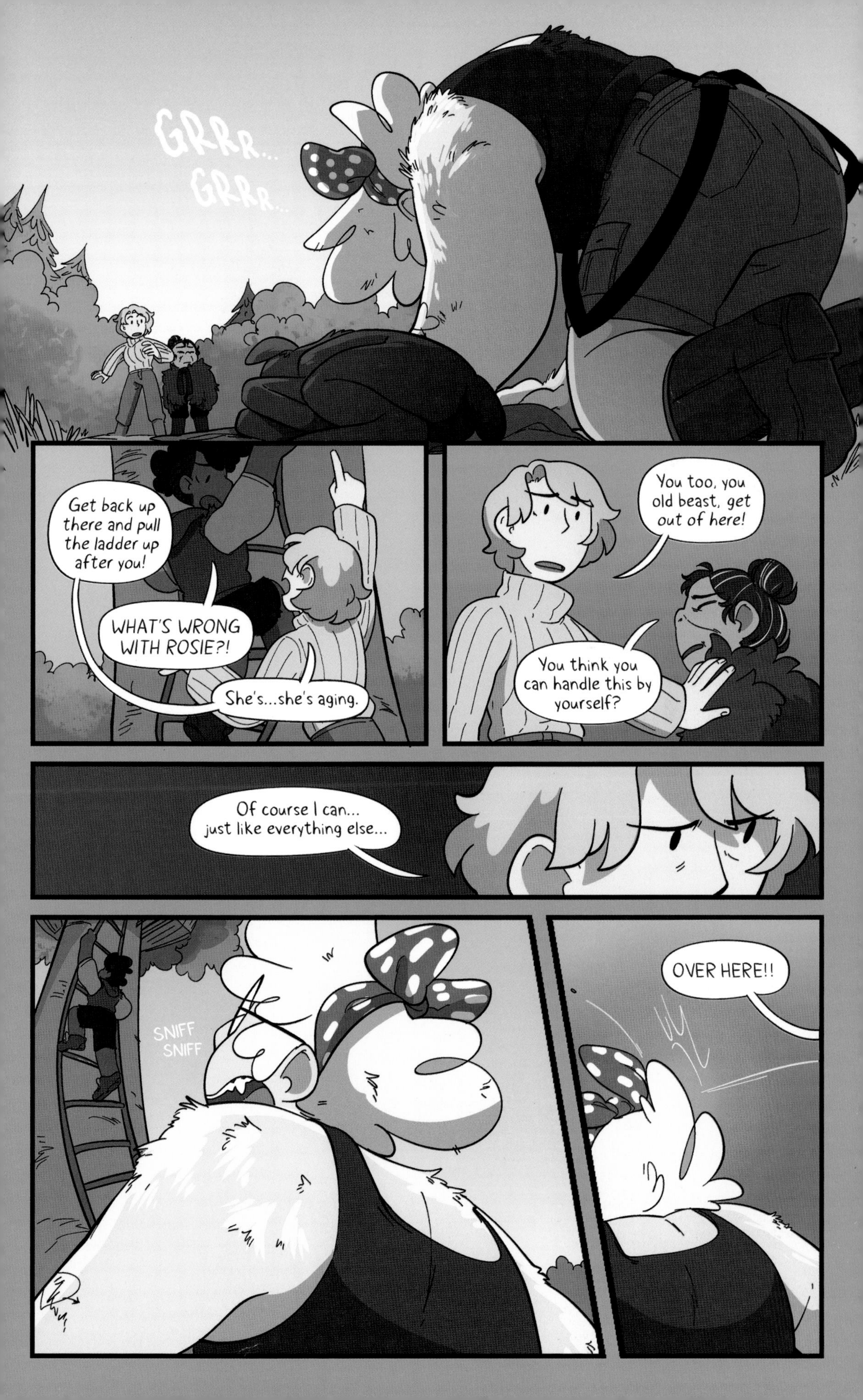
GRRR...
GRRR...
Get back up there and pull the ladder up after you!
WHAT'S WRONG WITH ROSIE?!
She's...she's aging.
You too, you old beast, get out of here!
You think you can handle this by yourself?
Of course I can... just like everything else...
SNIFF
SNIFF
OVER HERE!!

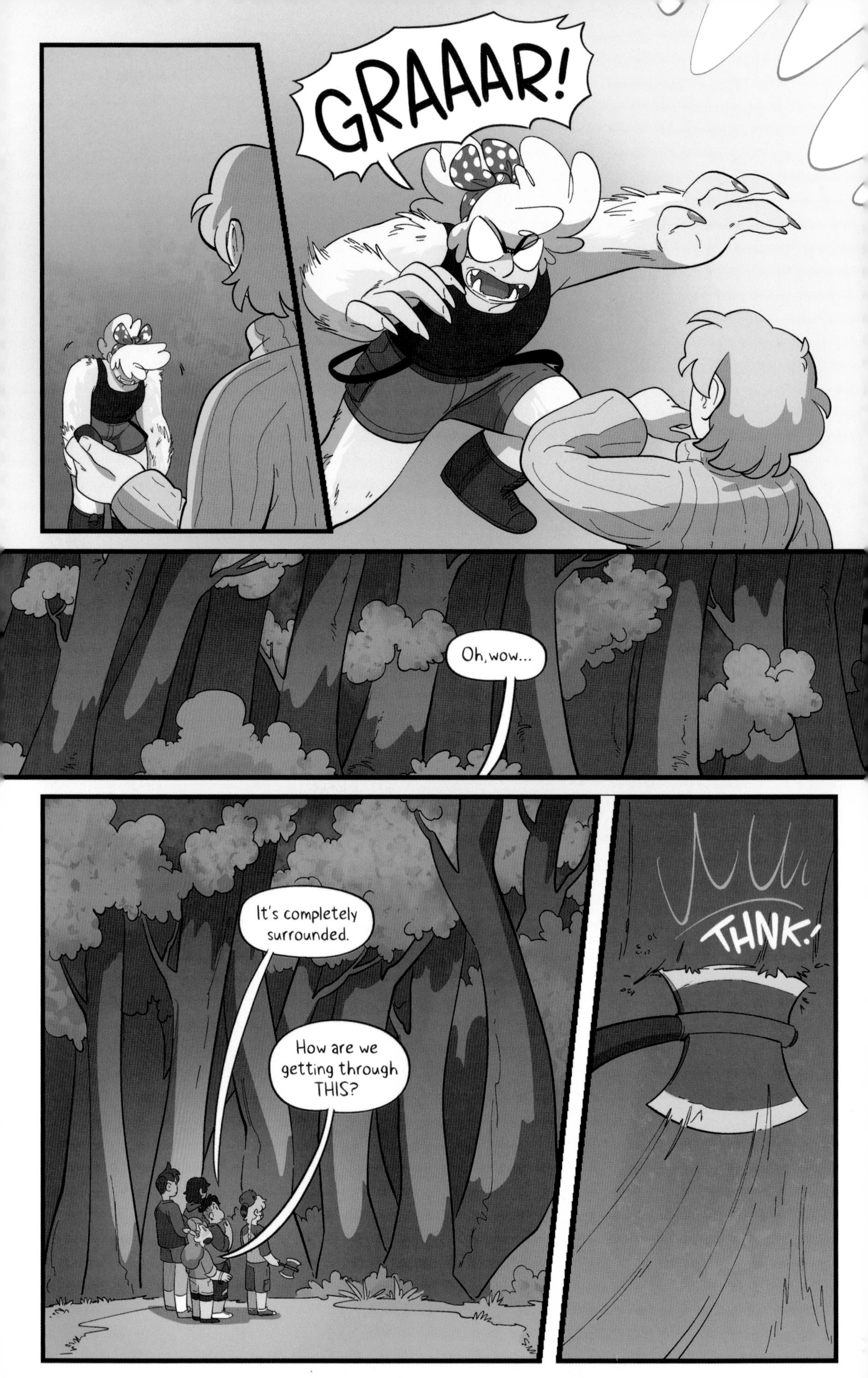
GRAAAR!
Oh, wow...
It's completely surrounded.
How are we getting through THIS?
THNK!

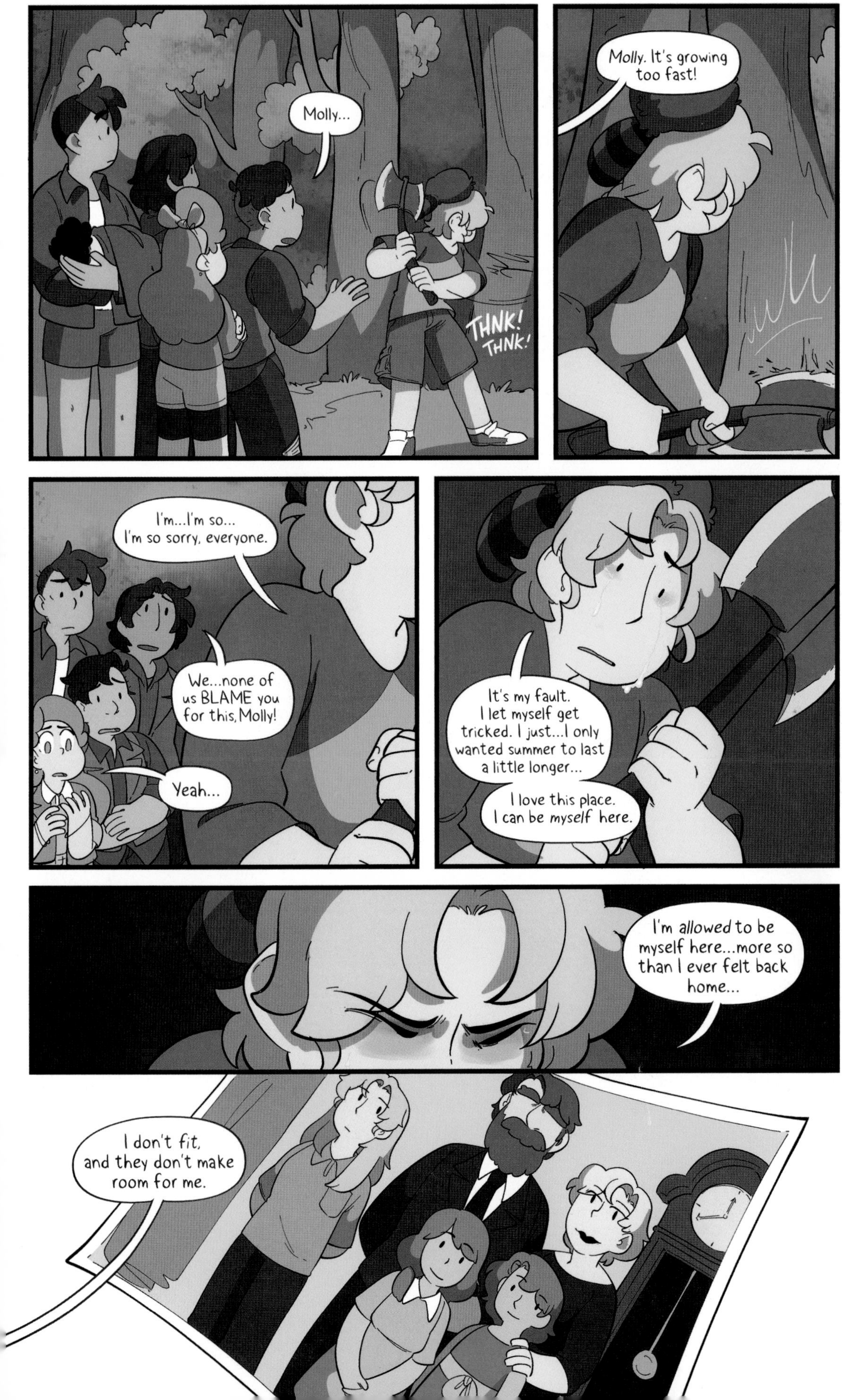
Molly...
THNK!
THNK!
Molly. It's growing too fast!
I'm...I'm so... I'm so sorry, everyone.
We...none of us BLAME you for this, Molly!
Yeah...
It's my fault. I let myself get tricked. I just...I only wanted summer to last a little longer...
I love this place. I can be myself here.
I'm allowed to be myself here...more so than I ever felt back home...
I don't fit, and they don't make room for me.

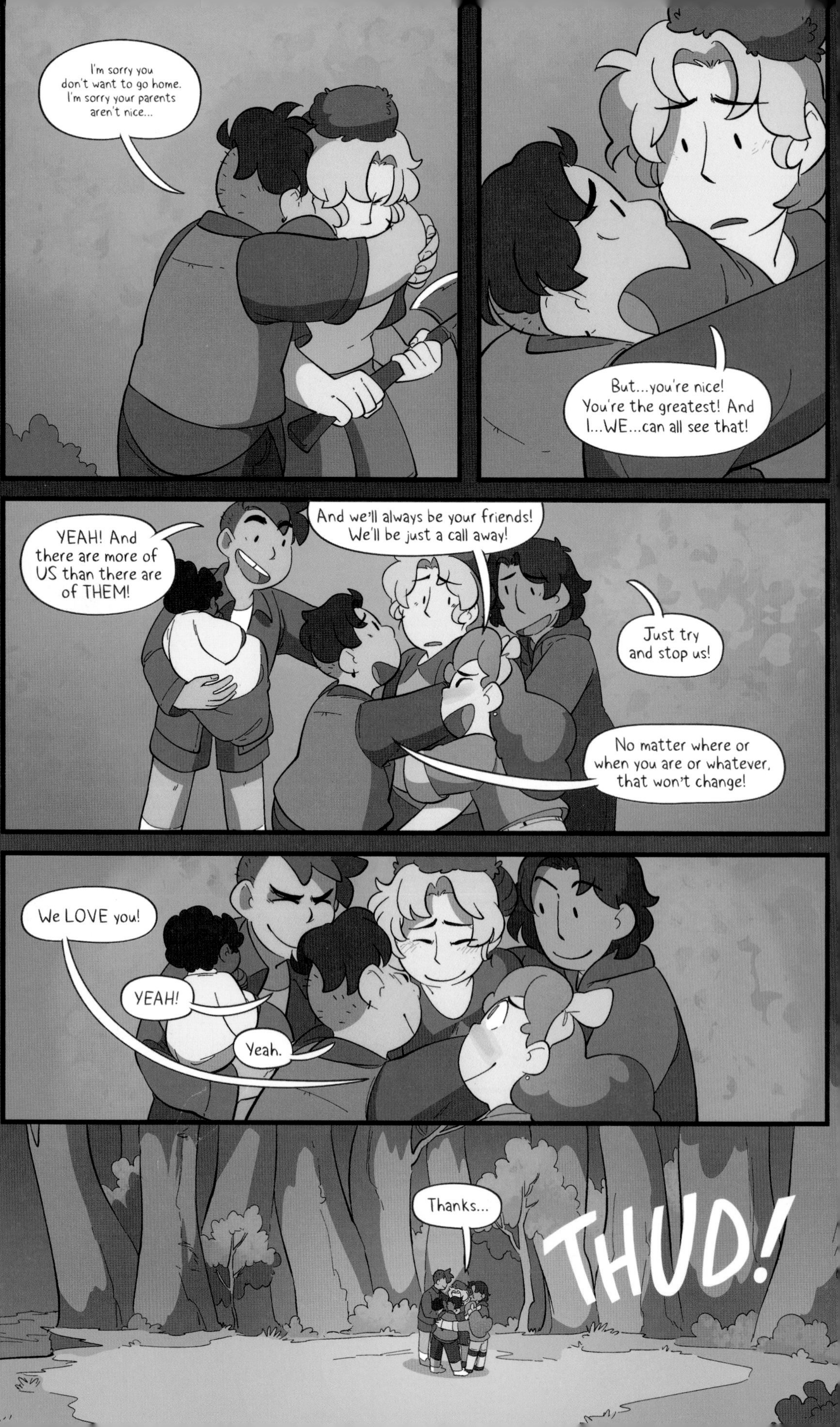
I'm sorry you don't want to go home. I'm sorry your parents aren't nice...
But...you're nice! You're the greatest! And I...WE...can all see that!
YEAH! And there are more of US than there are of THEM!
And we'll always be your friends! We'll be just a call away!
Just try and stop us!
No matter where or when you are or whatever, that won't change!
We LOVE you!
YEAH!
Yeah.
Thanks...
THUD!

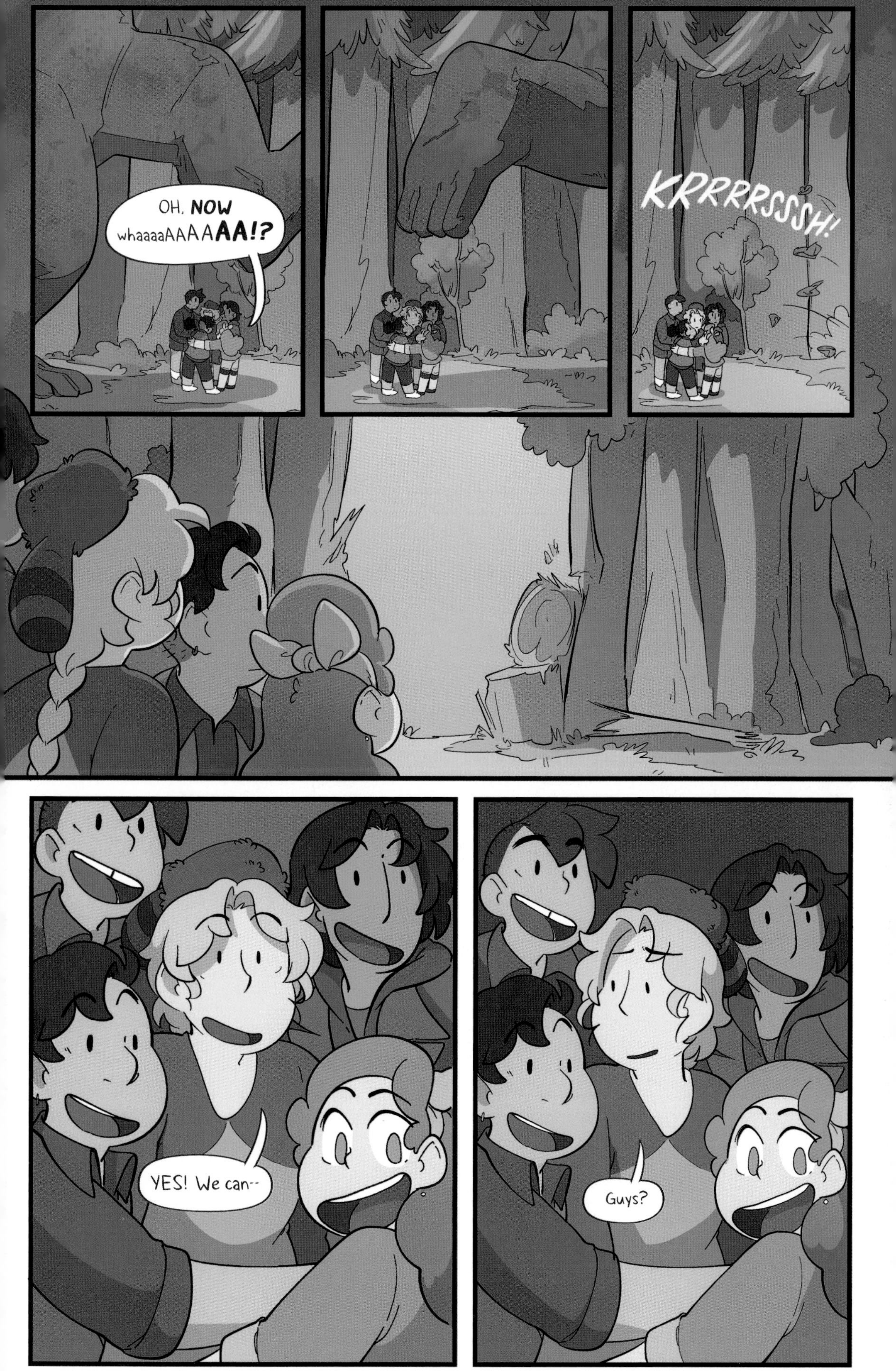
OH, **NOW** whaaaaAAAA**AA!?**
KRRRRSSSH!
YES! We can--
Guys?

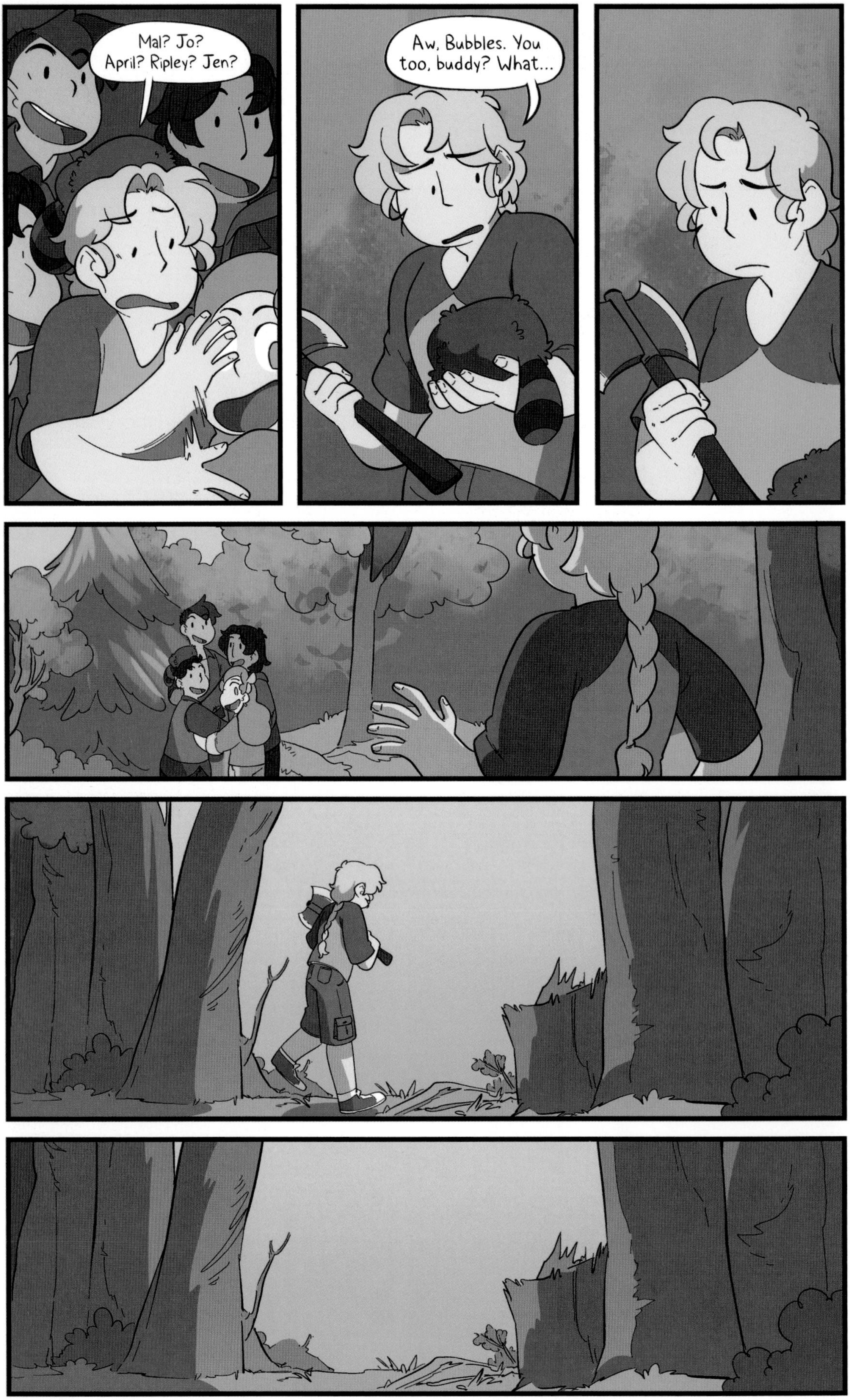
Mal? Jo?
April? Ripley? Jen?
Aw, Bubbles. You too, buddy? What...

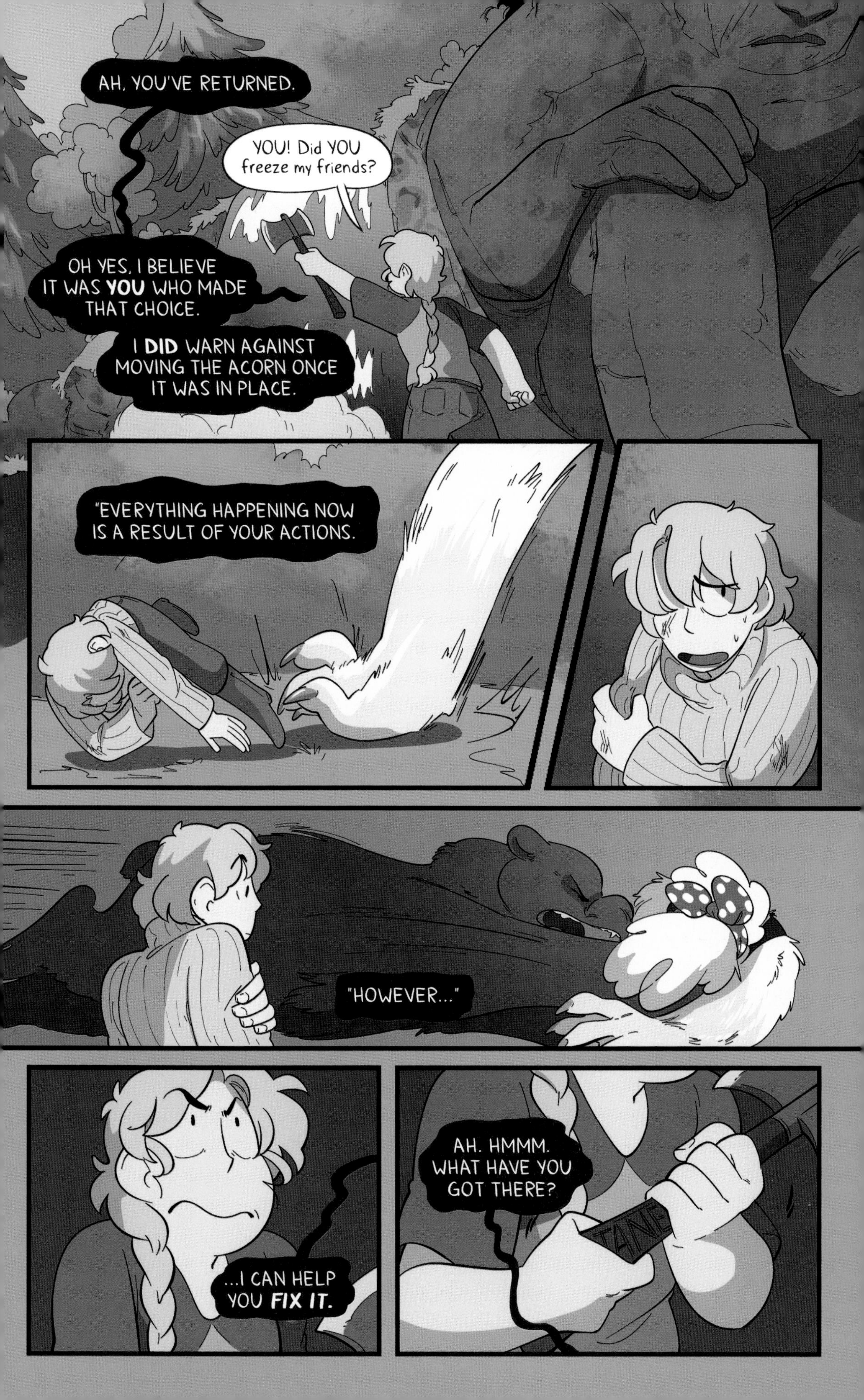
AH, YOU'VE RETURNED.
YOU! Did YOU freeze my friends?
OH YES, I BELIEVE IT WAS YOU WHO MADE THAT CHOICE.
I DID WARN AGAINST MOVING THE ACORN ONCE IT WAS IN PLACE.
"EVERYTHING HAPPENING NOW IS A RESULT OF YOUR ACTIONS.
"HOWEVER..."
...I CAN HELP YOU FIX IT.
AH. HMMM. WHAT HAVE YOU GOT THERE?
TANE

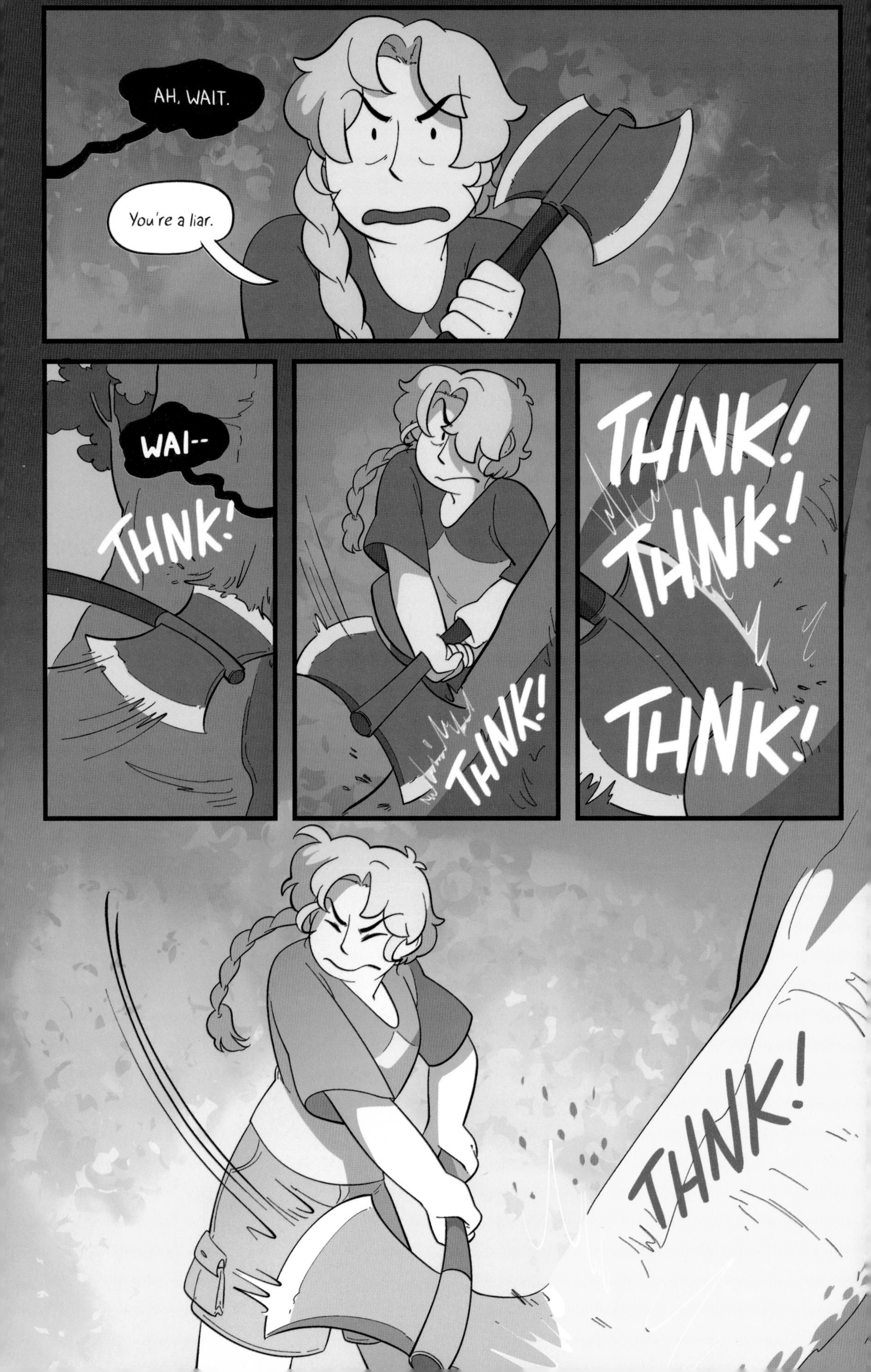

AH, WAIT.
You're a liar.
WAI--
THNK!
THNK!
THNK!
THNK!
THNK!
THNK!

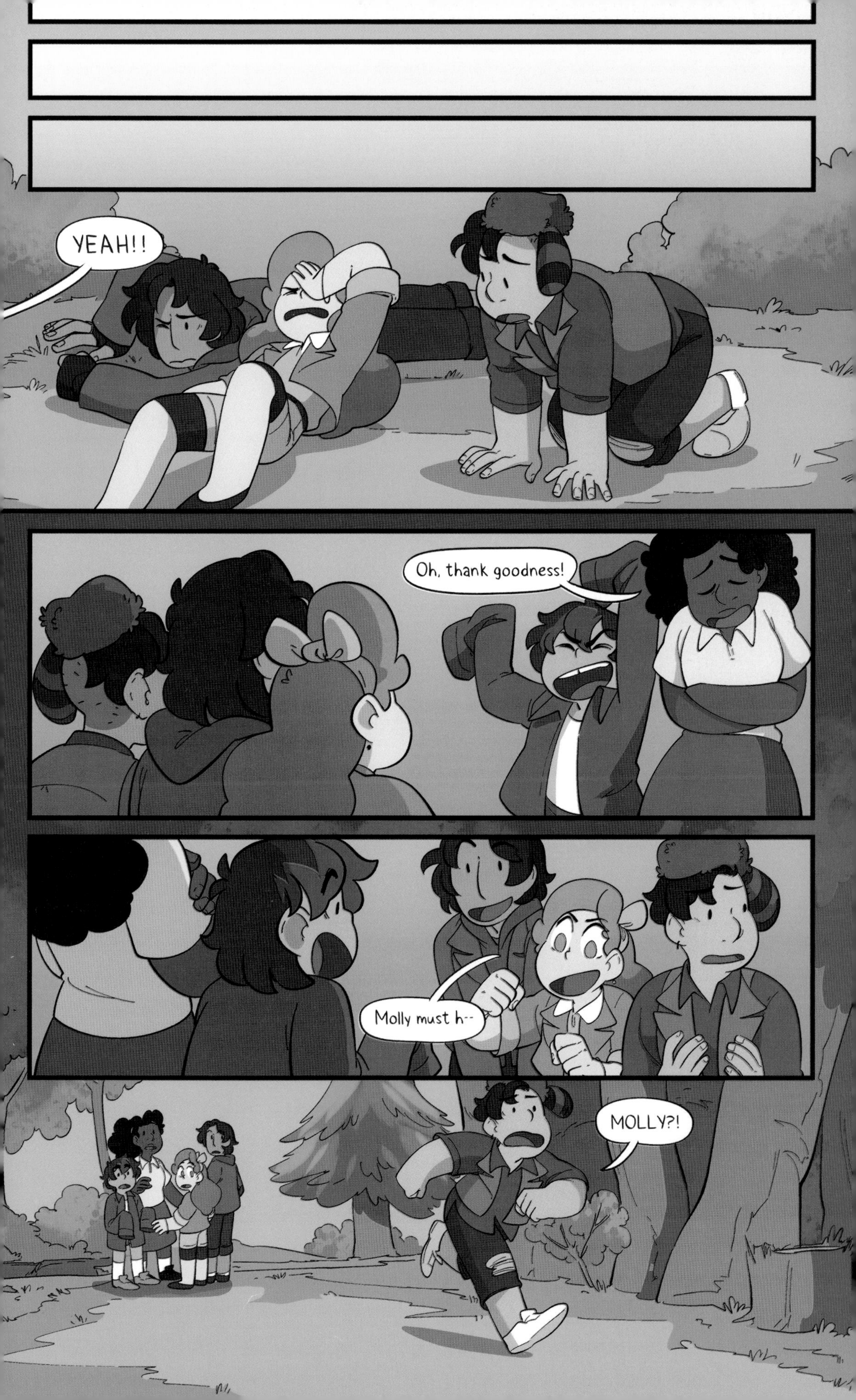
YEAH!!
Oh, thank goodness!
Molly must h--
MOLLY?!

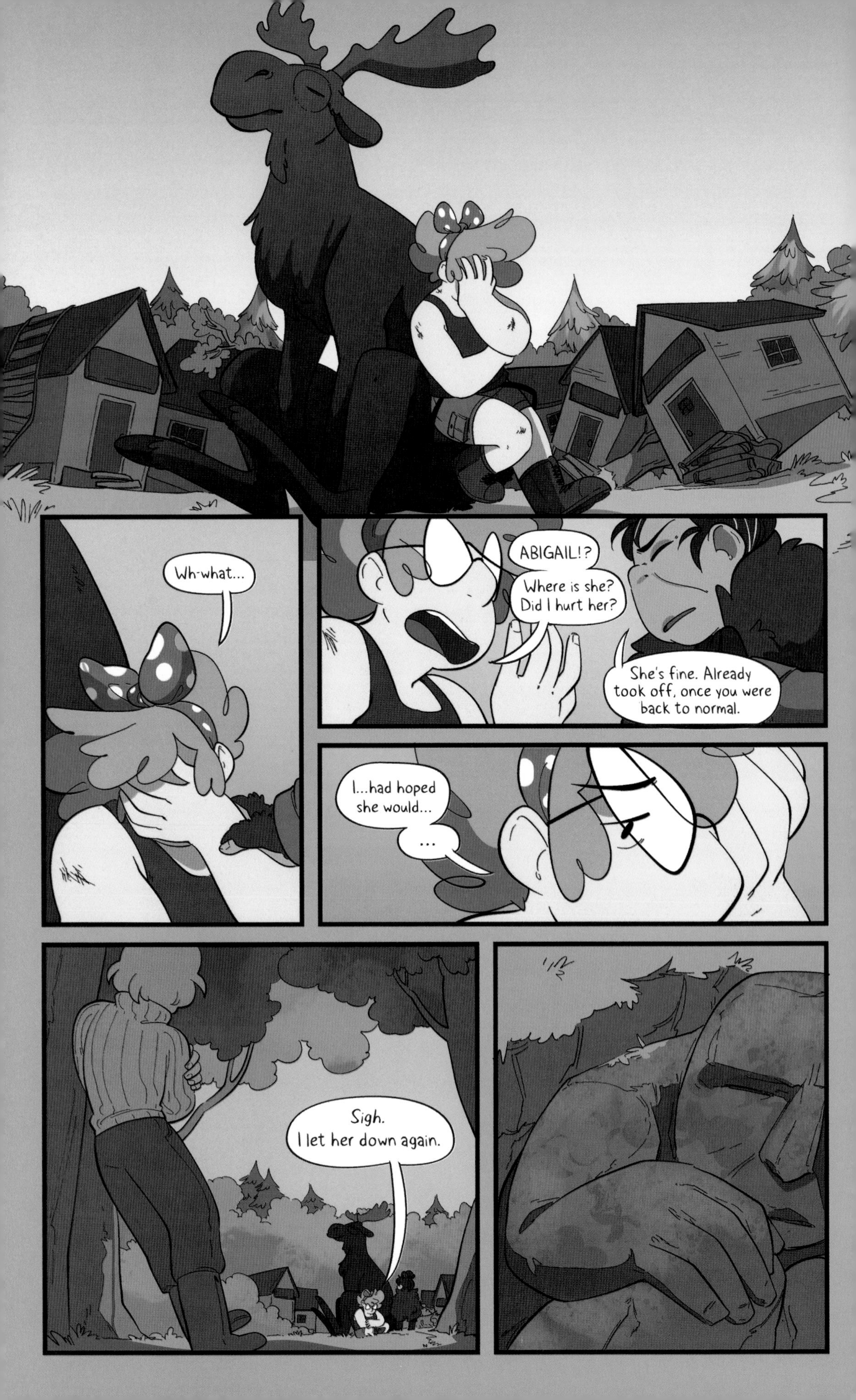
Wh-what...
ABIGAIL!?
Where is she? Did I hurt her?
She's fine. Already took off, once you were back to normal.
I...had hoped she would...
...
Sigh.
I let her down again.

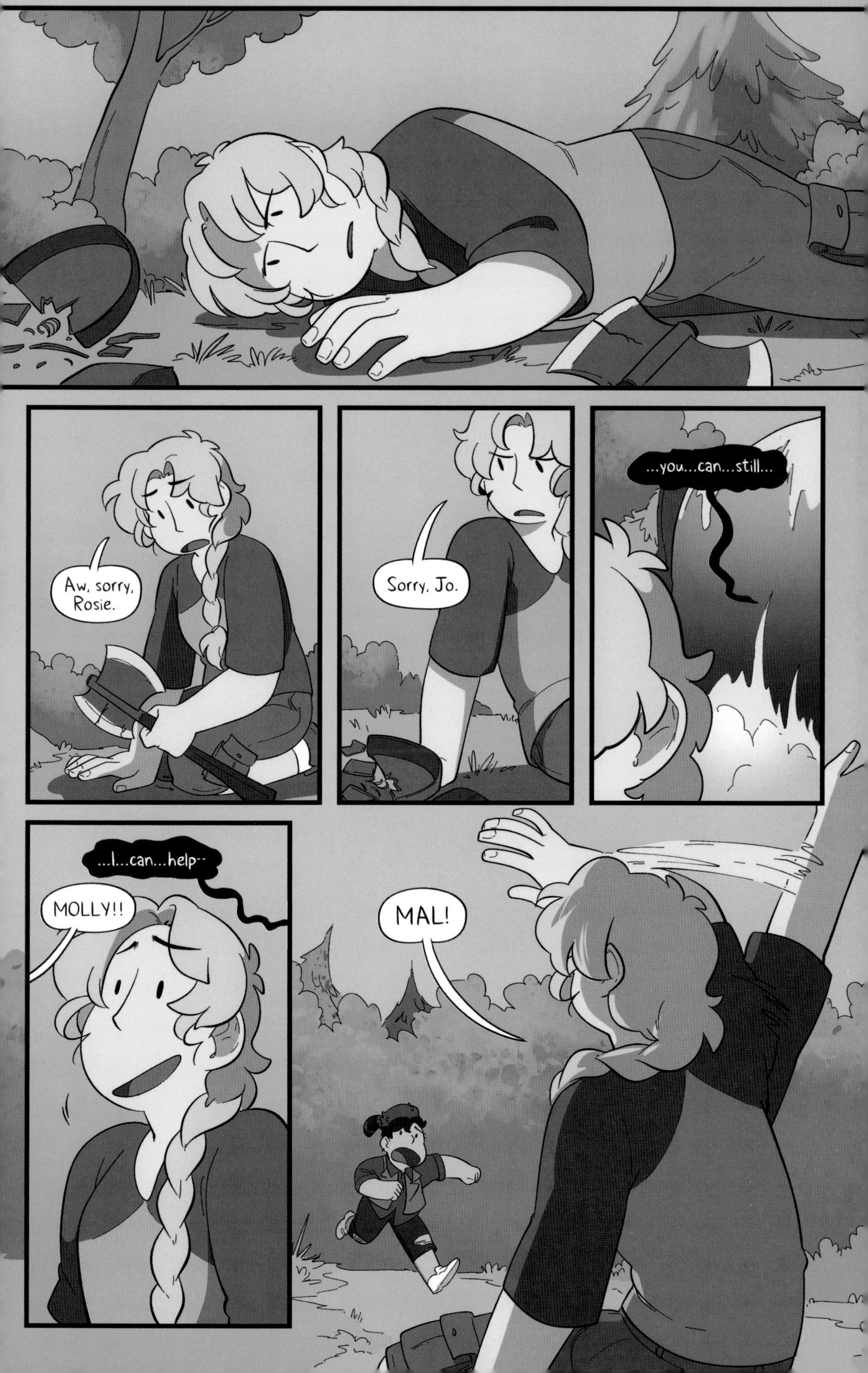
Aw, sorry, Rosie.
Sorry, Jo.
...you...can...still...
...I...can...help--
MOLLY!!
MAL!

YOU DID IT!

C'mon... let's get out of here.

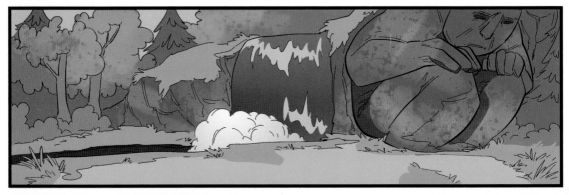

...this...is not over...

...see you soon...

TO BE CONTINUED...

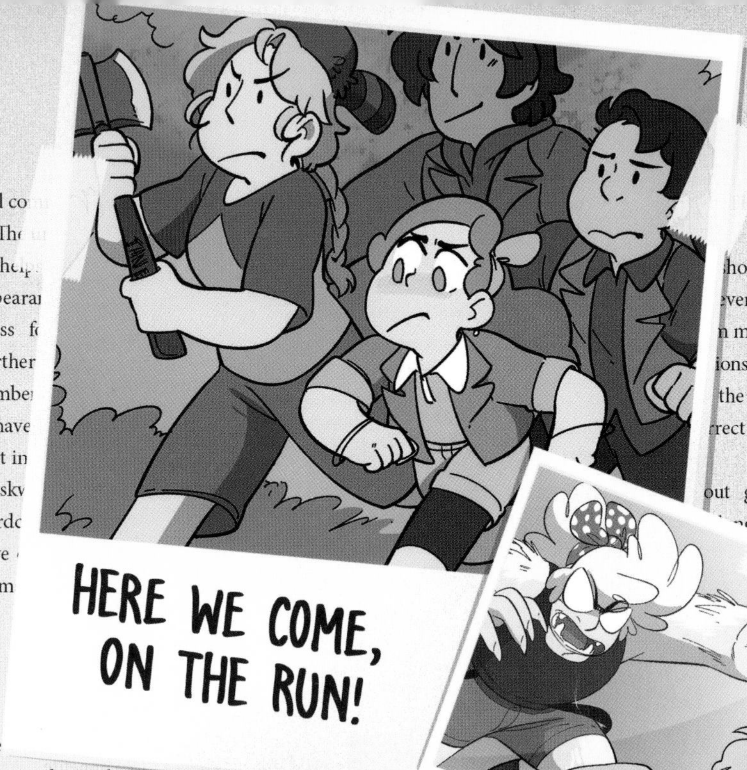
HERE WE COME,
ON THE RUN!

will co

The u

It help

appearan

dress f

Further

Lumbe

to have

part in

Thiskw

Hardc

have

them

HE UNIFORM

hould be worn at camp events when Lumberjanes n may also be worn at other ions. It should be worn as a the uniform dress with rrect shoes, and stocking or

out grows her uniform or ng to another Lumberjane. ia she has her her

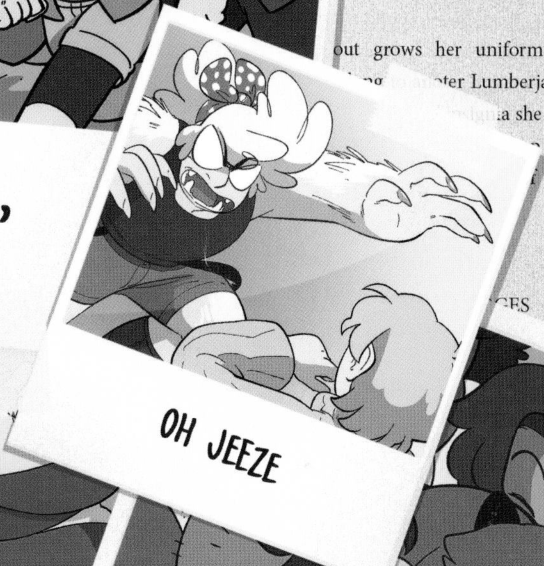
OH JEEZE

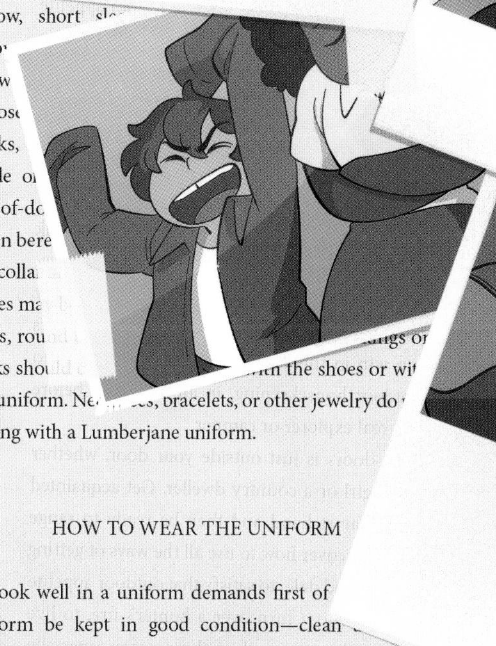

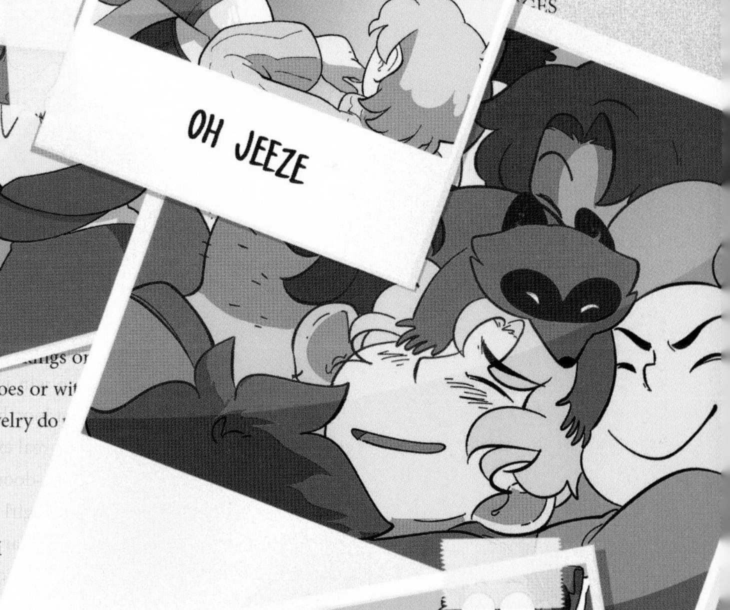

The

yellow, short sl

emb

the w

choose

slacks,

made o

out-of-do

green bere

the colla

Shoes ma

heels, rou kings or

socks shou with the shoes or wi

the uniform. Ne es, bracelets, or other jewelry do

belong with a Lumberjane uniform.

GES

HOW TO WEAR THE UNIFORM

To look well in a uniform demands first of uniform be kept in good condition—clean pressed. See that the skirt is the right length for your own height and build, that the belt is adjusted to your waist, that your shoes and stockings are in keeping with the uniform, that you watch your posture and carry yourself with dignity and grace. If the beret is removed indoors, be sure that your hair is neat and kept in place with an insonspicuous clip or ribbon. When you wear a Lumberjane uniform you are identified as a member of this organization and you should be doubly careful to conduct yourself in a way that will show everyone that courtesy and thoughtfullness are part of being a Lumberjane. People are likely to judge a whole nation by the selfishness of a few individuals, to criticize a whole family because of the misconduct of one member, and to feel unkindly toward and organization because of the

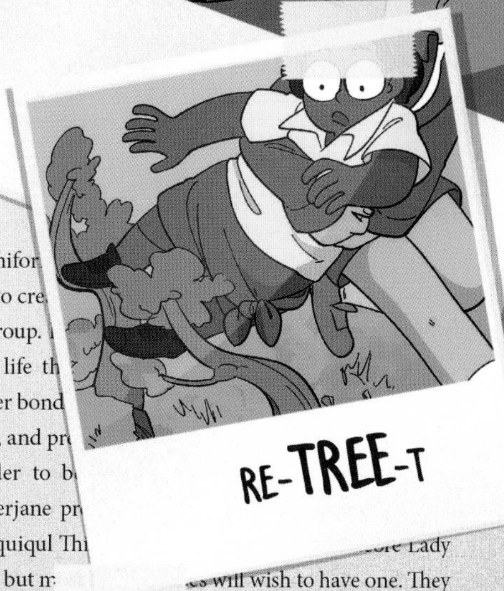
RE-TREE-T

The unifor

helps to cre

in a group.

active life th

another bond

future, and pr

in order to b

Lumberjane pr

Penniquiqul Thi

Types, but m es will wish to have one. They can either b , or make it themselves from materials available at the trading post.

COVER GALLERY

Lumberjanes "Out-of-Doors" Program Field

TIME AFTER CRIME

"Time is an illusion, never waste it!"

What did you have for breakfast this morning? What about yesterday? Three weeks ago? Six months? If you're anything like us, the further you go back, the more difficult it is to recall details, particularly for events as small and everyday as breakfast. Now imagine that effect across the vast span of history, and imagine how many little details have been forgotten or erased over the years. There are so many historical ideas and implements that we view through a skewed lens, or misunderstand, or simply don't know!

History, the long stretch of time that came before you, is unfathomably vast. There are countless ways to work on remembering or relearning the things that have been lost, via archaeology, paleontology, genealogy, anthropology, or any other number of "ologies" (like the most vital of all: apology), but it can sometimes seem that this work is all being done by adults, like scientists and researchers and librarians, and that there is little room for children. In the Time After Crime badge, we hope that you will take part in uncovering the history all around you and become a time traveler through memory!

Perhaps your mother has told you about how her parents grew up in houses that didn't have electricity, or how their parents didn't have so much as running water, maybe in a country far away from here. Perhaps you have thought about these distant relatives, so long ago and far away, and wondered if your life bears any resemblance to theirs. Did they like to play games, like you do? Did they eat the same foods as you? Did they read books that you like to read, or make crafts like you like to? Asking your parents and grandparents about their childhoods is a great way to get started, and if you're lucky, they may even have diaries, photos, or toys, to help give you a fuller picture of what their lives were like!

From there, you may decide to take this badge in a few different directions. Learning more about your family's history and creating a family tree can be a fun second step, but you may also enjoy grouping up with your troopmates to talk about your families' histories: where they came from, what traditions they hold dear. How does your family's history and culture compare and contrast to your friends? What can you discover about the past, and about yourselves?

Issue Forty-One
KAT LEYH

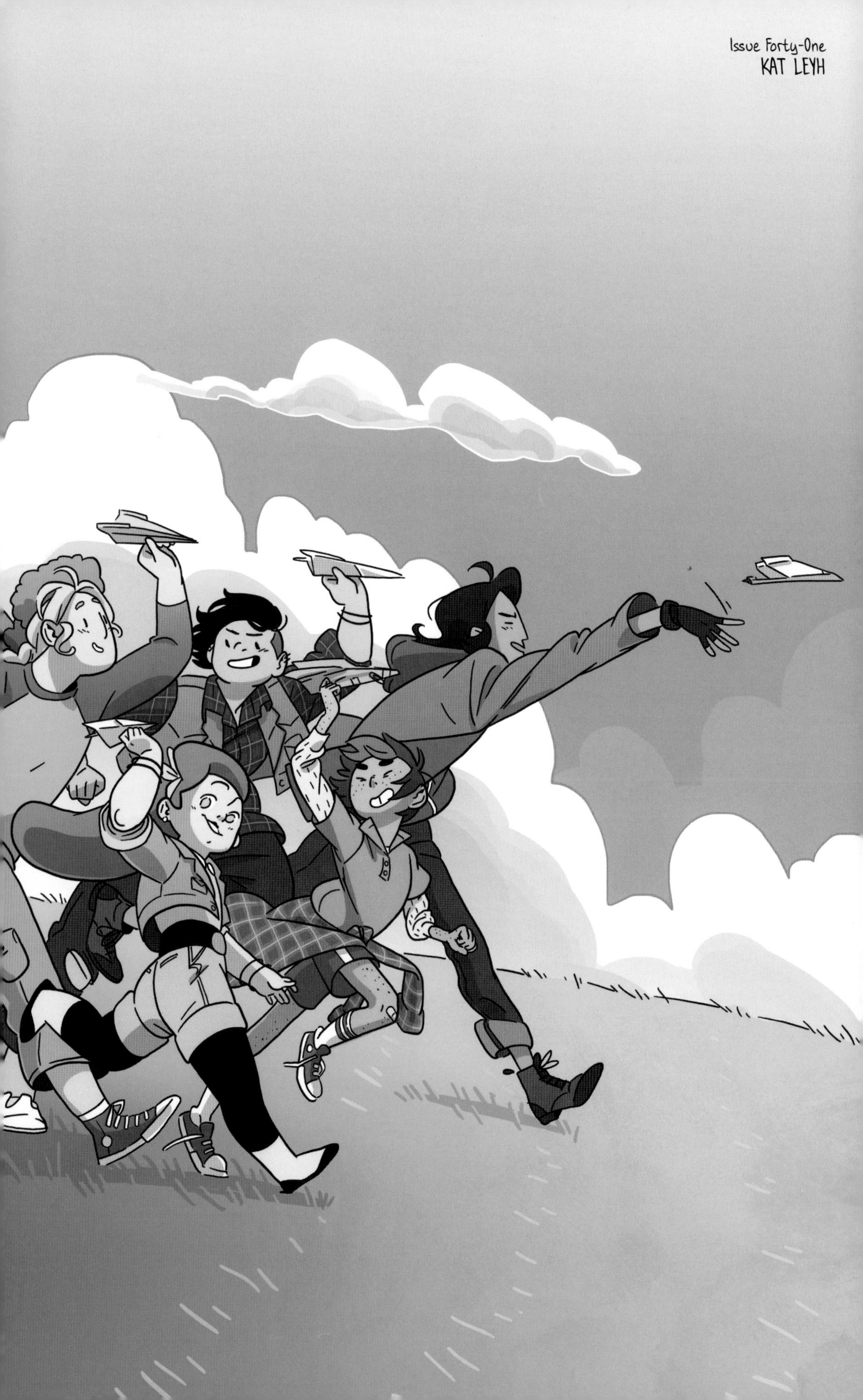

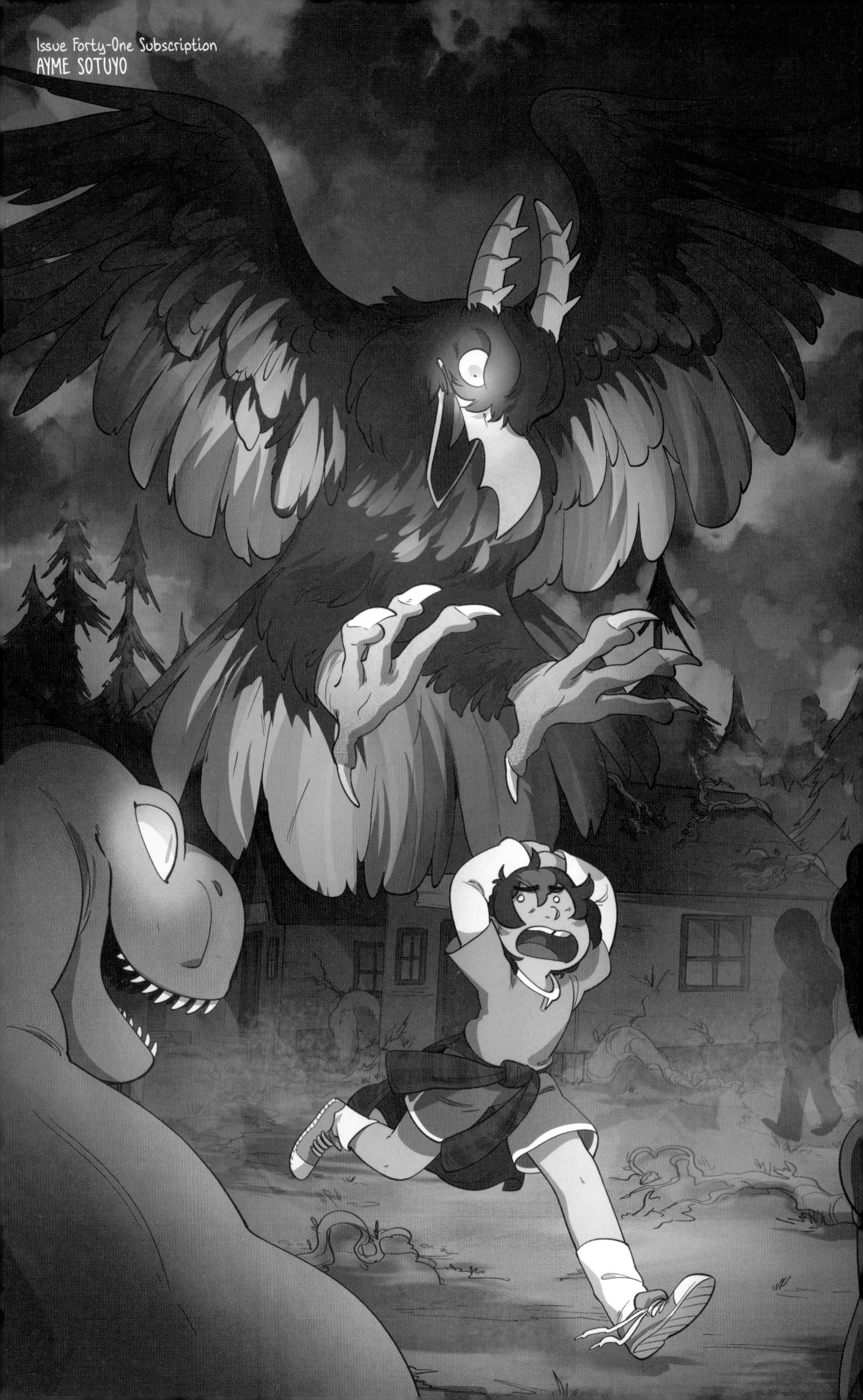

Issue Forty-One Subscription
AYME SOTUYO

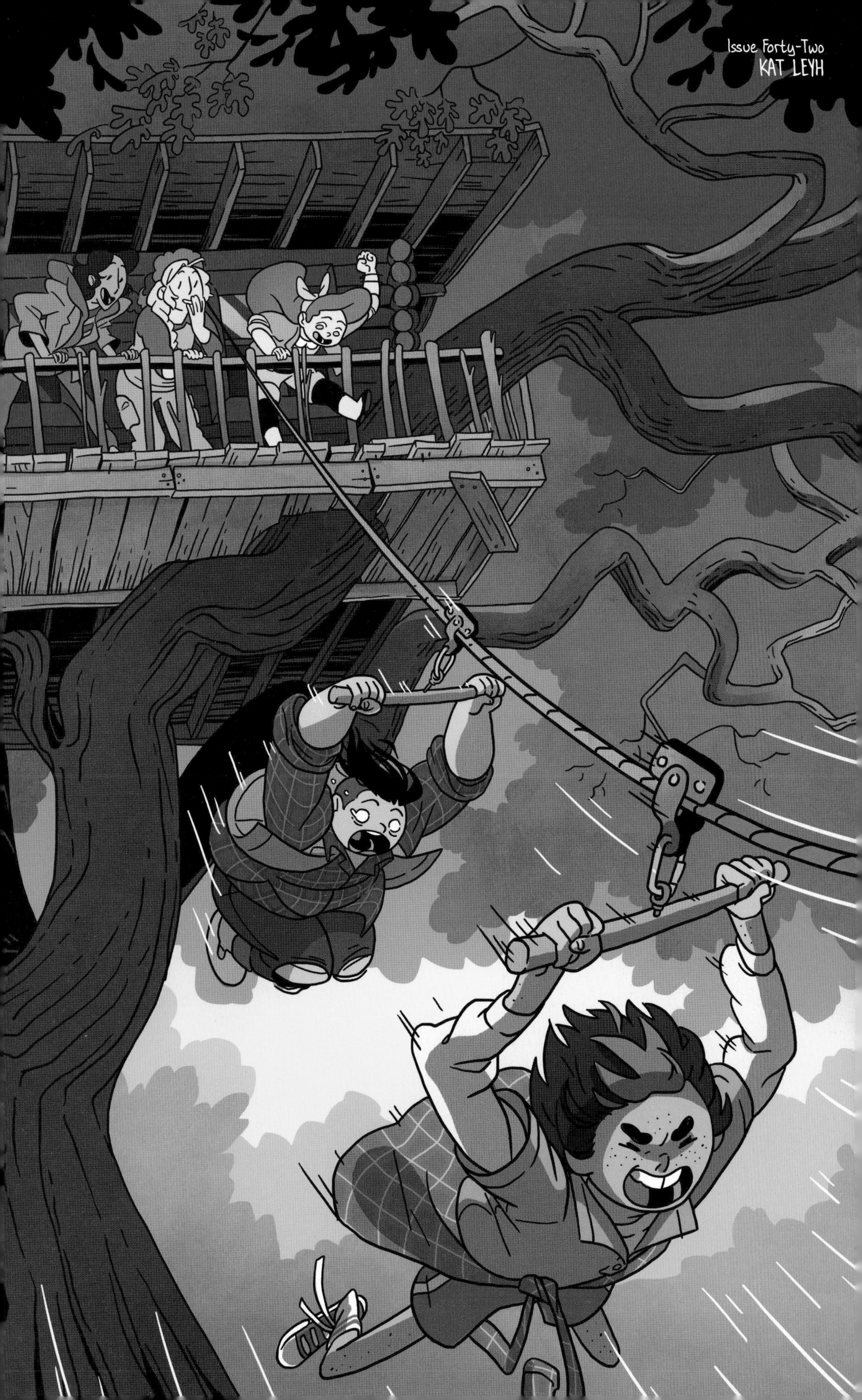
Issue Forty-Two
KAT LEYH

Issue Forty-Two Subscription
AYME SOTUYO

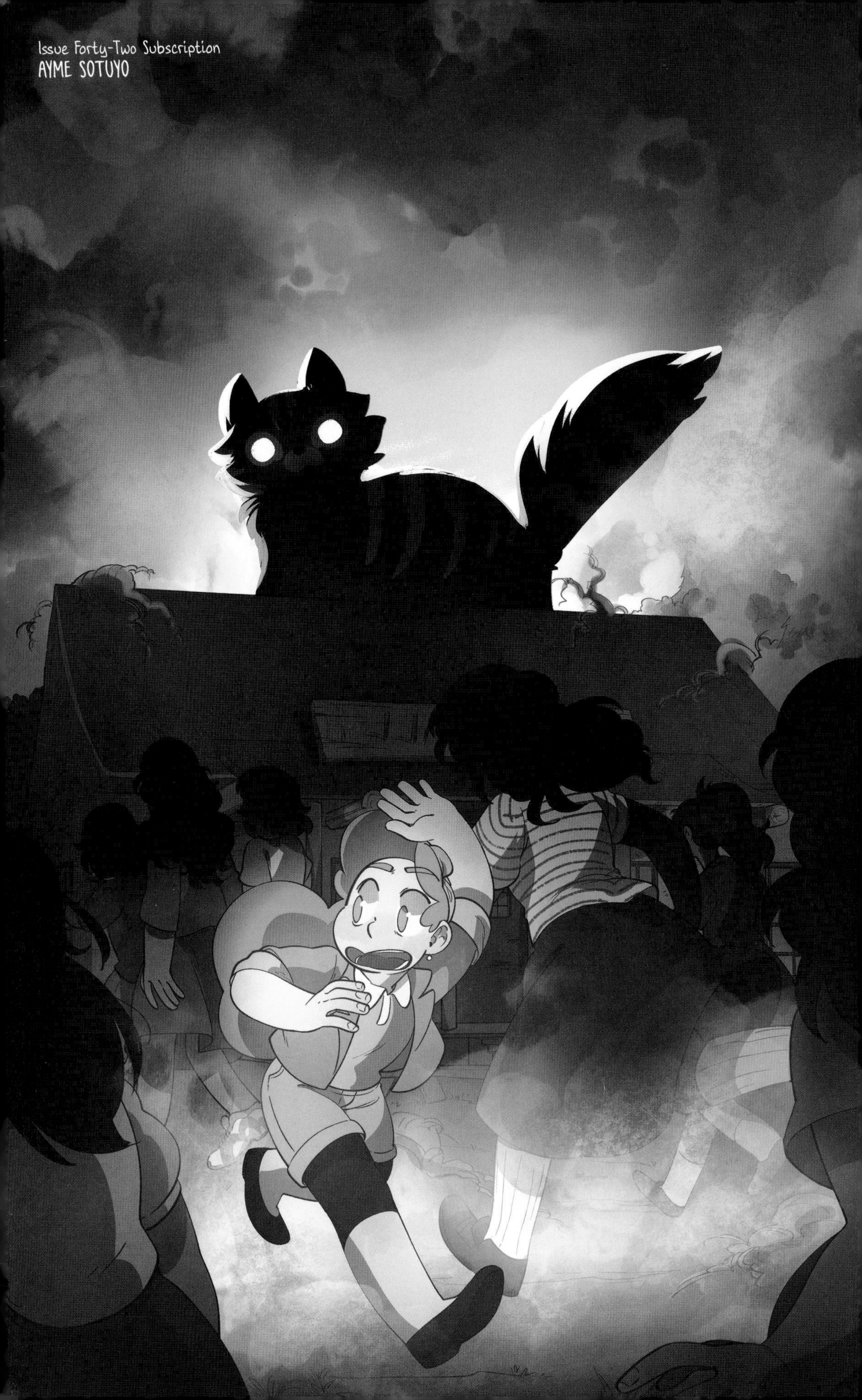

Issue Forty-Two Rose City Comic Con Variant
AYME SOTUYO

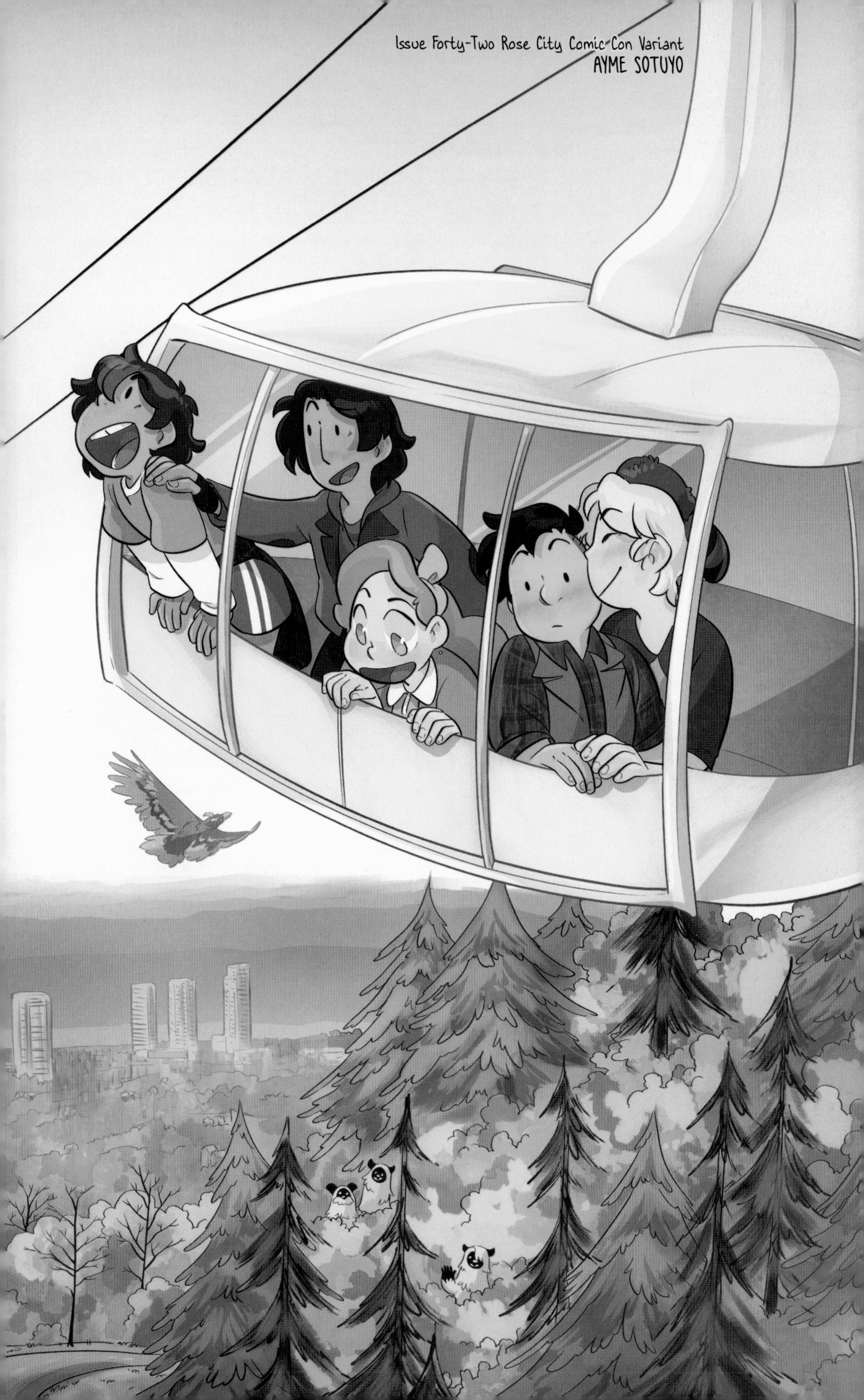

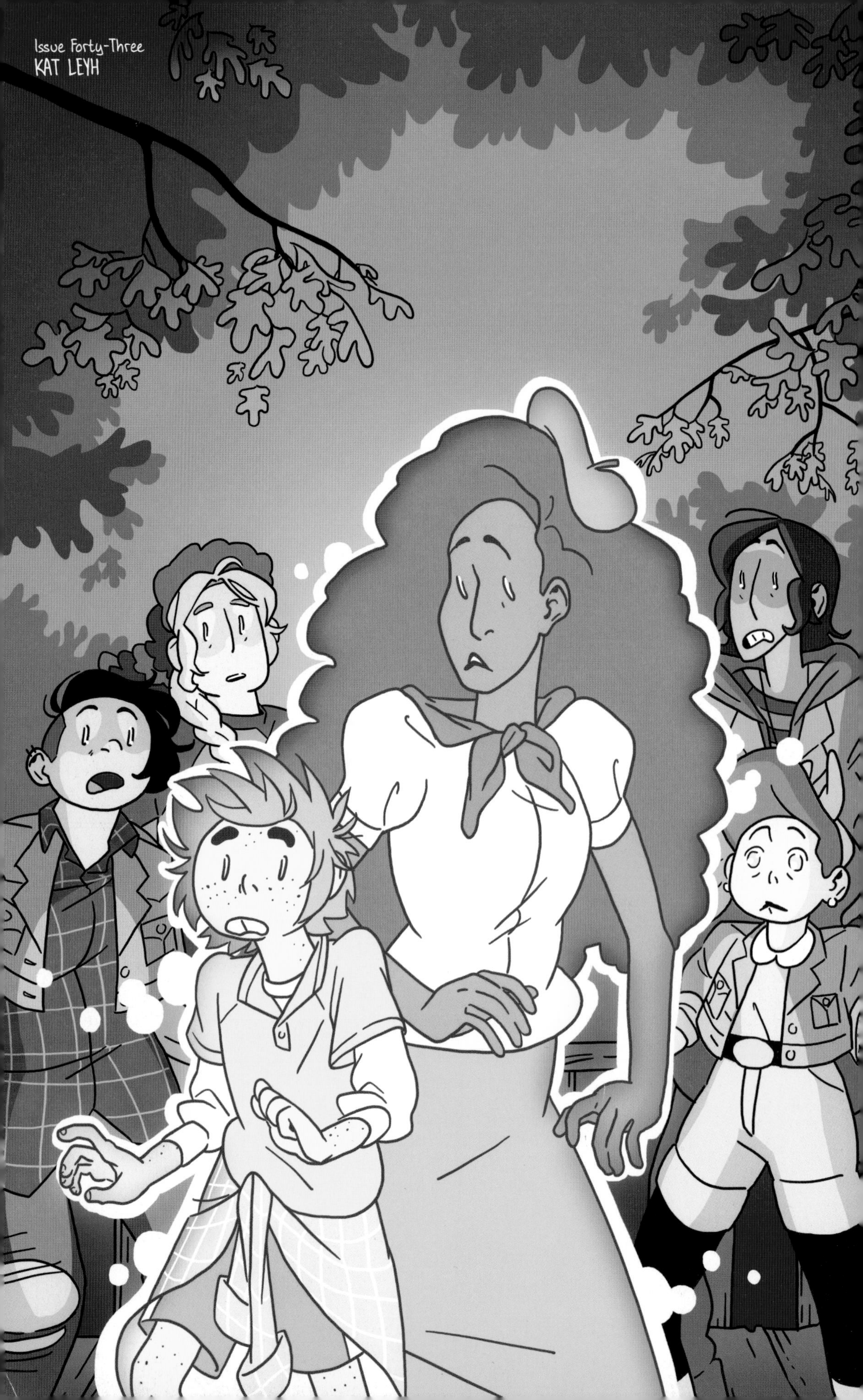
Issue Forty-Three
KAT LEYH

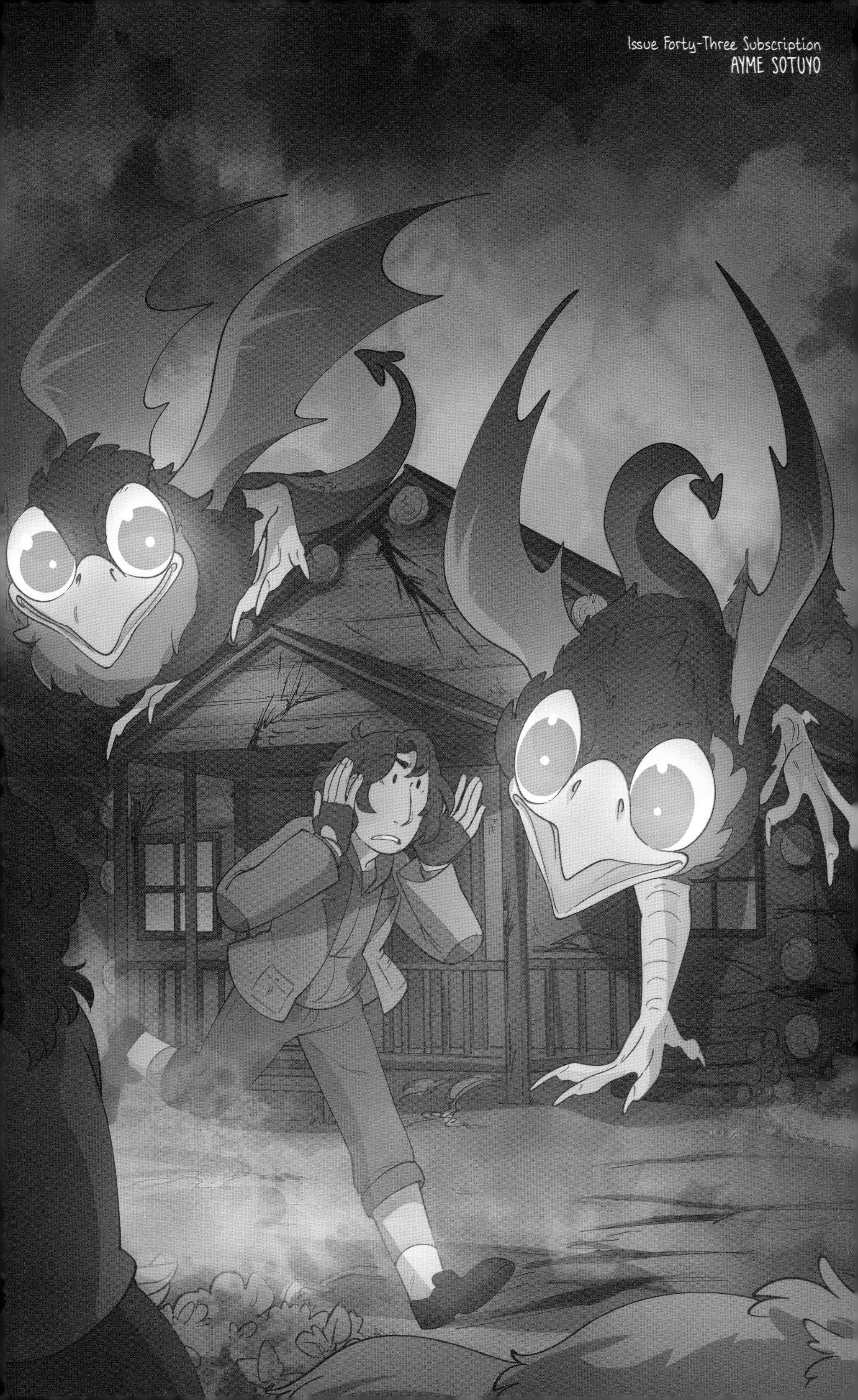
Issue Forty-Three Subscription
AYME SOTUYO

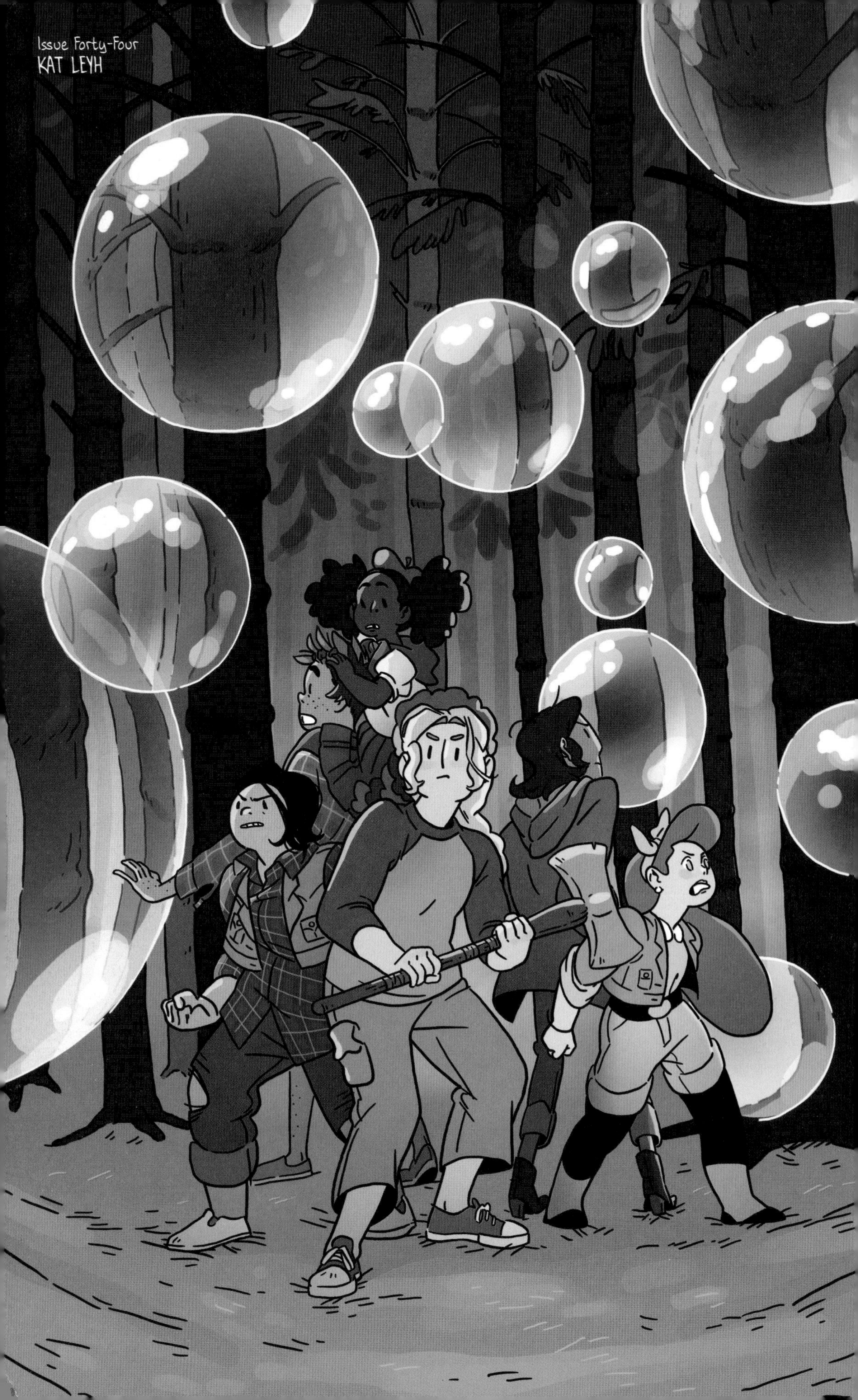
Issue Forty-Four
KAT LEYH

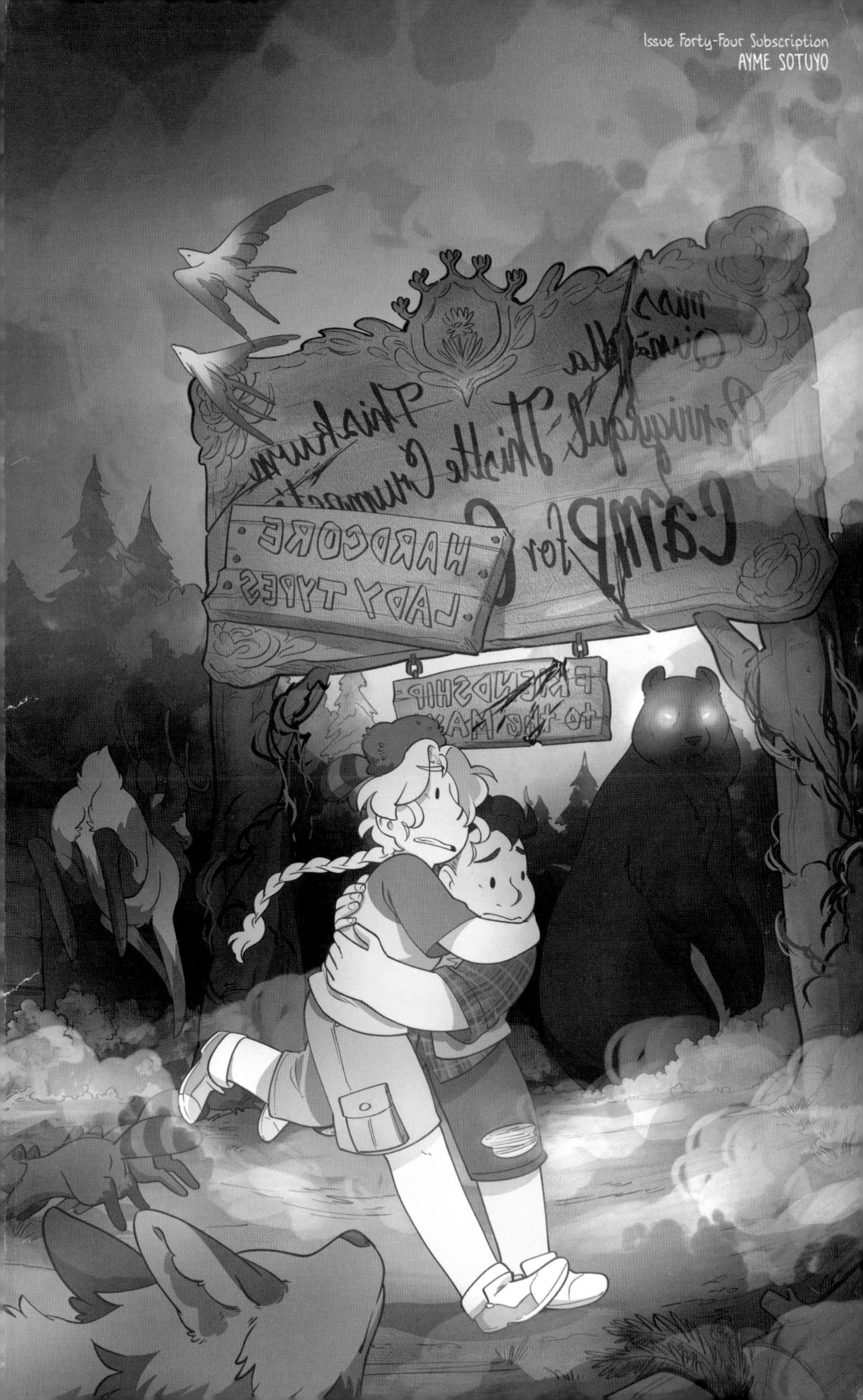

Issue Forty-Four Subscription
AYME SOTUYO

DISCOVER
ALL THE HITS

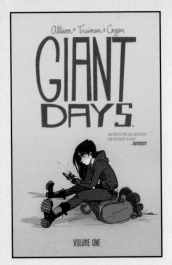

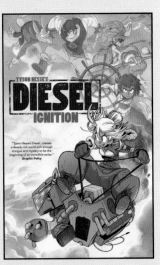

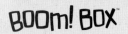

STEVENSON · ELLIS · WATTERS · ALLEN
LUMBERJANES
BEWARE THE KITTEN HOLY
NEW YORK TIMES
BESTSELLING SERIES

Allison + Treiman + Cogar
GIANT DAYS
VOLUME ONE

RIBON · FISH · PEER
SLAM!
VOLUME ONE

Hope Larson · Brittney Williams · Sarah Stern
GOLDIE VANCE
Volume One

THE BACKSTAGERS

TYSON HESSE'S
DIESEL
IGNITION

Lumberjanes
Noelle Stevenson, Shannon Watters, Grace Ellis, Brooklyn Allen, and Others
Volume 1: Beware the Kitten Holy
ISBN: 978-1-60886-687-8 | $14.99 US
Volume 2: Friendship to the Max
ISBN: 978-1-60886-737-0 | $14.99 US
Volume 3: A Terrible Plan
ISBN: 978-1-60886-803-2 | $14.99 US
Volume 4: Out of Time
ISBN: 978-1-60886-860-5 | $14.99 US
Volume 5: Band Together
ISBN: 978-1-60886-919-0 | $14.99 US

Giant Days
John Allison, Lissa Treiman, Max Sarin
Volume 1
ISBN: 978-1-60886-789-9 | $9.99 US
Volume 2
ISBN: 978-1-60886-804-9 | $14.99 US
Volume 3
ISBN: 978-1-60886-851-3 | $14.99 US

Jonesy
Sam Humphries, Caitlin Rose Boyle
Volume 1
ISBN: 978-1-60886-883-4 | $9.99 US
Volume 2
ISBN: 978-1-60886-999-2 | $14.99 US

Slam!
Pamela Ribon, Veronica Fish, Brittany Peer
Volume 1
ISBN: 978-1-68415-004-5 | $14.99 US

Goldie Vance
Hope Larson, Brittney Williams
Volume 1
ISBN: 978-1-60886-898-8 | $9.99 US
Volume 2
ISBN: 978-1-60886-974-9 | $14.99 US

The Backstagers
James Tynion IV, Rian Sygh
Volume 1
ISBN: 978-1-60886-993-0 | $14.99 US

Tyson Hesse's Diesel: Ignition
Tyson Hesse
ISBN: 978-1-60886-907-7 | $14.99 US

Coady & The Creepies
Liz Prince, Amanda Kirk, Hannah Fisher
ISBN: 978-1-68415-029-8 | $14.99 US